"Moving, ac[...]
to be widely [...]

Kate is Amanda's adorable baby.

Tom is her wonderful husband in a delight-
fully successful, two-career marriage.

That is why Sarah, who can have her pick
of families to work for, picks Amanda's.

For what Amanda has, Sarah desperately
wants. A baby of her own to replace the one
she lost. . . .

HUSH LITTLE BABY

"A strong, engrossing and disturbing story."
—Deborah Moggach,
author of *The Stand-in*

"Dark, scary, moving."—*The Literary Review*

HUSH
LITTLE
BABY

by
Sally Emerson

A SIGNET BOOK

SIGNET
Published by the Penguin Group
Penguin Books USA Inc., 375 Hudson Street,
New York, New York 10014, U.S.A.
Penguin Books Ltd, 27 Wrights Lane,
London W8 5TZ, England
Penguin Books Australia Ltd, Ringwood,
Victoria, Australia
Penguin Books Canada Ltd, 10 Alcorn Avenue,
Toronto, Ontario, Canada M4V 3B2
Penguin Books (N.Z.) Ltd, 182–190 Wairau Road,
Auckland 10, New Zealand

Penguin Books Ltd, Registered Offices:
Harmondsworth, Middlesex, England

First published in the United States by Signet, an imprint of New American Library, a division of Penguin Books USA Inc. Previously published
in a different version in Great Britain by Macdonald and Company under
the title *Separation*.

First Signet Printing, August, 1993
10 9 8 7 6 5 4 3 2 1

 REGISTERED TRADEMARK—MARCA REGISTRADA

Printed in the United States of America

PUBLISHER'S NOTE
This is a work of fiction. Names, characters, places, and incidents either
are the product of the author's imagination or are used fictitiously, and
any resemblance to actual persons, living or dead, events, or locales is
entirely coincidental.

For my daughter Anna

1

The first scene to show you is a familiar one: a woman leaning over her sleeping baby in its crib. It is a particularly pretty crib decked out in white broderie anglaise. The nursery is painted white, with a border of ducks around the top of the walls. Although the baby cannot be more than about three months old, she has plenty of possessions, including two teddy bears which sit at the foot watching her sleep with glazed black eyes, their arms outstretched. The baby's shelves are well stocked with books made of board, plastic books to go in the bath, and some classics, bought on the assumption that this baby will be a reasonable baby and will not tear up the works of Beatrix Potter.

The baby has a voluptuous curve to her lips, and cheeks touched by pink above a white nightdress. Her hands are perfect baby hands: soft and pink and curled up tight as though eagerly clutching onto life, as well she might. Everything is clearly organized to make her life as agreeable as possible.

The mother has a tender expression. She is in her early thirties, and smartly dressed for a woman at home with a baby, in a well-cut beige suit. Her hair is beige too, with a trace of blonde, shaped into a bob. Her features are small and quite pretty, and her body is boyishly trim. She is, to put it another way, no earth mother. But if you look again into her face, the tenderness overwhelms you. This mother loves this baby more than anything, and the love is so intense it is hurting her, in the way that love can hurt even before the lover deliberately hurts you.

The curtains bordered with ducks are drawn, enclosing mother and baby.

The doorbell rings. The mother jumps. The baby stirs. The mother presses down the Play switch on the tape recorder at the bottom of the crib. Nursery rhymes begin to play, soothing and, the mother hopes, educating the small baby as she sleeps.

"Sing a song of sixpence

A pocketful . . ."

The mother blinks as she leaves the twilight nursery and steps out into the brightness of her main room.

Behind her the windows stretch themselves across a view of the Thames. The boats drift up and down, and the sky shines down on the water, filling the room with space and sun.

In the nursery the baby murmurs and tries to push herself up but fails.

"Wasn't that a dainty dish . . ." sings the nursery rhyme.

She lets out a wail. Her mother does not hear the wail.

The baby lies with her blue eyes open.

The sounds of the day outside—cars, boats, building construction—grow louder.

"Jack fell down and broke his crown . . ." murmurs the nursery rhyme.

The baby closes her eyes and subsides back into dreams.

"You see," says the mother in the bright room beyond the nursery, "the great thing is that you can start immediately. The girl I chose originally was suddenly offered a job in Monte Carlo, and took it. Only the disadvantage is—it does make it all a little rushed."

As the mother talks, she tugs the ear of a pink rabbit.

"It's next Monday you want me to start? That is, if I get the job," says Sarah Adams.

Sarah is fine-boned, with coal black hair tied back in a ponytail, a wide mouth, and pale skin. She has her hands respectfully clasped, as though in church, and her handbag waits by her chair like a well-trained dog. In a navy skirt, cream blouse, and well-polished court shoes, she has an air of seriousness. *She is not like the other flighty girls I have seen,* Amanda tells herself.

"Yes, this Monday." She pauses.

The mother twists the ear of the rabbit. She is staring fixedly at some smudges on the window.

Mrs. Amanda Richardson looks down at her watch.

"You're a management consultant?" says Sarah.

Mrs. Richardson is still examining the blank face of her watch.

"I wonder how long Kate will sleep. She always sleeps well in the mornings," she says.

The phone cries out, sharp and insistent in this tranquil room, which seems for a moment to have lifted anchor and floated off down the Thames.

Amanda jumps up. She looks around as if she doesn't know where she is, or what is going on; then she straightens her face and her skirt and strides out to answer the phone in another room.

Sarah observes the familiar milky dribble which decorates the back of one of Mrs. Richardson's shoulders.

Sarah Adams waits, and listens to Amanda Richardson's voice.

"Yes, at once. Let me talk to him right now," says Amanda.

Sarah stands up, walks to the window, and looks out at a pleasure boat bouncing over the river.

"And check every chart," continues Amanda. "I mean *every* chart. OK?"

The voice is firm, decisive, different from the voice of the woman who had been sitting there dreamily.

As Amanda talks, the sun goes in and the Thames darkens with dirt and time.

On the opposite bank a large warehouse stares at Sarah, and a giant builder's crane stoops down to its work. A pigeon sits on the wall of the apartment's terrace and surveys the scene with the authority of a hawk.

Sarah smiles to herself, and the ordinariness disappears. The changeability of her face is one of the most remarkable features of Miss Sarah Adams.

"We are being paid in francs? That's fine. But the whole point of the presentation is ..."

Sarah Adams walks to the door of the nursery.

"Ding, dong, bell ..."

She puts her white hand on the door handle and opens the door.

"This job is getting out of hand. Geoff's got to pull his weight or ..."

Sarah enters the baby's room.

She stands over the baby.

"What a naughty boy was that
    To try to drown poor pussycat ..."

Sarah Adams touches the baby's cheek and feels the rose softness and smells the sweet baby smell of new life.

"Who ne'er did him any harm ..."

She goes to the wardrobe, across which floats Winnie the Pooh holding a balloon, followed by bees. Inside is a row of tiny dresses hanging on miniature wooden hangers. She lifts one out. It is made of pink cotton with white spots, and it has a lacy collar. It is waiting for Kate to grow bigger. There is something poignant about the dutiful row of dresses in the half darkness, waiting their turns. She puts back the dress.

She presses the wardrobe door closed and returns to the sleeping baby, who is pretending to suck milk as she sleeps, her fat lips moving sumptuously.

"When the bough breaks, the cradle will fall;
  Down will come baby, cradle and all."

The door clicks open.

Sarah sees Amanda's body taut at the doorway.

"What are you doing?" Amanda snaps.

"She's a lovely baby," says Sarah.

"Thank you," says Amanda, trying to let her hunched shoulders drop, her face lose concern. But somehow Amanda had not liked the way the girl had just wandered into the nursery.

On the glass table is a photograph of Amanda with her baby and her husband. It is a color photograph and it is glossy. The adults gaze out as though they've been embalmed into beaming corpses. The husband looks the more robustly deceased. Amanda and her husband have their cheeks pressed together and appear to be propping each other up while the tiny baby lies stiffly, cradled tightly in her mother's arms. It bears no relation to the baby in the nursery, whose breath comes quickly and surprisingly loudly, like a train desperate to go faster, to get speedily into life.

Amanda's confidence has been bolstered by the voices on the phone. She lowers herself with bureaucratic elegance into the chair, but her bottom quickly leaps up to the loud cry of a red squishy duck she has sat on.

She places the duck on the coffee table and sits down again.

"Your daughter, she really is a beautiful baby," says Sarah. "I wanted to have a proper look at her. I hope you didn't mind."

"Of course not, of course not," says Amanda. "It's understandable. Of course you want to see the baby you might be looking after. And I'm delighted you think she's lovely. You see, I had no idea I'd think she was so beautiful. To be honest, I'd never really liked babies. But I suppose one's own always seem beautiful."

"Oh no, she is exceptional."

"She's sweet-natured too," confides Amanda. "Really sweet."

Although there is again bright sunshine outside, a spotlight shines on a terra cotta statue in full warrior dress. The room is bare and white except that here and there the baby's toys and clothes lie around. A striped clown with a red hat sits on the dining table. A yellow plastic hammer lies on the floor beneath the table. A tiny sock curls up nearby.

Amanda takes the notebook into which she's been scribbling details about Sarah and stares at them. She is astonished at how hazy her mind is, as though she has borrowed someone else's. To become close to Kate so that she understands her and her needs, she has had to let go of her own identity and let her mind become at times like that of a baby.

"You know, I'm continually interviewing people for jobs at work, but ... I find it harder to decide on who is the right person to look after Kate ... so much harder."

"Of course," says Sarah in that deferential tone. She sits tidily, with her legs pressed together, as if to suggest that she will be a minimalist nanny, just someone to cope when the real mother is away, someone as neat and untroublesome as the terra cotta warrior. She will not mess up the room. She will just be the nanny, wearing dark blue, polite, efficient, and even decorative in an odd kind of way. Amanda has a strong sense of design, and Sarah's functional quality pleases her.

"It's rather distressing to have to leave her," says Amanda. "I didn't think it would be. Now, you certainly have a good reference from this job in France. Now, tell me again ... you were a nanny in France ... and since then?"

"I traveled," says Sarah.

The phone rings.

Amanda leaps up.

"Oh, I just *wish* they'd leave me alone," she says, then stalks out.

When Amanda has gone, Sarah walks over to the glass coffee table, where Amanda left the duck. She squeaks it a few times and smiles. She stares at the group photograph of Amanda, her husband, and the baby.

Amanda hurtles back into the room. Her pen must have leaked because she has ink on her fingers. She looks down at it.

"Crisis after crisis," says Amanda. "I really need someone who can start at once . . . I wish my husband were around. I'd like him to have met you, but he's in Hawaii—he's an astronomer. He works at home sometimes. But he won't be back until next Thursday, and I need a nanny to start on Monday."

"Yes," says Sarah, "the agency told me that. They told me everything they knew about you both. I thought you sounded suitable."

Amanda tips her head nervously to one side.

"You chose us, then?"

"You could say that. You see, it isn't hard to find jobs. So many mothers don't feel happy leaving a child with a young girl. Mothers often prefer an experienced nanny, someone who knows what to do in a crisis."

"I can see that. Mind you"—Amanda glances at the form before her—"you're only twenty-eight."

"I wanted to make sure you were a pleasant, happy family. That's why I asked for a photo-

graph of you all. And I thought you all looked
. . . nice."

"Er, thank you," says Amanda, sitting up a
little straighter.

"Of course, I presume I'll be on a trial period."

Amanda is not aware that she has formally
awarded Sarah the job of nanny.

"I believe we agreed on the phone that the
position is living out," continues Sarah. "Eight
o'clock until about seven in the evening, although you'll try to be home earlier."

"Your last position . . . I really must speak to
the people you last worked for," says Amanda.

There is a note of panic in her voice. She suddenly does not want to give this woman the job.
But she cannot work out why because she is simply too confused. She suspects it is because she
does not wish to give anyone the job. This is not
a good reason, she tells herself. She must go back
to work. She has reached a very high level
within the company by virtue of her hard work
and determination. The company needs her. She
must go back to work at the time agreed, or people will think she is unreliable. She does not
wish to let down those who need her. If she
weren't to return, it might jeopardize the careers
of other young women in the future. Anyway,
she likes her job.

She recalls her talk with one of the other part-
ners, Jeremy Harris, shortly before she went on
maternity leave.

"Of course I'll be back," she had said. "Three

months after the birth. To be honest, I don't much like babies. All those diapers."

"I quite agree," Jeremy had said, smiling conspiratorially, and she had felt tough, mannish, independent, in spite of the heavy contents of her womb, which at that moment delivered a sharp kick.

Jeremy was in his late thirties and had four stylish children of assorted heights who sat in a row on his mantelpiece in mock marble photograph frames. The children looked as though they had been purchased from an exclusive London shop.

"But," he continued, "they're marvelous as they get older. I wouldn't be without my children for anything. Lavinia, for instance, she is an astonishing child. She makes up the most terrific stories. I think she'll be a novelist one day, and she's only two now. Jocelyn goes to ballet lessons and, well, I have to admit she shows real talent. . . . She has a bit of a cold, so she hasn't been to her lessons this week, which is a pity. . . . But Winston, he never gets a cold."

Jeremy continued in this vein for at least five minutes, at the end of which he beamed at Amanda and told her he looked forward to seeing her in three months to the day.

"Now, darling, don't you go falling in love with the baby, will you? I know you can do it. You're not the type to give in."

Amanda had observed that men nowadays talk about their children whenever the opportunity presents itself. She knew the age, character, talents, ambitions, and medical history of every child belonging to her male peers in the company. Pictures of them were always being presented to her "just in case one of the clients might be looking for a suitable child model." They clearly felt that their affection for their children added to their images. They were caring men. They could blow noses. They attended school plays. They knew where the antiseptic was kept. The women in the company, however, kept very quiet about their children and would make up improbable excuses rather than admit that they were leaving work early for anything more domestic than an important client meeting in Manchester.

At least, Amanda feels, she can trust this Sarah Adams not to keep phoning her up at work. At least she appears to have a measure of authority. Some of the young girls who came to be interviewed were like babies themselves. One of them couldn't hold a cup without spilling its contents. Another was hugely fat with dimples in her cheeks and wispy hair. A third wore a pink jumpsuit which resembled one of Kate's. When they saw Kate they had all spluttered theatrically over her, saying wasn't she *sweet*, wasn't she a little *pet*, before quizzing Amanda about pay and the use of something called a "nursery car," which she had at first assumed was a child's toy.

Most had complained about their previous employer.

She had not wanted any of them to look after her beloved Kate, but had finally settled on a skinny, formal girl from Scotland who, unlike the others, did not look as though she was at any moment about to stick her thumb into her mouth and whimper. But the girl had phoned, in high excitement and a great state of apology, to tell Amanda about the job she had landed in Monte Carlo.

First thing the next morning, Amanda had called the agency Nanny, Nanny and had been recommended a Miss Sarah Adams.

In a fulsome voice Camilla from the agency read out the reference from France, written in stilted English.

"Sarah Adams is an intelligent young woman with dignity. Our four young sons adore her, especially the baby, and we are desolated that she has decided to leave us for the university. We hope that she will return to see us, as we will always be very happy for her to be at home with us in Paris or in the country. We do not hesitate to recommend her for any job with children. She loves all children and has a good rapport. She believes childhood should be the best time of life. She likes to have her privacy, and has reserve with adults she does not have with children."

"Well, that certainly is a glowing reference," said Amanda.

"And I checked the reference," said Camilla perkily. "The whole family loves her . . . and the wonderful bit of luck is, she can start immediately and wants to live out," gushed Camilla. "There's no one else on my books who comes close to her."

"I'll have to see her first."

Amanda knew that at times domestic employers gave good references in order to get unsatisfactory employees out of their houses and into someone else's.

"Of course. I'll send her right over. The only thing is . . . she wanted . . . well, she wanted a photograph of you all before she came over. If you could just messenger one over perhaps? . . . She particularly wanted to see one with the baby."

"Well, I suppose it won't do any harm just to interview her," Amanda had said, and arranged for one of the family photographs to be messengered over to the nanny agency. As Amanda was accustomed to having things sent by messenger all over London, she did not think this an especially odd request.

"Now, how long were you with the French family?" asks Amanda.

"A year. I particularly liked looking after the baby. I find babies . . . comforting. You could phone the family anytime—the number's on the reference," says Sarah. "Only sometimes they're at their Paris flat, and sometimes they're in the country. You might get a caretaker who doesn't speak English. Actually, only the husband speaks good English and he's often away. But you could try."

The baby wails and Amanda leaps up to attention, dropping on the carpet the rabbit she has been caressing.

"What time should I come on Monday?" says Sarah.

"About eight," replies Amanda as she hurries to the nursery. She emerges with a victorious expression, the baby in her arms, just as the phone begins to ring.

Sarah steps forward, offering to hold the baby while Amanda answers the shrill phone. Amanda holds her more tightly. The baby has enormous blue eyes which look at Sarah as though she were someone she used to know but hadn't seen for years.

The phone shrieks on and on.

"Could you possibly let yourself out?" asks Amanda.

2

This scene shows a figure standing by the side of the River Thames. The figure wears a black scarf over her head and an old duffel coat which could well have been purchased at a flea market. The figure moves restlessly from foot to foot, and the shoulders are slightly hunched. Below the duffled person, on the shingly beach, some barges are rusting to the accompaniment of excited seagulls practicing their soars and shouts. The beach also features a wide variety of rubbish, including an old tire, some empty cans of soft drinks, various bits of wood, and the left hand of a glove.

Over on the opposite side of the river, builders' cranes stalk the landscape like prehistoric creatures, raising their monstrous heads behind the rows of warehouse flats. A number of predatory buildings, run by customs officers earlier in London's history, lean over the river as though about to snatch up unsuspecting smugglers. But the boats which bob past the houses now as the figure watches are disappointingly innocent, full of smiling tourists and the crackle of cameras. Up, down, up, down; although the river is rough and threatening, the little boats have no fear.

From the side of a pleasure boat some tourists wave. The figure does not wave back. One of the tourists has a red head scarf. There is something cheery about her red scarf in the midst of all the gray water.

The figure walks along the wall above the water and comes to where some steps lead down to the river.

Some of the bottom steps are worn away. The staircase suggests that anyone can easily walk down or up as they please, passing from one element to another as though from one floor of a department store to another. The water is disturbed by the difficulty it has in getting up onto land, and each time it has to sink back to its own element, the river is angrier. But the staircase remains, taunting it unremittingly.

"Don't do it, darling," shouts out a man painting a window high above. The figure does not acknowledge his greeting.

The figure walks back to above the shingly beach, from where she can see better the large warehouse building. She sits up on the wall. She takes out the photograph of the Richardsons from her pocket.

The father, Tom Richardson, sprouts out behind Amanda Richardson, who is sitting down cradling Kate Richardson. He is in the picture yet not in it. The picture is actually of a mother and child. The father is an extra. He has wild hair and an amused, almost puzzled way of standing, with an arm on his wife's shoulder, as though to say, look here, I know I'm an impostor, I know I shouldn't really be here, but there we are, these things are expected. His brown eyes are transmitting a certain charm, an inappropriate, boyish charm which conflicts with the masculinity of his bone structure. The only grown-up in the photograph is Amanda, who wears a sensible smile apart from a skirmish of maternal love in her eyes. She manages to combine gentleness with vigor. She appears to be wearing gray silk, and her hair to be made of some other shade of silk. As for the baby, well, the baby can hardly be seen. It's a young baby, not yet quite in focus.

From the emerald gates of the Tower Wharf apartments comes a man with hunched shoulders. He is not able to walk straight. As it is only 11:00 A.M., she does not expect to see anyone drunk. He is well dressed and yet everything about him strikes her as somehow dissolute. He sticks out his chin belligerently. His skin is ruddy. As he has only just stepped out into the cold, the cold cannot be responsible. He wears brogues and a tweed suit.

Emerald gates. The Wizard of Oz. The man looks a little like a wizard.

He stumbles and nearly falls on the rough ground of the unfinished car park.

He manages to open the door of an orange Renault after a great deal of fumbling. He tips himself into the car. The car roars backward, then forward, and out down the narrow road between the two towering rows of warehouses converted into city dwellings.

The next man who comes out of the building is tall and young. He has the legs of a circus clown on stilts, and indeed walks rather stiffly. The most extraordinary thing about him is his attire. He wears a dinner jacket with tails and a bow tie. He has a startled yet gleeful expression, as though he has lost his inhibitions somewhere and doesn't know where.

She looks quickly down at her hands. He is someone in the mood to talk to strangers. She wants him to go away, but he is approaching her.

He grins at her.

She doesn't look up.

He takes a step toward her. He frowns, then turns and walks along the road, stumbling occasionally, through the overhanging wharfs.

She is certain that could not be Tom Richardson. She looks again at the photograph. No, Tom Richardson is older than the man in the dress suit.

She feels sad for the young man. It must have been such a good party last night, Friday night, and now he is walking along a hard road to an underground station, his shoulders a little bowed.

Sarah's hands are cold. She stands up. She moves from foot to foot. A seagull rises up skittishly above the rusting barges.

She looks up at the balcony which she believes must belong to the Richardsons' flat.

She is glad that Amanda Richardson has not stepped out onto the balcony. But probably she would not have recognized her, because today Sarah feels quite faceless. She has withdrawn her features, her personality, from her face so that she is just a woman wrapped in a black scarf.

A Coca-Cola can lies wedged in the mud. A radio is blaring out from some builders on a nearby site.

She wonders what is happening inside the flat. Is Amanda Richardson now watching Kate as she sleeps?

Sarah can almost smell that intoxicating scent of sweet young baby and feel the drowning softness of her skin.

She looks down at the beach.

Another pleasure boat goes by, and a number of hands wave in her direction.

She can see the Tower of London crouching farther along the river. Around it stand tall, modern buildings lightly sketched in. Anyone with a good eraser could simply rub them out and start again. But the Tower is solid, part of the damp air and the chill.

She walks away.

She walks and walks and doesn't know quite where she is walking.

How tatty people look, she thinks. London is a bad movie directed by someone who has never been to London: red telephone kiosks, helmeted policemen, and old people with hunched shoulders in shabby coats.

Everything that she sees seems to be happening a long time ago, and that is reassuring. It is as though what had happened to her hasn't happened yet, and maybe it needn't happen.

She finds herself on the grass of a large playground, observing the small children with their mothers, and some fathers on weekend duty. It is a particularly fine playground, with an area for older children which could train a brigade of paratroopers.

One father is dressed in a black trilby, dark glasses, raincoat, and black leather boots. He is ushering around a merry fat child with food all over its mouth. The father crouches in the sand of the infant play area and helps his son make a sand castle. After a while the man stands up, dusts off the sand, places his hands in his pockets, and ambles off a little way.

"Dad," screams the boy, "please can I go on the swings?"

Unhappily the father proceeds back and lifts his son over to the swings. He stands next to a plump lady with a beaming face and an ancient coat, and they both push their children.

All the women at the playground have immense smiles. When they address their children they crouch down, look straight into their eyes, and grin before saying anything.

Another of the fathers wears a fringed black

leather jacket, cowboy hat, and cowboy boots with silver heels.

The women nearly all wear enveloping coats, as though attempting to look like the elephants and teddy bears which receive such acclaim and affection in children's books.

It was the same in the playground she used to visit in Chiswick, near the river in West London: women with children dressed fat, while fathers sought to express that they were important people who just happened to be taking their beloved children out for the day.

She used to like taking Alice to the playground. Alice is her little girl. Sarah loves Alice.

Some days they would go to the zoo.

Sarah and Alice used to watch the penguins standing around in their black and white suits discussing politics, swaying back on their heels before flying down deep into the water, flapping their wings.

Sarah picks up a brown sycamore leaf and tears off the brown parts to leave the skeleton behind.

A boy with the face of an imp is on a seesaw with his mother.

"Bounce higher," he shouts. "Bounce higher and higher."

A toddler in a bobble hat nearly the size of his body sits with his legs stretched out, and watches the sand run through his fingers.

A fat baby crawls over the sand on all fours, crying. As he crawls, his head moves anxiously from side to side like a tortoise. He is looking for someone. His mother's feet appear a little way before him, and the speed with which he moves his feet and hands increases as his cries of loss decrease. Soon he is in her arms.

Everything seems to hold its breath.

Then the child gives his mother a good strong shove with his powerful arms, she lets him go free, and he is off in the opposite direction.

Over on the other side of the playground, bigger children climb through the jungle of frames and ropes as sparrows scatter excitedly around them.

A woman comes to sit by her.

"Great playground, isn't it? My little one wants to spend all her time here. She's the one who looks like a polar explorer, in purple. You can always meet someone to chat to here."

Sarah runs her hand over the skeleton of the leaf.

The woman has a round face which would no doubt have been charming ten years earlier but is merely pleasant now. Lines have been scrawled on the forehead, red color has been splotched too hectically on the cheeks. It is as though her unruly toddler (who is now pushing over some more mild-mannered lad) had been let loose on her mother's face, which is what perhaps has happened, in a way.

The woman smiles devotedly.

"My little Rebecca has such energy," she says

as the little boy whom Rebecca attacked rushes sobbing to his mother.

Sarah recalls a nursery rhyme about Rebecca. The rhyme starts in her head:

A Trick that everyone abhors
In Little Girls is slamming Doors.
A Wealthy Banker's little Daughter
Who lived in Palace Green, Bayswater
(By name Rebecca Offendort),
Was given to this Furious Sport.

She would deliberately go
And slam the door like Billy-Ho! . . .

Sarah blinks and shakes her head slightly to try to shift the words from her head. Rhymes molest her at unexpected moments. She finds herself wishing to turn to the amiable woman, who wears sensible lace-up shoes as though life were a sensible, lace-up matter. She wishes to turn to her and say:

"Multiplication is vexation,
Division is as bad;
The Rule of Three it puzzles me,
And fractions drive me mad."

The woman begins to deliver a speech about the problems of finding a good school in the area. As she talks, Sarah watches a small blonde girl methodically pick up leaves from the sand on

which the play equipment rests. She places a
small portion of each leaf in her mouth and
chews it thoughtfully. Her mother, over on the
other side of the playground, is reading a thick
paperback.

Sarah's favorite skipping rhyme as a child was
the one she taught Alice.

My mother said.
That I never should
Play with the gypsies
In the wood. . . .

"Which child is yours?" asks the voice of the
woman at the playground.

Sarah blinks. For a moment she is not sure
where she is.

"My child isn't here," says Sarah.

As she walks away, she notes shadows hurled
onto the pavements. The dandelions have dust
on them.

She returns to the hotel where she is staying,
near King's Cross station. The room contains a
dark wood wardrobe, a bedside table in the same
junkyard wood, an armchair, some dishrag curtains, a picture of a horse, and an antique chest
of drawers. In the hall downstairs is a photograph of the Queen and Prince Phillip in a cheap
gold frame. It hangs, tilted slightly to one side,
above the registration desk. The crimson flock
wallpaper is peeling. The Sunrise Hotel smells
of bacon all day.

Sarah takes out a pile of photographs from the chest. They are all photographs of Alice. When Sarah reaches the bottom of the pile she starts all over again.

Alice is smiling as she sits on a swing. It is a smile of radiant happiness.

But in spite of the smile, Alice, with her thin limbs, gives an impression of fragility, as if she could be crunched up in the palm of a hand, a tiny bird. She has high cheekbones, questioning pale green eyes, and shoulder-length mousy hair which falls in snaky curls, as though it has just been tightly plaited, then released. She has a wide mouth.

Sarah can hear her voice. She is repeating the riddles Sarah taught her:

"Little Nancy Etticoat
 In a white petticoat
  And a red rose.
 The longer she stands,
 The shorter she grows . . ."

"Now," says the querulous voice, "can you tell me the answer to that?"

There is nobody replying. Perhaps Alice is speaking to her dolls.

"Yes," says Alice, "that's right. A candle."

Alice's bedroom is covered with queer child's drawings, mostly featuring stick people drawn in red crayon. Her dolls sit in a row on her bookcases as though attending a road-safety lecture.

One doll has become separated from its head, which lolls beside the body as though hoping for a reconciliation. All have oddly stern faces. Her father gave her a Barbie doll, and even she is stern, in a frivolous kind of way, as she sits naked on the top of the bookshelf. Beneath her are picture books, tales of courageous mice and foolish bunnies, of circus girls and seaside adventures, all in marked contrast to the life Alice lives in the large, sad house overlooking the river at Chiswick.

The most beautiful doll, Martha, which Sarah gave her, is the only one more or less fully dressed. The others are in various stages of undress, their knickers and dresses and socks having long been abandoned in some corner of a cupboard. Martha wears an extravagant straw hat and white, flouncy clothes, yet even this doll with its porcelain body and rosebud lips has an air of someone in serious disagreement with her surroundings, and has lost a leather shoe. But Alice accepts her and her other more disheveled dolls out of politeness and lack of alternatives, just as people accept unsuitable friends throughout their lives.

On the facing bookshelf is a more wholesome collection of soft toys which includes a dirty polar bear, an unloved sheep, four teddies, one shaggy dog and a pink pig who was the favorite soft toy at the time when Sarah left. The dolls and toys gaze at each other from across the room—rival football teams.

" 'Runs all day and never walks,' " continues Alice's voice in Sarah's head.

" 'Often murmurs, never talks.

It has a bed, but never sleeps,

It has a mouth, but never eats. . . .'

I'll give you another clue, it's wet . . . can you really not guess? . . ."

Alice stares out the window and watches the boats go by on the River Thames.

Alice is missing her mother. It has been over a month since Sarah left.

Alice wears just a T-shirt with a teddy on it to go to bed. Sarah hears Alice's voice:

"The wood was dark,

  The grass was green . . .

  Up comes Sally

  With a tambourine . . ."

Down below, the tops of people's heads hurry along.

3

Let me stop a moment to introduce a little-known character, the chief character in so many real-life scenarios, although severely neglected in literature and plays. Let me introduce THE BABY, at present fast asleep in her crib, eyes fluttering to the universal tune of Brahms' lullaby, looking mild and peaceful. THE BABY is a figure of enormous consequence, never to be underestimated. Watch a baby of a few weeks kick its legs. Oh, the power of that soft skin and appealing blue eyes. Lovers—beware of babies. The baby wants the mother all to itself. It doesn't want the father with his bristly chin. Go away, Father. Go back to your work. I shall wake my mother at night. I shall stare searchingly into her eyes. I will need her so much she will forget all about you. And you will be left alone in your bed. She will cease to buy clothes for herself. She will buy them only for me. I will suck at her breasts. I restore her and destroy her. She will wash the creases of my fat thighs. She will long for me to sleep, and when I sleep she will

long for me to wake. She is in love, you see. Shhh
... it's the secret women never tell. You were
just the booby trap nature set up to send her
hurtling into my arms. All the makeup she put
on and the pounding music you listened to, and
the hot kisses you shared, it all leads only to me,
the beginning and the end of things, a new age-
old bald person, a Buddha giving meaning and
taking it all away.

A young girl's wriggling hips, the roar of a mo-
torbike, the tightness of black leather, it all leads
to a nursery decorated with pink pigs.

And the funniest thing of all, the really hilari-
ous thing, is that few guess it. Most adults believe the central drama of existence is love
between a man and a woman.

In fact, we run the show. We send men out to
work with briefcases when they would like to be
explorers. We twist and turn families with our
gurgles and our cries. We make even the most
sensible childless women go broody and sad in
the coolness of the night. We make a woman
with three impossible, horrid children want a
fourth and destroy herself completely. We make
men stay with women they don't love, and we
make men leave women they do. We make people
completely happy and absolutely miserable. On
warm, drunken summer days we make lovers
forget to remember.

Beware of babies. Joke about their dirty diapers, disparage their eating habits, laugh at their
elderly expressions, complain about the way

they wake you at night, but never underestimate their power.

They are the third person in many a bitter love triangle, they are the menders of many broken lives, they blink their blue eyes and the world turns in obedience.

This particular baby, Kate Richardson, is certainly no exception. Ravishingly innocent, momentously tiny, she is making her steely mother into her slave, or trying to. Her mother is attempting to fight back. It will be interesting to see who wins, and to judge whether whoever wins really has won.

4

"Good morning," said Sarah to Tom Richardson the following Friday, addressing herself courteously to him with a nod of the head. He shook hands firmly. He was tall, with a face which looked as though it might have been created from rock by a drunken sculptor. The knife appeared to have slipped now and again and left ridges from the nose to the chin and across the forehead. It was an assertive face, which softened when it smiled.

"How marvelous to have you here," he said intensely.

Sarah smiled. She was reassured to be part of such a setup. It helped modify her despair. She wanted the family to be like their photograph.

"She's a lovely little girl," said Sarah happily.

"Thank you," said Tom. "We think she's quite magnificent."

"And I love the atmosphere of the flat . . ."

"I'm glad you don't find it gloomy. Some people do." Tom Richardson spoke seriously, although what he was saying was frivolous. "If

38

you're bored, make lists of the names of the boats. Yachts have romantic names like *Fleur de Lys,* motorboats are generally called *Hasty Fred,* but dirty little tugs have grand names. I noticed one entitled *Cleopatra* only last week. As for tankers," he continued with a flourish of a hand, "they have frisky names like *Toots* or *Bouncer*— and of course the launches are all *Princess* somebody. Most entertaining."

"Ah yes. Well, I doubt if I'll be bored," said Sarah. "I've been . . . traveling . . . a bit recently, so it's good to come to somewhere stable."

"I never found out where you'd been traveling," said Amanda, walking through to get a baby's bottle from the table over which a breakfast had been shipwrecked: half-eaten toast, opened jars of marmalade, half-finished cereal among a listless teddy, a jar of applesauce, and the striped overweight clown who had already lost his red hat.

"Our interview was a little disrupted," explained Sarah with too much poise.

She realized she was behaving more like a cocktail party guest than a nanny, and smiled and turned away from the broad-shouldered man in jeans.

"Well," he said, "help yourself to coffee. Grand to meet you," he said. "But I'd better get on with some work." He maneuvered his large frame forward, then swerved to the right. His giant's hand swept a book from a bookshelf which was inset into the wall. He then frowned, ran his fingers through his disordered hair and reversed, vanishing in a quick sideways movement into the study.

Amanda walked through to get the red rattle from the floor by the sofa.

"Tom works continuously," she said. "Work is his leisure pursuit. I was the same," she continued. "Until I had Kate." She shook the rattle. "If only I could persuade myself she was work rather than pleasure, I'd be fine. Puritan upbringing, I suppose. What kind did you have?"

Sarah thought, but by the time she had formulated a reply, Amanda had returned to the nursery.

There were a few prints of former famous cricketers in the area by the door, one with a red handlebar mustache.

She was left in the main drawing room, with its curious shadows and rows of bookshelves.

Sarah listened to Kate cry. She had been working here for four days now, and had already grown fond of Kate. The first day she had screamed, not the baleful cries of an unhappy baby but screams of fury. But she was getting used to Sarah now.

Sarah took off her raincoat. She walked over and hung it up on the coat stand. The sun had gone in. Sarah liked the melancholy light which invaded the room.

She liked the contrast between the resolute flat, with its glass dining room table, and the river, which made a mockery of human confidence.

Even the coat stand had a poignant air. It stood there so smartly, but the coats which hung from it were limp, and Kate's little pink woolly hat sat on one hook, a fluffy caterpillar. The black umbrella was ridiculous too, so comical and traditional like some old joke with rabbits and top hats.

The magazines on the coffee table were plump and shiny, smelling of good paper and pleasure.

The other smell was that of fresh coffee. Despite the dementia of morning with a baby, Amanda had managed to make coffee.

A vase of daffodils sat beside the magazines on the coffee table.

Amanda stalked out of the nursery carrying her daughter cradled in her arms. Amanda took large steps. She was trying to appear the efficient mother, but Kate let her down by struggling. Bits of baby flapped around—hands and feet chiefly, but also a cardigan which hadn't been done up.

Amanda was dressed in a coppery silk blouse and fawn trousers which emphasized her slimness.

Feeling the tension in her mother, Kate whimpered.

Amanda looked down at Kate. At once her brisk expression crumbled, as though her face were being demolished by a giant ball and chain. What was left after the impact was only a featureless softness.

"I have to leave you," she told Kate tenderly. "There is no question of my not leaving you. I have a job. I have responsibilities. We have a mortgage."

From the study, Tom turned on Holsts's "Jupiter" very loudly.

"He plays that half as a joke, half to inspire him," said Amanda, and then she stopped. "You see, it's called 'The Planets.'"

"I know," said Sarah.

"Oh ... not everyone does, you know," said Amanda, embarrassed.

Kate's face suddenly crumpled like a scarlet piece of tissue paper, and her mouth rose into a colossal sob.

"Oh," said Amanda, as if in pain. "I can cope with complaining colleagues ... but my own daughter. Her cries are like daggers. I can tell you, it's an awful feeling."

"I'll take her for a while, shall I, Mrs. Richardson?" said Sarah.

"Oh, thank you," said Amanda regretfully. She passed her daughter to Sarah.

Kate stared sulkily into Sarah's eyes. Sarah launched into her repertoire of baby entertainment, which included winking, sticking out her tongue, and making her cheeks go pop. Kate's tearfulness changed to amazement. But then she decided she was appalled after all, and sobbed and sobbed and sobbed while her mother rushed around the flat like some crazed top, spinning around to pick up something, then spinning around again to get something else from the same direction she had just left. All the papers, the pen, the address book, the baby photographs, were shoved into a briefcase which bulged so much it indeed began to look not unlike a baby. She clasped the briefcase to her.

"Are you ready, darling?" she yelled. "We really must go."

Tom came out of his room with an expression of someone undergoing serious psychotherapy, disturbed but elated. "I really do think I'll get the book done by the end of next month," he said. "And then I'll be able to devote more time to you and Kate."

Amanda walked over to him and kissed him on the nose. "If we're still here by then," she said. She turned to Sarah. "He came back last night from two weeks in Hawaii. It causes a certain friction."

Sarah nodded.

"Well," said Amanda to Tom. "She has to know us in order to understand Kate and Kate's moods, don't you think?"

"I suppose so," said Tom. "Excuse me ... there's just something I must check." He dashed back to the study.

"The book will take him at least another six months," said Amanda. "It's a layman's guide to theories of the beginning and end of the universe. He believes that all the greatest ideas are very simple, and there's no need to write down to people. The problem is he writes very simply, with very simple words, but it's all totally incomprehensible. His last book did well, though, but it's his research he cares about most. He claims he's writing this book for the money, so that we can buy ourselves a country cottage. He says we'll spend weekends playing amid roses. The problem is, he can't buy the time to go with the cottage," said Amanda. "And he has no idea about money."

She took her coat from the coat stand.

"Tom," she called.

He rushed out, grabbing Amanda by the arm and his coat from the coat stand.

"Goodbye," called Sarah.

But Tom and Amanda had already gone.

Kate cried. She cried so much that Sarah deposited her in her buggy and covered her with a blanket and took her for a walk, up and down the dusty streets until she fell asleep. She woke up much calmer and almost pleased to see Sarah, who was good with babies.

Sarah wandered through the flat, into Tom's study, into the kitchen, absorbing an atmosphere she couldn't quite put a name to. She took a book from his shelves: "The greatest mystery is why there is something instead of nothing, and the greatest something is this thing we call life. I am entirely baffled by you and me. We were both there near the beginning. The atoms in our bodies were made then, yet their sum now, in a living thing, is greater than the whole—perhaps the universe is the only way it can be for us to exist."

She read the words again.

Outside the river was greeny-gray. Seagulls rested on barges dappled with white droppings. Little tugs and cheerful little yachts hurried along, bobbing up and down. The distant buildings were hazy—faraway memories—and through the soft pastel shades danced cranes, urban ballerinas.

She liked the underlying sense of control here in this flat; the tablescape paintings on the wall of the kitchen, the confident use of white. The chaos of the breakfast table was superficial, Sarah felt. Amanda was someone you could rely on. Here Sarah felt safe, as though the river would not at any moment reach out and grab her, as though her despair was something transitional, as though the reality of things was perhaps this well-formed family unit, headed by a reassuring man and a capable woman who managed well the two contradictory parts of her nature, that of the mother and the ambitious figure in the public world.

5

Late on Saturday Sarah walked to Chiswick and stood outside the big old house where Alice lived with Sarah's husband, George Stewart. Sarah listened to the noise of the water, and saw people moving behind the half-closed curtains.

She too had had a baby once, and she too had been enslaved. She used to give her kisses like a butterfly, fluttering her eyelashes over the baby's cheeks.

Sometimes when she was playing with Kate she even for a short time forgot about Alice's frown, that pained little crunched-up frown.

6

Amanda found work more amusing than before. It now seemed a comedy show put on for her benefit.

She sat at her huge desk and acted out her part as a partner in a company. She wore high heels. She swiveled on her high heels. She answered the phone with authority. She worked harder than ever to try to cover up the fact that she wasn't really there. She kept a picture of Kate in her drawer and looked at it furtively every now and again.

She phoned Sarah every half hour, but if anyone came in while she was talking about Kate, she changed her tone of voice and pretended she was on a long-distance call.

The image of the company was very contemporary, but they held their board meetings at an antique mahogany table to suggest that the company only pretended to be elegant and modern; it was wonderfully traditional when it needed to be.

At two the next morning, Kate woke up and filled the flat with indignant cries.

"I'll get her," said Tom, sitting up straight in bed.

Amanda blinked at him in surprise.

"Well, it's certainly my turn," he said.

He leaped up, his hair even more disarrayed than usual, and grabbed the bottle of formula milk from the bedside table. His naked body lolloped off in the direction of his daughter's cries.

Amanda tried to get back to sleep but couldn't. Her mind drifted around peacefully with images of work and of Kate.

After about a half hour, she got up and went to the nursery, which was deserted. She found Tom and Kate in his study. Kate was watching Tom with her wide eyes, while he held her securely—bottle in hand—his eyes directed at a page of his writing propped up against his computer. The only problem with the scene was that the nipple of the bottle was inserted not in Kate's mouth but up her nostril.

Amanda sighed. She walked over to Tom.

"They don't get milk that way," she said as his glazed eyes stared at her, then blinked as he looked down.

"You know," said Amanda, "I think she thinks you're funny. Look at her eyes. They're trying to laugh. I think she thought it funny to have a bottle stuck up her nostril."

"I am sorry," said Tom to Kate. "I really am. I was just a bit ... distracted. Oh dear, where would the milk have gone?"

Amanda laughed. She would have had to suck

to get any milk. "Don't worry about it. I don't suppose even Kate can suck milk with her nostrils."

"I'll just do a bit more work, then, now I'm awake," said Tom.

"You know, darling," said Amanda, "I dislike those who follow fashions, but nevertheless I do wish you'd sometimes behave a little more like the New Man."

His big shoulders shrugged. "I try . . . I try. . . ."

Behind them, steamers hooted like owls over the black river.

"I never said I was a New Man, did I?"

"I never asked. Next time before I get married, I'll take my husband to a nursery and see how good he is at looking after babies and children."

"Good idea," said Tom, pointing at the words he'd been studying. "Do you think this sounds okay?" He read: "Many people are pessimistic about humanity because to them life and intelligence seem an insignificant part of the universe. But it's quite conceivable that even if life now exists only here on Earth, it will eventually spread through the galaxy and beyond. Life may well not be an unimportant trace contaminant of the universe. One can regard the preservation of our world as a matter of cosmic importance.

"For despite our own species' unprepossessing characteristics, it may have potentialities. If you had clobbered the first fish that crawled onto dry land, you might have destroyed the potentialities of all land-based life. Similarly, if we snuffed ourselves out, we'd be destroying cosmic possibilities. We could well be all the gods the universe has."

"Very good, darling. Of course it's very good," said Amanda. She stroked his hair. "There's no doubt about it, you're very clever."

She wandered off to put Kate to bed.

7

There are days when everything shows off the glory of being itself, and this was one of them. Even the metal rails of the balcony glittered delightedly in the sunshine.

Sarah kissed Kate on the head. It was like kissing warm feathers. She closed her eyes as she kissed her because that made the pleasure more intense. She stroked Kate's arm, then made a circle with her fingers in the palm of the baby's hand.

Babies and children made Sarah feel calm. Besides, the baby added color; a smile there, that heavy-lidded ecstasy as the baby fell asleep, all was voluptuously shaded.

This was no doubt the ideal place to stay for a while as she regathered her strength and worked on getting Alice back.

Sarah took her out onto the balcony. Kate gazed in the direction of the sky with an expression of astonishment. It was quite warm and Kate wore a flowered dress which came down below her rounded knee. The sky poured into Kate's eyes and made them even bluer.

A cloud passed across the sun, and Sarah pointed, remembering how many times she had pointed out things to Alice: look at that cloud, look at the moon, look at the shape of that leaf . . .

The seagulls pranced around the barges aground on the stony beach below. Occasionally the gulls would surge up into the air like young men showing off their aeronautic skills to terrified girlfriends.

On the way to work she had seen a boy in jeans throw his arms around a girl in jeans outside King's Cross station, and the rest of the world became their backdrop. He was tall, she was just a bit smaller; both were fairly good-looking, but the beauty of their embrace had nothing to do with their wholesomeness. The couple's hug was not passionate or tortured; it was just radiantly happy. His arms had embraced her so well, and the girl had curved herself into them.

And then, on the down escalator, a big black man had been carrying a tiny black baby in a white woollen outfit. On the step above, his wife, her tummy still plump from the birth, peeped over his shoulder at the tiny creature, and the expression on her broad face was so delicate it had made Sarah turn away.

She had read an article which said after oil spillages eventually nature readjusted itself to the new circumstances and simply grew different plants and animals in the area.

As she stood on the balcony with the breeze

from the river skittering over her face, the
thought that nature could cope with a lot of pol-
lution kept rearranging itself in her mind.

But when she moved back into the flat, she
heard a child crying. She frowned. She knew
there aren't any other children living in this
building, and then she realized it was Alice
crying.

Sarah was still holding Kate, who was struggling, irritated by the way Sarah had turned
from softness to a statue. Sarah put Kate down
abruptly on the carpet. Lying on her back like a
tortoise which can't turn itself the right way up,
Kate bellowed.

Sarah sat down on the sofa. She could still
hear Alice sobbing. Sarah put her hands to her
ears, but the noise continued, and not even the
relentless rhythm of the nursery-rhyme tape
could smother it.

"So there was an end of one, two, three,
    Heigh ho! says Rowley,
The rat, the mouse, and the little frog-ee . . ."

She began to walk up and down the room. She
could even hear Alice's characteristic sniff at the
end of a bout of crying.

She stood over the glass coffee table, where a
copy of *Country Life* lay open, displaying a photograph of a gray stone Cotswold house swathed
in morning sunlight and surrounded by a box

hedge; the pathway to the door of the house was through an arbor of roses.

Sarah wished the crying would stop. She wished she was not quite so painfully close to Alice.

She hated the crying of children. Once Alice had had a convulsion from a high fever, and Sarah had taken her to the hospital in an ambulance while Alice stared fixedly in front of her, beyond consciousness.

For four days the fever had shot up and down, and at times Sarah had thought Alice would die. It was there she first found just how close she was to her. She had to leave her for a few hours, and all at once, in the middle of those hours, she knew the fever was worse and rushed back to the hospital to find Alice's temperature dangerously high. Wherever Sarah was, she knew how Alice was. She would know at once when Alice was distressed. She was so close to Alice, she felt they were one.

In the hospital Alice had lain in a crib, shivering with cold one minute, her eyelids droopy like some sad flower from a night garden. A few minutes later she would start to get flushed and hot, and Sarah would dab her forehead with a tepid sponge. The small figure adrift in the middle of the crib would cry, a little as she was crying now. Sarah would give her apple juice in a bottle, and switch the fan on so it blew directly at her to cool her down, which made her cry more.

Sarah stayed the night in the hospital ward, and it was like bedding down in hell. The first two nights she sat all night by Alice's crib, finding a tortured pleasure in her inability to distinguish Alice's pain from her own. She *was* Alice. She no longer existed except as the person who loved Alice.

On the third day she happened to see herself in the mirror, and she was surprised to see herself there. It wasn't anyone she recognized. If she had seen Alice there, she would have been less surprised.

When Sarah returned to the house in the middle of the third day of Alice's fever for an hour or two, it had seemed extraordinary that the newspapers which lay on the kitchen table weren't full of information about Alice. They contained irrelevancies about political maneuvers, terrorists, and wars. The flat without Alice was derelict, as though it hadn't been lived in for years. It seemed to Sarah even then that there was only Alice in the world.

Sarah's husband was a well-known barrister, George Stewart, a man of great charm and ruthlessness, known for his ability to sway juries and for the bow ties he always wore. He was as usual busy on a case during this terrible period of Alice's sickness, and only visited for a half hour here and there. He claimed later he couldn't bear to see the child suffering. It wasn't that he didn't love Alice. He did. He just didn't love her enough.

On her fifth day Sarah went down to the canteen for something to eat, and when she came out she saw a little blue tit prancing about on the snow, which was spread in patches over the earth. There was something about the extreme optimism of its movements, and the upward tilt of its head, which made her break down. When she got back, the doctor said he thought Alice was through the worst and could go home now.

Sarah picked up Kate and held her in her arms, and rocked her over and over, telling her that she loved her. But Kate remained fidgety and unconvinced.

She rocked her with more warmth and sang, "Hush-a-bye, baby" which pleased Kate, and after a while Alice's distant sobs too seemed to subside.

Sarah placed Kate on the floor. She sat by the coffee table. She tore an edge off the photograph of the Cotswold cottage. She tore another bit of the picture. Then she tore that piece of paper in half.

She dialed her lawyer's number.

The man's voice was toneless.

"Are you sure?" she said. "I mean, there must be some way. I have plenty of money. It's not a problem."

There was now only about half the cottage left.

"I just want her. Alice. Or at least to be able to see her. . . . Surely? He says I'd kidnap her. He says I'm mentally unstable. It's just absurd. I just want a normal life with my daughter. She happens to need me. She doesn't even much like her father. You are supposed to be on my side. Besides, she's my child. Why, keeping her from me will *make* me mad."

She still didn't like to think about the day when she had left the house. Alice and she had taken their little motor boat, *The Princess*, out that day, on the Thames, steering through the barges and the tugs and the pleasure boats to their secret place, a boathouse at the end of a friend's long garden. Alice loved to play in there with Sarah, who allowed her to look after their key to the rusty padlock. Alice kept it in her little red suitcase.

Alice and Sarah would take the boat right up to the boathouse, with its chipped turquoise paint, and Alice would unlock the padlock, then they would guide the boat into the darkness of the empty boathouse and imagine they were floating through an underground cave. There were stone, slippery ledges around the water. Sometimes Alice would pretend Sarah was an ogre and say she would lock her in the boathouse and never let her out. When they had finished playing, Sarah would let Alice use the key to lock the padlock, then let her steer the boat back home. There was something about the boathouse, with its lapping waves and dankness, which intrigued them both.

Alice liked to be with her mother on the boat, winding over the river, up and down.

"Let's go faster!" Alice would say, pink-faced,

wind in her hair, eyes bright, hands clutching the sides.

Sometimes she would lean out to try to see imaginary sharks in the Thames.

"Be careful you don't fall in," Sarah would say.

"I've got my lifejacket on," Alice would say. "And anyway, I'm a good swimmer."

George had kept *The Princess* locked up in their own boathouse on the front lawn, over the other side of the road, by the river.

When Sarah had left the Chiswick house that last night six weeks ago, she had first put Alice to bed and told her that she would be away for just a few days. She had agreed with George that she and he needed some time apart, and he could not leave the house because he had his work to do.

"Don't leave me," Alice had said drowsily. "We had such a lovely day."

She had been lying with her head on her pillowcase, her eyes blinking at Sarah. Sarah had held her hand. George had always arranged everything, and she thought he'd arrange this trial separation for her too. He had stood in the hallway stroking her hair, saying over and over again, "It's all right, it's all right. I'll make it all right. Just have a rest."

He had been so plausible, as always. His lawyers within a day had traced her—she'd gone to her parents—to tell her he had organized an exparte denial of her rights of access to Alice.

She had been playing cards with her parents at the time and had just played the ace of spades.

"Why would he do this?"

"He wanted Alice," her mother had said, turning over a card. "If you try to see her, he'll get you put in prison. I always knew he was like this."

Sarah had closed her eyes tightly, as she was closing them now.

Her mother and father had never had much to do with Sarah. They had boxed the odd little child up in her room. She had been plain with frizzy hair and had suffered from a sense of dislocation, a changeling child. But then she had grown prettier. As a teenager she used to go to discotheques alone and stand around, waiting, and eventually some boy or some man would come up to her, and she would dance, and would feel a hand on her bare thigh, and he would press her close to him, and outside in the black street they would kiss, her tongue pushing down into his throat, and he would take her home, and she would enjoy the danger of the strange room in a strange place. Perhaps she had been looking for love. That's what people said, that women have sex in order to find love, as though love could be found in some corner of these strangers' rooms. It was true, she would look around in the darkness, or the light, of the rooms when the men left for a moment, as though searching for something, some kind of pattern, some arrangement of furniture, something in the way the light fell, which would explain her desolation and give it substance, which in those days, before she had Alice, was what she thought love was, desolation given shape and form.

When she opened her eyes, for a moment she wanted to shake Kate for not being Alice.

Sarah swept Kate up from where she was howling on the floor. But Kate noted the tension in Sarah's body and continued to howl.

"Be quiet, darling," said Sarah.

Kate howled louder and louder and louder.

"Please be quiet," said Sarah again in a colder voice.

Kate appeared to be fighting Sarah. Her little fists were clenched and her face was scarlet.

Kate was growing hot in Sarah's arms.

Sarah took her out on the balcony. Sarah swayed her from side to side a little roughly, and Kate introduced a short intermission in which she stared at Sarah without crying while she decided whether Sarah really had any malicious intent.

And once she had stopped, she forgot to go on crying. Instead she just sobbed a little, not remembering why she felt miserable and feeling vaguely discontented about that too.

"I'm sorry," said Sarah to Kate, kissing her. "I really am sorry. I won't hurt you, really I won't. I won't let anyone hurt you."

8

Tom turned up at one o'clock in the morning.

"Darling," he said loudly into the darkness. "Darling. I'm back."

"Mmm," she rumbled.

"I'm going to be a Cambridge professor! I've been offered a job as a Cambridge professor! All those splendid libraries! Punting along the backs!"

"What are you talking about?"

Amanda had worked particularly hard that day and had found it hard to switch to looking after Kate, who had been restless.

He sat on the edge of the bed, taking off his bow tie. He had been to a black-tie dinner at some gentlemen's club. It had sounded so tiresome she hadn't gone. Besides, she hated leaving Kate more than she had to.

She managed to sit up.

Their room was starkly attired: white linen curtains which let in too much light, a Berber carpet which was too rough on the feet, and pictures on the wall which were too tasteful. Life was suddenly a great deal more elaborate.

He took off one of his black brogues and threw it into the open wardrobe.

"Cambridge! It's one of my favorite places," he said.

"You're not making sense," she said.

He took off the other and threw it into the wardrobe.

He turned. "You and I, my darling, are going to move to a delightful house in the Cambridge countryside. They think I'm brilliant, dedicated, just the chap. What about it?" He grinned. Even in the half-light the openness of his face was apparent.

"You have been offered a Cambridge professorship?"

"It's the best place in England for cosmology. The still center of the turning world."

He tossed his bow tie into the air.

He began to dance around the room, humming, "I could have danced all night . . ."

"Tom . . ." insisted Amanda. "But, Tom . . ."

He stopped his dance and pretended to peer over his invisible partner's shoulder.

"We live in London," she said. "We have a flat, remember? Two jobs. We have friends. Who offered you the job? Which college?"

"Don't worry, my darling. I have the letter in my pocket." He began to look around anxiously for his jacket, which he had chucked over the oatmeal armchair. He located the jacket, seized it, and took out the letter with a flourish. "By the way," he said, studying the armchair instead of the letter, "you realize this room is a period piece, a testament to our narrow-minded youth. Already the oatmeal armchair has sick stains. And we thought life would continue forever as it was—no sick stains on oatmeal armchairs, no recession, the steady-state theory of existence."

"Can I see the letter?"

"Oh, it's just a letter, one of those things with black type on white paper. The letter is of no consequence. Bang, bang, bang, went a typewriter somewhere typing out our future!"

"If the letter is of no consequence, why are you hugging it like that?"

"We have a different future! Future, as I point out in my book, is what matters." Tom began to march up and down, in dress shirt and trousers and socks, running his hands through his hair every now and again as though composing a major opera. Amanda watched. Every now and again he would swivel around and address a remark fiercely to her. "It's why we humans matter! It's why Kate matters more than us. She has more future. Here in England we pay more attention to the past than the future. That's why we don't care about babies and children. We no longer believe in the future. Once a nation concentrates too much on the past, it's finished. The whole of space and time spreads before us ... and we humans are possible inhabitants of the whole of the universe, and the whole of future time, yet people spend most of their time discussing the Second World War and Agincourt!"

"Tom, it's one-thirty in the morning. I was up with Kate until twelve. Can we discuss this tomorrow?"

He sat on the bed with a bounce.

He gazed at her.

"How beautiful you are. How perfect life is."

"Darling, come to bed."

He took off one sock, then another. He threw them over to the other side of the room. They came down to land by the door, where Amanda would later pick them up.

"How's Kate's cold?" he said.

"Much better," said Amanda.

"You don't seem especially elated."

"Please, I am utterly exhausted. I have to go to work tomorrow. I'd like to discuss it tomorrow."

Tom took off his shirt, then his trousers, and leaped into the bed. Amanda was wearing one of his old shirts. He wanted to make love, but she was not enthusiastic. She just wanted to sleep. She had spent most of the evening stroking and caressing one little human being, and she did not have the physical and emotional energy left to go through the same sort of thing with another eager human. Fortunately, he fell asleep abruptly once she had murmured that she was just too tired.

9

Sarah lay in bed. She could see Alice tossing and turning. For comfort Alice's right hand caressed the edge of the patchwork quilt Sarah had made for her.

In the half darkness her animals and dolls watched her from their shelves, sinister guards.

Sarah closed her eyes tightly. Alive was dreaming. Alice was too warm. Alice could see flames.

She had never had nightmares when Sarah put her to sleep. But now Alice had a new mother, Trisha, a cheerful, calculating young woman with boundless energy for her own pursuits. In other words, the stepmother (well, a girlfriend of her father's really). Trisha employed a nanny to look after the quiet child with the possum eyes. The nanny also had boundless energy for her own pursuits, which were chiefly having sex with as many young men as possible.

Meanwhile, Alice grew sad. It was as though someone had scooped out her heart with an ice cream scoop. She needed her mother. Of course she needed her mother.

Alice flayed around in the flames. Her foot was caught, so she couldn't escape.

"When I marry a prince, I'll keep you in a secret room and not tell him because he wouldn't like me loving anyone more than him," Alice had said earnestly what seemed like months ago. Sarah had just been reading Alice's bedtime story, a fairy tale of cruelty and bravery of the kind Alice liked.

"Once upon a time," Sarah had read, "and a very good time it was, though it wasn't in my time, nor in your time, nor any one else's time, there was a girl whose mother had died, and her father had married again. And her stepmother hated her and was cruel to her and never let her have any peace. . . ."

That day Alice had sat on her bed, thin knees, thin arms, a distressed tilt to her head, as if she knew what Sarah didn't know, that soon this whole life here, with its breakfasts and trips to school and laughter in the garden, would be dissolved.

Sarah could hear Alice's voice talking to her now. She could see the water she was sipping and feel her puzzlement.

"I think about you all the time," said Alice. "I can't sleep because I think about you. I told you once that you were velvet lightning, and you are."

Alice was sitting up in bed.

Alice caressed the blue ribbon edge of her

blanket. Her slender hands were the same shape as Sarah's.

Alice's clothes hung on a rail. In the half darkness they were people chained together in a row.

"I don't know what's true and what isn't. At school Miss Taylor told me dinosaurs were real. Until then I hadn't believed in them. I thought they were just monsters, and of course I don't believe in them," she said uncertainly.

"The thing is," said Alice softly, "that children don't know about the world like grown-ups do. We don't know what is in our imaginations and what is real ... of course I know there aren't witches," she continued in a confident tone. "But the world itself could be ... anywhere." She shrugged her thin shoulders. "In the middle of a red duck, or in the belly of a tomato, or at the foot of a giant eating bread and honey ... and I wouldn't know.

"Trisha kissed me last night," said Alice. "I wiped it away. But still she left a red mark all over my face, like blood. I get scared at night. I get that lonely feeling. I feel I'm trapped inside a ... chocolate egg. When I hear her voice it's like ... barbed wire.

"One day I woke up and you'd gone. I'm afraid one day I'll wake up and the house will have gone. . . . I can see a snake on the floor now, curled up by my old dolls' house. It is purple and red and watching me.

"If I scream, Daddy will come. If I scream really loudly, will you hear me?"

10

"Oh, Amanda, we can afford to live on one salary for a while," said Tom as they strode together, with Kate in the buggy, through London zoo. They were meeting some friends for lunch later at a restaurant by the canal. It had not been easy for Amanda to persuade Tom to come. He wanted to get on with his work, but she was tired of treating the baby like a baton in a relay race: one person takes it until he or she gets tired, then hands it on to the other. She wanted to do things as a family. That was the romantic idea: a man and a woman and a baby taking Sunday morning walks. Tom treated his life as an enormous bramble bush he was struggling to get through. Occasionally he would pop his head through a gap in the brambles and try to burst out, crying out that he'd finished a paper, or a book, or had just had an extraordinary idea, but then he would pop his head back in and continue to fight the brambles. Nobody but she knew this about Tom. When he was out, he appeared eccentric but vigorously sociable. But that was merely because whatever he did, he did vigorously. He wanted to be a vigorous father too, but the brambles got in the way of it. He frequently said, "When I finish this book . . ." "When I finally get this idea clear in my head . . ." and offered her fantastic visions of the three of them taking holidays in exotic lands, wandering hand in hand to buy freshly baked bread, spending all his free time changing diapers, singing lullabies, making sand castles, and taking Kate to puppet shows.

The friends they were meeting also had a baby, but the wife, Jennifer, had given up work and was tediously sanctimonious about it. Still, she tried not to be, and would at least keep saying unconvincingly that she thought it fine to continue to work if you had someone good and completely reliable looking after your baby.

They stopped.

A giraffe turned its head to one side and gawped at them.

"Look, Kate, giraffes," said Amanda. "Look at those long necks."

Kate gurgled and kicked her legs.

"We don't need a lot of money," said Tom.

"Oh, but we do. The amount of money we have will make a direct impact on the type of life Kate has: the holidays, the schools, the memories. You personally don't need any money. You could be stuck in a hut at the end of someone's garden and be fine so long as you had sex occasionally. But not all of us are so cerebral, and children certainly aren't."

"Thank you very much," he said, and sounded genuinely hurt.

"Oh, Tom," she said, putting her arm around him. "It's just that I have a job. I like the job. I have a certain status. I don't want just to throw it all in and become a don's wife."

"It would be heaven . . . you'd like it. You could have a nice little garden, grow your own strawberries—"

"Tom, I don't know if you've noticed. We have, after all, only been married five years. But I'm actually not that kind of person. I'm a person who wears suits and goes to work. I wouldn't even recognize a strawberry plant."

It was a warm day, and the animals didn't seem very pleased about it. The giraffe that had befriended them kept digging at the ground with one of his hoofs as though trying to dig a hole in the ground to get back to wherever it came from.

"Let's see what she thinks of the monkeys," said Amanda. "Imagine, it'll be the first time she's seen one."

An ape glanced contemptuously at Kate and she stared back in amazement, then fell asleep.

The lunch by the canal was good: fried goat's cheese, beautifully cooked lamb chops, a gooseberry sorbet. It was served by supercilious waitresses in a restaurant by Camden Lock, from where they watched brightly colored barges go by.

"Oh, I've never been so happy and so exhausted," said Jennifer. "Since having Titania, my life has been complete."

"She won't talk about anything else," said David, her husband.

"Well, most of your friends only talk about cricket and television," said Jennifer, a sleek young woman with a round face. She turned to Amanda.

During the lunch, which concentrated chiefly on the domestic problems of David and Jennifer and Titania, including the baby's defecatory habits, Tom drank rather too much and Amanda had to get the car and drive him home.

"It's the stress of not knowing whether or not you'll come with me to Cambridge," he explained as she took him to their bedroom and made him lie down. "Oh, and I forgot. Jonathan's invited us over for next weekend . . . I said yes."

Jonathan came from an incalculably rich family and had made himself a figure in the field of corporate law. He had weekend house parties in the grand old style.

"What about Kate?"

"She could stay with Sarah. Sarah's marvelous with her. We could have a romantic time together."

He was lying on the bed with his eyes closed. She felt herself to be one of the Lilliputians and he Gulliver, a giant. The cover on the bed was white-and-apricot-striped linen, and it too had already received a good share of baby stains.

"You go. I'll stay with her."

He opened his eyes. He stretched out his hand to her.

"Or, of course," she said, "we could take her too."

"People won't like it."

"That doesn't matter. All those politicians and those journalists—she's who they're working for."

"They don't know that," said Tom.

"Well then they're blinkered, pompous fools too full of their own importance to recognize the importance of anything unlike them," said Amanda.

Tom closed his eyes again. "I'm going to sleep," he said.

11

Kate yawns. She is wearing a stretch toweling outfit with a Peter Rabbit motif. With her bald head and serious expression she is a minor deity, observing the human vanities and frailties around her. That she should be dressed in anything with a Peter Rabbit motif is outrageous. But of course they don't know any better.

Look at them both. Amanda's hair so well cut, her clothes so well fitting. Look at Tom in his racy green sweater. Look how well they've observed the fashions of their time and learned to copy them.

The newspapers lie on the floor, the headlines yelling out scandals and resignations, in love with change.

Kate lies in her mother's arms, watching the movement of the curtains by the open window while her mother eats. Kate's decision to watch the movement of the curtains appears to be one arrived at after years of thought, and yet she has no years. She has no years and yet she seems to know everything there is to know. She has the practicalities left to learn—how to change a plug, how to cook a white sauce, how to walk—but everything important she knows.

It isn't easy to describe what she knows because she has no language to think about what she knows. She knows that life is sweet, inexpressibly, gloriously so. But these adults' words don't capture the extent of her understanding. Look into her eyes. Look at the laughter, the seriousness, as she tries to turn her head to see more, to take in more. Her eyes are fresh and blue.

On the wall is a picture of a lonely girl on a sofa. Kate knows about that too. It is all in her eyes.

A wineglass glints on the table.

A few months back and there she was, curled up in her capsule, ready to arrive, tiny hands all wrinkled from the long, magic float in amniotic liquid. Knees up, hands around the knees, someone jumping.

In the womb she was old, her face ancient and wrinkled, an elder from some forgotten race.

Sometimes she floated around and around.

"I wonder if she's thirsty," says her mother, but Kate hears only the pleasant murmur of her mother's voice and likes the movement of her body as she speaks.

In the womb Kate sucked her thumb.

They watched her on the screen.

They have a picture of her in the womb,

a black and white map of an undiscovered world.

The womb used to be a private place, but now people gather around, relations, friends, and watch the baby before it's even born, as it swims in its secret chamber.

Some never do get born, of course. Some die before they're born, so all they've known is that long, tumbling swim.

At first it seemed Kate had come to them from a long way away, but now she seems to have forgotten the journey as she adapts to this place where she will spend her life.

Kate is trying to keep her eyes open, but a sleepy content is creeping over her and the eyes are flickering. She gives a toothless practice smile before she falls asleep.

Kate's face changes as she sleeps and dreams. It is hard to know what she is dreaming of, perhaps of her future, perhaps of her mother's breasts, perhaps of that long swim into life.

When she wakes, her father puts her face-down on a rug and starts trying to teach her to crawl. She stares at him. He moves her knees into position. He tries to move her arms. He shows her how. Doesn't he know anything? What Kate is achieving now—the lifting of her head, the grasping of objects—is all unfolding from within her at an incredible speed. She is not learning by receiving information from outside. The information all comes from within herself.

"Come on, darling," he says on his hands and knees, shuffling forward with his mane of hair.

Kate picks up a rattle and examines it with curious eyes while her father crawls over the floor.

12

Sarah took a taxi to Chiswick and, with Kate asleep in the stroller, stood outside Alice's school, a red brick Victorian house with notices stuck all over the bay windows.

She could see in her mind Alice bowed over a book, her earnest face frowning a little as she moved her finger from word to word, trying to read a story about a mermaid:

"Once upon a time, there was a mermaid who fell in love with a human being . . ."

She stood for a long time, in the sunlight, and then walked away.

13

On Saturday morning Tom, Amanda, and Kate drove off for the weekend to Jonathan's house in Cambridgeshire. Kate slumped in her baby seat, fat limbs spreading everywhere, and screamed rhythmically as they negotiated London traffic. Kate disliked traffic jams and lights and complained whenever the car stopped. She also complained whenever the car moved. Tom played the cassette recorder loudly and at traffic lights pretended he was conducting. He was a fast, haphazard driver who frequently seemed to be trying to make the car dance to the sound of the music. Before the birth Amanda rather than Tom used to drive, but now she liked to be able to keep an eye on Kate.

The cries became more insistent. Neither Tom nor Amanda spoke for a while, but both became steadily more irritated.

Kate struggled in her seat belt as though trying to escape.

"Maybe she has colic," said Tom.

"Do you know what colic is?"

"It's a tummy upset."

Tom yanked the car into a right-hand turn and halted abruptly outside a house.

"I think you should sit in the back with her. You'll both be happier."

"Please don't be cross about it," said Amanda.

"I'm not cross, darling," said Tom. "Why should I be cross about a sweet little baby yelling? It would be unreasonable of me. It's just that if she continues to do it, I might turn around and throttle her."

A dalmatian was watching them from the first-floor window of the house, his head to one side.

Amanda unstrapped herself.

"I just can't look after her properly from the front seat. I can't turn around properly," she said.

Amanda kissed Kate even before she closed the back door. She smothered her with kisses.

"Could you close the door properly, darling?" said Tom. "It's a bit dangerous to drive off with it wide open."

Kate paused to watch her mother close the door.

They drove on. Amanda felt Kate's forehead to see if it was warm, and it was, because Kate has been crying so much. Amanda opened the window and a gust of wind blew into Kate's face and made her start crying again. Amanda fumbled in her bag for medicine to try to bring down what she had now decided was a fever.

"She probably feels carsick," said Tom. "I did

when I was a child. She probably takes after me."

Amanda found this idea obscurely annoying.

"I was never carsick," she asserted.

(The actual reason why Kate was crying was because the seat belt rubbed her tummy. As she had grown bigger, her parents had failed properly to adjust her straps. Her inability to express the reason for her displeasure made her displeasure worse.)

After putting a teaspoon of medicine through Kate's trembling lips, Amanda inserted a bottle of diluted apple juice. (This would of course make her tummy even bigger, and so make the problem even worse.)

"What will you do with her while we eat?" said Tom.

"She can be on my knee."

Kate was quiet now as she sucked on her bottle ferociously.

If Kate had not been quiet, Amanda would have been incapable of consecutive thought, as Kate's cries drilled into her mind, splintering all logical ideas and thoughts and sentences.

Tom began to sing "Jerusalem" with gusto, and to conduct it with one hand.

Amanda gazed out the window at the flat landscape, out of which occasionally sprouted a gray church with a tall steeple.

Amanda made a funny little noise like a "humph."

Tom was driving at seventy-five miles per

hour. Amanda thought it was ridiculous of him to drive so fast with Kate in the car.

"Could you please slow down?" she said.

"Have you thought any more about moving to Cambridge?" he said as he slowed down abruptly.

"Only that it would mean changing my life completely."

They arrived at the gates of Jonathan's house. It was just after twelve-thirty. The weatherbeaten gatehouse had a sulky air which did nothing to prepare visitors for the glorious good nature of the Jacobean mansion, except perhaps to increase the shock upon first seeing it, its curved chimneys reaching up to the skies, as though stretching contentedly for another wonderful day. It had been built in 1592, so its continual good nature was surprising. Most old buildings tend to store up certain resentments over the years.

They drove up through an avenue of sycamore trees bordered by morose sheep.

"You know," said Amanda, "this is my kind of place."

"I know," said Tom.

"Bit showy, perhaps?" she said.

"Showy? Nope. It's exactly what I'm looking for."

"Well, on a Cambridge professor's salary we should be able to afford one of the flower beds," she said.

Kate cried as they carried her through the door. A butler greeted them. He nodded at Kate, as though to acknowledge her and to pretend she was a normal human being who wasn't fat and small and screaming, rather as someone might politely acknowledge a drunk.

"Hello, Robert," said Tom easily. "Is Jonathan in?"

"Hello, sir. He's out hunting, sir."

"Oh, well," said Tom.

Tom immediately vanished into Jonathan's study. He stood urgently pulling out books and turning them over as if he'd never seen a book before.

"I'll change Kate," Amanda called. He took no notice.

"I insist on dealing with Kate myself," she said. His head bowed deeper into a book.

"I want to give you a real break from her this weekend. You deserve it," she continued.

"Thanks, darling," said Tom, not looking up.

The butler smiled and walked with a stately tread to the car to get the bags.

Amanda marched upstairs with Kate, and Kate's bag, and her handbag, to their usual room.

Amanda placed Kate on the bed and laid out the plastic mat which formed part of the shoulder bag. Kate's scarlet and blue striped suit was wet. Amanda had intended to stop somewhere to change the diaper but couldn't bring herself to carry Kate into a dirty garage smelling of urine and grapple with her on a stone floor.

A frantic quality to Kate's crying gave Amanda

hope that Kate was tired. Quite often an abrupt cessation of crying followed desperate cries.

While holding Kate on her hip, she tied the white broderie anglaise bumper from Kate's crib at home around this splendid old mahogany crib to make Kate feel more at home.

A bunch of white tulips stood on the chest of drawers.

A little above the flowers, on the white wall, was a self-portrait painted a long time ago by their host. The person in the painting was sad and lost and had skinny white arms the way many serious young men do.

Jonathan used to make regular, and agreeable, passes at Amanda before she had Kate.

Kate stopped crying. She made funny little movements with her mouth, as though sucking. Her lips were wet and curved, the underside of a snail.

All at once Kate frowned. She was not where she was used to being. She whimpered. She cried out again.

Amanda picked her up and patted her. Kate regarded Amanda with dangerous kitten blue eyes.

"There, there, darling. It's okay."

She continued to cry.

Amanda stood up and walked with her along a corridor, empty except for the occasional pile of curtains, which lay at the sides of the oak-paneled gallery as though they had fainted in folds.

While Kate paused in between screams, Amanda heard a giggle.

Jonathan and a young woman with blonde hair and the squashed nose of a pekinese emerged from one of the oak doors, his arm around her waist. Her features were in disarray, as though he had kissed her and by doing so moved her nose too far to the left, while the mouth had slipped down her face. Seeing Amanda and the baby, she tried to gather up her features, while Jonathan just gave Amanda a grin.

Kate wailed.

"Hi there," said Amanda, then she took the noisy Kate swiftly along the corridor and back into the bedroom.

With her free hand she switched on Kate's little brown tape recorder containing one of her nursery tapes. Amanda had bought it with her mother from a toy warehouse a few days before Kate was born. She had had difficulty preventing her mother from investing in a particularly charming pink two-wheeler bike for Kate.

"I have nowhere to keep it," Amanda had said. "And it'll be five years before she needs it."

"Five years goes quickly. You'll be amazed. Look, I'll store it for you in my attic. Oh, darling, do let's get it."

I didn't get a bike until I was at least ten, Amanda had thought as they waited interminably at the checkout desk. But she accepted that this was the way of things, and that from now on her mother's purchasing power would concentrate on possessions for her first grandchild rather than her only daughter.

Since Kate's birth, Amanda had often asked her mother what she had been like as a child, but her mother just said, "Oh ... you were a very quiet child."

To the sound of "I had a little nut tree and nothing would it bear ..." Kate fell asleep in Amanda's arms, cheeks still flushed from crying and the battle she had fought not to go to sleep.

Amanda placed her gently in the crib.

"Darling, what are you doing? Do come and have a drink," said Tom, standing at the door.

"What am I doing?" she groaned.

Kate stirred.

Tom came toward Amanda and put his arms around her. Octopus arms, winding around and around.

He kissed her behind her ear.

"I'll be down in a minute," she said.

Kate lay with her head to one side and her hands raised in little fists on either side. She wore a pink sleep suit, and her oversized bottom, layered with diaper, was stuck slightly in the air.

"She's so beautiful when she sleeps, isn't she?" said Amanda, and outside she could hear the wind humming in the trees. Tom put his arm around her shoulder.

His hand caressed her upper arm.

"Sorry to be grumpy in the car," she said.

He kissed her neck with tenderness.

This wasn't an edgy expression of sexual desire. What he was suggesting here, as they stood together, the trees whispering outside, the light from the countryside entering the room with its four-poster bed, was an expression of their mutual solid affection: a man and a woman with the child their love had created, making love once more, calling on the countryside to witness this deep-seated, entirely appropriate, love. And of course that was the trouble, the wholesomeness of it all, the simplicity, watched by the clear light of the Cambridgeshire countryside. Tom and Amanda backed onto the bed, with its lilac silken canopies. Probably this is why you need wealth as you grow older and more secure, she thought, in order to buy yourself the respectable excitements of silk and canopies.

Afterward, he had a quick bath and he dressed and told her she was beautiful and that he loved her. Then, looking amazingly happy and about ten years younger, he gamboled out into the corridor, calling out to her not to be too long.

She ran her fingers through her hair. She smeared on some lipstick and sprayed on her scent. Nowadays she carried a much reduced array of cosmetics in her bag, since she had to carry so much for Kate.

She put on a black cotton dress and stuck two silver earrings through the holes in her ears. She put her hand on her hip defiantly.

She listened to Kate's snorting, snuffling breathing. She didn't like to leave her. Supposing she woke and didn't know where she was? But there were no cats in the house, and the dogs were outside, so she couldn't come to any physical harm. Amanda told herself she would sense when Kate was awake, and anyway would keep popping up to see if she were okay.

She proceeded down the hallway, down the sweeping staircase, past the Great Hall laid for lunch, and through the wooden door into the drawing room with its window seat overlooking the park. Tom smiled at her from the other side of the room, where he was gesticulating about something or other. He became more intellectually active after sex, whereas she became less so.

His smile and his flying hands and laughter dominated the room. He had a circle of people around him. The words came hurrying out of his mouth like passengers rushing off a burning plane. Some words fell over each other. His craggy face and footballer shoulders made him look more like a builder than a cosmologist.

Apart from the circle around him, there were two satellite groups of two people, conversing sporadically.

Jonathan was not yet in the room. He made a point of not coming down for drinks before lunch until everyone else had arrived. Those who had not visited the house before became uneasy at not having their host in case they had somehow been impolite in not seeking him out. This helped to build up tension so that his eventual arrival had an effect. Such small dramas were illustrative of a skillful stage managing by Jonathan, who treated his life as a play he both directed and starred in, in contrast to many people who only have walk-on parts in their own life story.

Amanda knew a few of the guests. She knew Tony Smithson, who was tall and blundering but clever, especially on foreign policy, the area he covered for his newspaper. His flesh had not been tailored to suit his body. His face had been particularly badly designed. It was embedded in a penumbra of extra flesh, almost as though someone had pushed it too far in. His eyes gazed out in alarm as if to demand instant assistance with the bully who was doing this to him. He had a pair of square glasses, which did nothing to disguise his horror. He used them partly to see but also to attempt—unsuccessfully, as it happened—to give himself a more aggressive air.

Tony had a plump stomach which clearly wanted to escape from the restrictions of daily life, and was making a dash for it over the top of his trousers.

The trousers were imitation elephant's legs: they were bountifully creased.

"Hello, Amanda," he said, bumping into a chair as he moved toward her.

He butted her at the side of her face, which was his version of a kiss.

"How are you?"

Tony had a good-hearted air. Amanda liked him. She meant to ask him about his recent travels, but instead she found herself telling him that she had her baby with her.

Tony, who wasn't married, nodded. His eyes wandered to where Tom was standing talking to one of America's leading physicists. He looked longingly in that direction, and Amanda took him by the arm into the group surrounding the physicist, who was talking to the floor.

"I so much wanted to know what you were saying that I dragged poor Tony over," she said.

"This is my wife, Amanda," said Tom.

"James Peterson," said the physicist. "My name is James. How do you both do?"

Amanda had actually met him before, but he was shy and didn't dare look at her and therefore didn't recognize her.

James's face seldom unraveled out of a deep frown, as though he were constantly wishing he might disappear. He spent most of his time gazing at his shoes, perhaps in the hope that his feet might vanish first.

His voice was so soft it was almost inaudible, and because of his shyness, the closer anyone moved toward him, the more he edged away, thus making conversation with him a bizarre mating dance.

Over on the other side of the room was William Softon, whom Amanda had sat next to at dinner on her most recent visit there, when she had been so enormously pregnant that no one had taken much notice of her, except to glance at her tummy in alarm.

William Softon was a Conservative MP who was always a bit melancholy when visiting Jonathan's house, for he would very much have liked to own it to sit in the most important position at the table.

He spoke with enormous confidence about nothing in particular and paused, with a little smile, as though listening to thunderous applause.

He looked a little like a seal, with a big top half tailoring away to small feet. He wore hats a lot, since he was getting bald, and open-necked shirts, but seemed uncomfortable in them. His long nose tilted slightly upward, as though awaiting the arrival of a multi-colored ball.

William Softon was talking to Rachel, a woman with bleached white hair and an intelligent face.

William was not aware that Rachel was left-wing and that she had one of London's sharpest tongues. Indeed, he did not really know much about other people. He always meant to find out all about them, just as soon as he'd finished whatever it was he had to say.

Rachel had that grim, pleasant expression which meant she was building up to say something really unpleasant.

She leaned forward, with a feline smile and metallic eyes.

"I think you are one of the most pompous oafs I've ever met," she said, turning and walking away.

He watched her walk away.

Amanda pretended she had not heard this exchange and asked William if he had had a nice journey.

William stood there blinking his eyes.

She remembered as a child the swooping faces which used to come down at her demanding kisses, and how ugly they had been and how frightening.

"I said, did you have a good journey?" she insisted, as though William was hard of hearing.

"Oh yes, Amanda," he said. "Terrific."

The blonde, pekinese-nosed girl was talking to Tom.

She was standing close to him, and he was grinning at her—that open, innocent grin, bending his head down sympathetically. For a moment he looked to her wholly lovable in his canary yellow sweater, his unlikely hair, his jeans, the clumsiness of his movements. He was talking avidly, gesturing, frowning, hands shooting out here and there like someone breakdancing.

She wondered if the pekinese woman had come with anyone.

Laughter came out of the girl's perfectly painted lips.

"Hello," said a man's gleeful voice, "may I introduce myself? My name is George Stewart."

The gentleman wore a pin-striped suit and an air of mischievous good humor. Sunlight glinted on his round glasses. He was a little overweight but agreeably so, almost as though his weight was a joke, like his round glasses and the scarlet bow tie which adorned his neck.

"Are you here with anyone," he asked, leaning back on his heels.

"With Tom, over there," she said. "And you?"

"With my friend Trisha. I'm a barrister and I'm doing some work for a friend of Jonathan's, so he asked us here. Have you been before?"

"Yes. It's beautiful, don't you think?"

"Indeed," said George Stewart.

14

Kate is not sleeping well in these new surroundings. The crib found for her has a bolt missing at the bottom right-hand side, and so the mattress slopes downward very slightly. Kate is restlessly moving her hands and her feet. The previous inhabitants of the crib—the babies of regular visitors here—had also noticed its peculiar tilt, but by the time they were old enough to complain they were no longer in it.

The mattress is hard and covered in plastic which has creased up into hard ridges. It is like sleeping on craggy mountains, only of course it isn't like anything to her, because she has nothing to compare anything with.

15

Alice stood by the window looking out. She wondered how long it would be before her mother came and saved her. She knew it wouldn't be long. She knew her mother would come for her in the end.

At school the teachers asked her what the matter was, but she wouldn't tell them. She wouldn't tell anyone but her mother. And what she wanted to tell her mother was that she missed her. Her father and Trisha fought too much. Their words came out of their mouths like worms. She didn't like the way her father's mouth was loose and slobbery when he drank.

She looked at a photograph of her mother as a child. She had been just like Alice was now. Alice was Sarah, and Sarah was Alice.

Perhaps she could climb out the window and escape that way. But she knew she was still too young. Even if she got away, what would she do then? She didn't know enough about the world, she knew that. She couldn't read the signs on the streets. She didn't have money. She didn't really know which were the bad men and which were the good. Mind you, adults didn't really know that either. People thought her father was good, but she wasn't sure. A man who her father said was a lawyer like him had come to see Alice and asked her about her mother. She had sat facing the lawyer in the drawing room. The paintings on the walls had watched them: the sheep, the horses, the people, especially her father's portrait. Alice had stared at her feet, as she had seen little girls do in films when they didn't want to talk. She had been wearing a dress covered in roses that her mother had bought her, and as the man talked to her she kept thinking of going into the shop with her mother and her mother laughing. Her mother had a beautiful laugh. Alice just kept nodding her head as the lawyer talked, hunched up on a chair in front of her. He wore black shoes like beetles on parade.

"Of course, your mother has a lot of emotional problems," he was saying. "Was she ever cruel to you? And what about her tempers?"

Alice didn't want to reply to the awful man's questions. He had a silly mustache which jumped up and down above his mouth. So she just sat staring at her shoes and nodding.

She tried not to listen to what he was saying. He had a spiky, hedgehog voice. She just kept nodding her head.

At school she worked hard to learn more, even though the teachers disapproved of children reading early. But Alice didn't want to be a prisoner in childhood. She wanted to be able to read the letters of the alphabet with which adults told each other secrets by writing.

Of course her mother had tried to phone, Alice knew that. But they wouldn't let Alice talk to her.

Nobody knew all kinds of things about the new nanny and Trisha, how they told her she was too old for a night light, how Trisha slapped her sometimes when no one was looking.

She knew the teachers were confused about her, because she was clever in lessons and took in information. And yet Alice hadn't been happy talking to the teachers or the other children since her mother had gone. "She is not quite here," she had heard them say to each other. And of course she wasn't. She was with her mother. She loved her mother. And she would soon be with her mother in real life, she knew it. And then everything would be all right. Her mother was clever. She would find a way to save her. Or maybe her mother would just come back and Trisha would go, and that would be that.

At school Alice drew pictures with crayons.

"She only uses blacks and browns and reds," said the teachers to each other.

"Why don't you draw a nice cheerful picture?" asked one of the teachers.

"I don't want to," Alice said.

The teachers had looked at each other, and reading those kinds of secret glances was like trying to read long words. Alice wanted to be able to read difficult words.

She didn't mention her mother to anyone—not to the teachers, not to the lawyer, not to her father—because she feared that by mentioning her to anyone, she would change her so that she was no longer the same mother whom she last saw.

Alice did not like Trisha. On Friday she was wearing a green dress with red splotches. She came back from lunch very late, she wobbled on her heels and words kept escaping from her mouth; then she looked surprised, as though she hadn't known they were coming out. She began to look as though Alice had painted her: the red lips, the head, which kind of hung to one side, the thin arms, the messy dress.

"I'm hungry," Alice said. Trisha followed her into the kitchen.

Trisha watched as Alice poured herself a bowl of corn flakes and took a bottle of milk down from the fridge.

"You've spilt some, darling," said Trisha.

"Only a bit," said Alice.

Alice switched on the television.

Tom was thinking up ways of killing Jerry. He slammed a chair on his head, but the mouse escaped. Trisha smiled. She was watching Alice.

"You know, you're too pale, Alice. You should get more exercise," she said.

Tom was putting a gun into the mouse hole.

"I really should like to be friends. But you don't make it easy for me," said Trisha.

Jerry ran very fast, on tiptoe, and stuck a pin into Tom's bottom.

Alice smiled. She liked television. She liked the way it closed off everything else. There was just the brightness and the picture and very simple things happening. All around the television everything was complicated and puzzled. The coffee mug from which Trisha was drinking had birds flying around it, twirling and swirling.

Tom had Jerry by the tail and was about to drop him out the window.

"You should go and play at friends' houses," said Trisha. "It's good to have friends. It makes you socially well adjusted."

She threw her words down as though she were throwing them into a big bowl, and as they reached the bowl they began to lose shape and become something else, a kind of sloppy, melty unhappiness.

Jerry was eating a piece of cheese while Tom crept toward him.

"I'm going to marry your father, you know," said Trisha. "I love him. And I'm really very fond of you. I think you're a lovely little thing."

Alice nodded.

Perhaps I should find a way to stop all this, thought Alice. *Perhaps it was all Trisha's fault,* she decided. *Perhaps I should stand up very big like Elizabeth Taylor when she was small and be very brave like children in films and say, "You must bring my mother back."*

The cartoons were over and now there was

some horrible game show where children had to knock bottles down. She had finished her snack. She wanted to go to her room now and see if she could try to talk to her mother again.

She put her bowl in the dishwasher and began to walk away.

"Where are you going?" said Trisha. "I wanted a proper talk with you." She swayed. She was worse than a witch, thought Alice. She took potions to change herself into somebody else.

She liked her like this even less than her more ordinary self.

Alice turned. She felt that Trisha wanted to tell her something.

"Who did you have lunch with?" said Alice.

"Oh, a friend of mine." She smiled in a funny kind of way. "It was a lovely lunch."

"I hope you ate a lot. Can I go now?"

Trisha followed her a little way down the hall, swaying like someone on a boat.

Alice went on walking. She wished she could take Trisha apart, crayon her here and there, then glue her together properly, so that she looked like her real mother.

She had told her father that she didn't want him to marry Trisha, but he hadn't listened. He'd been busy preparing some case, and had looked at her over his spectacles and smiled.

She had her little red suitcase ready, anyway, with four pairs of knickers, two vests, a toothbrush, and the key to the magic boathouse. The suitcase was hidden right at the back of her wardrobe. At night she would watch the people down in the street below and try to turn each one into her mother. She wondered if maybe her father had killed her. It had been so long now. She had thought her mother would come for her sooner. She wondered what was stopping her mother from rescuing her.

She wanted to go again to the magic boathouse with her mother.

16

A tapestry hung at one end of the dining hall, in which some pretty deer were being shot by a huntsman. The tapestry was faded, which helped to drain the horror out of the scene so that the killing resembled a dance.

Jonathan sat on his carved oak throne in the central position at the table, and opposite him sat Tom.

Tom was talking, elbows spread over the table.

"You see," he was saying, "in the seventeenth century the mechanistic philosophy of nature ascribed all creativity to God—"

"I agree with Jacques Monod," said Jonathan. "Chance alone is the source of every innovation: pure chance, absolutely free but blind. . . ."

On the wall facing Amanda, a painting of an elderly nun glared down at her.

She was sitting beside Jonathan, who reminded her of a square Mexican statue, sitting unchanging, determined, and somewhat grumpily through decade after decade.

On her other side sat the mercurial figure of

George Stewart, with his red bow tie and smell of cigars and pleasure. He had a restlessness about him as he drummed his fingers on the table softly.

Curious how often ugly men can be attractive, Amanda thought as he leaned toward her and seemed to ask her to tell him everything possible about herself, as if nothing in the world mattered more. His fingers tapped, his eyes sparkled, his interest was intense—and flattering.

"What about your views on the evolution business?" he said.

He had a round face, with reddish cheeks. Behind his thick lenses his eyes were intelligent and sympathetic. His clothes were just a bit rundown, as though he'd had them a number of years.

"Oh, I don't know, but I do see some kind of magic in it all, something more than chance."

"I know. I have a small daughter."

"Oh, do you?" said Amanda.

"Yes. Wonderful child. Six years old. I adore her."

"I have a new baby," said Amanda. "Well, quite new . . . three and a half months old. Not old, anyway. She's here. Did you bring yours?"

"No. I left her with her nanny."

"Is Trisha . . . ?"

"Her mother? No, I'm afraid not. Unfortunately, her mother ran off."

"Good heavens."

He leaned close to her, and again there was

an aroma of cigars and pleasure. His warm eyes exuded understanding.

At the other end of the table his girlfriend, Trisha Hunt, was behaving in a frothy manner, giggling and fluttering her eyelashes at Tom. She was made of eyelashes and lips rather as Tom was made of huge hands, a huge jaw, and too much hair.

"She wants custody."

"I thought women always got custody," said Amanda in a squeak.

"Not always."

"Of course," she said, "you're a barrister. That must help."

He shrugged. "My wife . . . was an unsuitable mother."

"Oh, my God," said Amanda shrilly. In her mind she saw a black car arrive and take Kate off. "I . . . thought it was one of the advantages of being female, that you got the children."

He was still contemplating her with entertained sympathy.

"Oh, I do a lot of divorce work, and that is far from always being the case. Now that fathers are taking so much of the burden of parenthood, they are also receiving some of the rewards."

"You changed diapers, did you?" she said.

"Never," he said, and smiled.

"So," she continued, "you mean the mother doesn't see the little girl?"

"No, she doesn't. My contention is that if she were allowed to see her, she'd grab her. As I say, she's not a reasonable person. God knows what she's up to at the moment."

"I see. What does the little girl think?"

"Oh, she thinks she misses her mother. But she'll get over it. Better off without her."

Amanda attempted to eat her salmon mousse. She couldn't do it. She put down her fork. She thought of the mother. She felt terribly sorry for her.

Amanda whispered to Jonathan an inept excuse about going to the bathroom and left the table..

She ran across the hall and up the stairs to the bedroom where Kate slept, nearly knocking over a maid as she did so.

Amanda stood over her baby, lying on her back, pink face to one side, limbs spread out, a satiated Roman emperor deep in fat slumber.

The mother must have watched her baby as Amanda was watching hers now, she thought.

She leaned over and smelled the soft, exotic smell of fresh baby. She half closed her eyes with the pleasure of it, and then walked back down the stairs, across the wood-paneled hall, and through the grand dining room doors.

Her mousse lay untouched on the plate. The butler had been waiting for her to finish before clearing the plates away. She nodded at him.

"I actually have this tapestry on loan. Shall I keep it?" said Jonathan to her, nodding at the hunting scene in front of the minstrels' gallery.

"Oh, do," she said. "I love scenes of slaughter, don't you?"

Over on the other side of the table was a Russian playwright who couldn't speak English. He sat there with a blank expression. He was watching everyone's faces, searching for clues.

"Are you enjoying England?" she asked him.

He smiled unhappily at her.

The young scientist who sat beside him, who was also an interpreter, turned to the Russian and said something.

The Russian, Sacha, talked for a while.

"Sacha," said Alan, "says he loves it here."

Alan resembled the head boy of a public school. He had a thin face, lovely dark eyes, and well-cut hair. He had an air of confidence, which was not overconfidence but a perfect acceptance of himself. With it came a certain well-considered sadness. His chin jutted forward slightly.

Every few minutes a high-pitched cry of delight came down the table as the pretty Trisha was amused by something somebody said.

Jonathan's interest had drifted away from Amanda and onto Tom.

The guests' subject was now Theories of Everything. "It's the physicists' term for the theory which would explain the violence of the atom, the existence of light, the pattern of the tides, everything. Another word for it might be God," continued Jonathan. "The physicists are seeking to reduce God to a formula—to a theory. Suppose they go to all that effort and come up with the equation: 'I am what I am'?''

Trisha giggled.

"I must say," remarked William Softon, the seal-like man, who had earlier told everyone about whom he knew at the White House, "I don't find these theories so hard, but then I always was interested in physics and chemistry at school." He bounced the words on his nose, as if each one were worthy of applause.

"Just think," drawled Rachel, "how appallingly unfair it would be if all the really huge topics were only understood by unimaginative people, the kind who managed to concentrate at school on Bunsen burners."

The seal man looked puzzled.

"But of course you find it hard. Why, some of these are immense ideas. Immense," said Tom, throwing his arms apart so that Trisha spilled some of the contents of the wineglass she was holding.

"Sorry," he said to her.

"That's why," he continued, "you don't understand them. Some scientists don't. The Superstrings theory, for instance, is really a piece of science from the twenty-first century which has somehow dropped into the twentieth."

"I think you're very good at explaining things," said Trisha as the butler handed her a napkin to wipe down her dress.

Tom grinned one of those engaging grins which took over the whole table.

It occurred to Amanda that Tom might well have knocked wine over Trisha on purpose. The idea cheered her up.

"Well, my area is more the problem of the missing mass," said Tom.

"Tom is an expert on beginnings—on how the universe began, on how life started here on earth, aren't you?" said Jonathan.

The silver candelabra were vast and ornate, decorated with a swarm of gods and goddesses, nymphs and dryads and one or two goats, all clambering up, or perhaps having an orgy.

It is curious, thought Amanda, *that at the same time as I experience some loss of self, I feel gloriously happy, much happier and much, well, nicer, than ever before. The private part of me is content, even though the public is somewhat confused.*

After lunch, Amanda went up again to see Kate, who was awake in the crib and intent on a patch of sunlight on the wall. All at once Kate frowned, a Churchillian, after-dinner frown, and then that passed as though it had never even been there, as though it were just another ripple over her skin. Then she tried boredom and pouted her fat lower lip. That too passed quickly. Next came puzzlement, creasing her untouched forehead, tracks in new snow. She seemed to be shuffling randomly through the many masks she would wear in her life, rehearsing.

"Hello, darling," said Amanda, and Kate turned her head and gurgled and waved her arms in greeting, enormously pleased to see her mother.

Through the window Amanda could see a cypress tree down below with its great arms outstretched, and the tiny people moving over the grass, playing their games, pieces of a chessboard. The leaded glass divided the outside world into panels, each one a tiny picture. In one picture she saw Jonathan walking with Tom across the sweeping lawn, both with their hands behind their backs and their heads down, portraits of importance, no doubt discussing the Cambridge job.

In another picture she saw George Stewart with his girlfriend. The girl tottered as she walked. Amanda watched as George let go of his girlfriend's hand and walked off toward the house.

In another picture Rachel, who had a reputation for state-of-the-art sexual technique and unquenchable sexual enthusiasm, was leading young Alan into the vegetable garden.

Amanda carried Kate out into the corridor, past the open doors of rooms: in one a woman's slip lay strewn on a bed, silk and puzzling, asking some kind of impossible question; in another a large pair of brogues was displayed in first position by the bed, as though some oversized and invisible ballet dancer were practicing his pliés. Near the shoes, a suitcase lay on the floor, the clothes crawling out of it.

Kate's head rested on Amanda's shoulder.

If only I could carry her all my life like this, close to me, as her head peeps out, observing. But one day she will be too heavy for me to carry for long, too grown up and too heavy.

They entered the door of the tiny chapel.

At the far end a white dove carved from wood looked toward them, its head to one side.

The dove was delicate and questioning. It was waiting here, fluttering here, among the pale blue walls and the golden stars on the ceiling above, and it suggested that this was the reality of things, this gentleness, this hope, this extraordinary tenderness in the tilt of its head.

Amanda caressed Kate's soft head. The top of her skull had not hardened yet; it was still soft, still in the process of becoming.

"Hello," said George Stewart, standing in the doorway. "I-I feel we have a lot in common. I don't know quite why. And I wondered, would you have lunch with me one day?"

He seemed nervous standing there, his hands in his pockets, and she was sorry for him.

"Of course," she said.

"Good," he said. The brightness returned to his eyes, and he turned away. He lumbered down the corridor, panels of gray light falling before him, but at the end he swiveled and waved.

17

On Saturday night Sarah couldn't sleep. She was feverish. She sat up. For a moment she thought she heard Alice's high-pitched voice calling her. She was convinced Alice had found her way alone over the London streets and up the stairs, guided like some cat or dog by love. She held her breath to listen for the rat-a-tat-tat on the door. She got up. She looked out of the window. The cars swished back and forth.

She unlocked the door, stood on the stairs, and called "Alice!"

There wasn't an answer, only the burble of a radio from another room.

She walked back. She sat on the bed. She dressed in black trousers, black shirt, gray coat. She walked down the stairs and out into the night. She hailed a taxi.

Her breath misted up the window. She rubbed it away.

It was raining, and the streets shimmered and the houses were without lights. Everyone was in bed, covers over them, while outside the hard rain splintered over the roads.

Traffic circles and fast roads, night fun fairs for adults.

She examined her white hands.

The taxi driver talked to her as she sat back on the black leather seats.

He asked her where she was going so late at night.

She told him she was going to see her daughter.

"You're too young and beautiful to have a daughter," he said.

"Thank you," she said.

He had a broad, lonely face and a mustache.

She looked out at the houses and blocks of flats with dark-eyed windows.

She saw Alice's face everywhere. Even a little girl on an advertising poster at a distance looked like Alice.

She closed her eyes tightly.

She tried to think of Alice's face and for a moment couldn't remember it. Alice had had so many different faces: that of a baby, of a toddler, of a child.

The driver dropped her off near the house where Sarah used to live.

He leaned out the window. "Are you all right? Are you sure you're all right?"

"Of course," she said, and ran off down the street.

The air was dank and familiar. She hurried

past the solemn houses standing looking over the river.

She stood in front of the house where she had lived.

I stood in the moonlight. Outside the window. They cut me off with their telephones and their forms. My darling. Sleep stirs in her face.

Sarah's head was full of stories—little Kimberly who was killed by her father, the sisters who were locked up in a spare room and starved to death, a child who was shaken so much her back broke like a hinge, Hansel and Gretel, whose parents abandoned them in a dark wood.

She hoped Alice was safe up in her room.

Sometimes when she thought of Alice, she saw her face like a Russian icon in her mind: the face in the center was pinched, frail, white, only the eyes were haunting, but around the face were jewels and gold, a frame worthy of Alice's elaborate heart.

She looked up at the window of the room where Alice slept. She could see the glow of the night light pressing against the flowery curtains. She sat on the wall.

Irritatingly, querulously, she heard, "Humpty Dumpty sat on the wall, Humpty Dumpty had a great fall . . ." in her head.

A group of four boys came reeling down the mall, talking in loud voices. They stopped and swayed in front of her.

"It's late, love, you looking for trouble?"

She tilted her face. She had the same face that Alice had, lying murmuring on the white pillow.

"I'm not looking for trouble," she said with a certainty that confused the four lads, who lurched on through the night while she watched them go.

Sarah knew that George had changed the locks and the number of the burglar alarm and that he'd told everyone she was crazy, even the schoolteachers. He'd warned everyone she must be kept away from Alice. He told them about her nervous breakdown. But she had only lost control with him a few times, and those were all before she had had Alice. The first time was after discovering one of his affairs. She had thrown a plate at him, then another, then another. In those days she had loved him and even desired him. The plates had crashed agreeably on the stone floor of the kitchen.

"You're being ridiculous," he had said, turning and walking away.

Ivy climbed up the old bricks of the square, unforgiving house.

Inside there were oil paintings on the walls, and books on the shelves crammed with the intricate patterns of dead men's minds. It smelled musty. Even the potpourri on the mahogany hall table never managed to drown that musty sense of an unresolved past.

In the drawing room there were silver trinket boxes on the mantelpiece, vases overflowing with flowers on the tables, a whole sense of a distinguished and complex past into which she had never fitted. She had been just a play of light on a carpet, an interesting decorative effect in a room, a symbol of something.

In the drawing room was his portrait: how florid he was, how smart in his bow tie, in oils, plush and red and substantial, while the light, sudden rain swam against the windows and the trees whispered of accidents and alarms.

The high-backed sofas sat elegantly on the carpet, discreet ladies taking tea.

In the kitchen Alice's red and black drawings of stick people hung on the white walls.

Everyone loved George Stewart, admired George Stewart and his lovely riverside house which displayed such taste, wealth, and authority. He was, after all, a brilliant barrister, a charming raconteur, a terrific entertainer.

"You're absent. You've never been here with me," he had said one day before one of their endless parties. "Emotionally, I mean."

He had stood before her, with his fists clenched and his face as red as his velvet bow tie.

"I don't know what you mean," she had said.

"Except when you're with Alice. Then, if I catch you when you think I'm not looking, then you lose that monochrome expression. With her you're a normal person. You're perfectly real . . . but the rest of the time . . ."

"I-I just find all this entertaining . . . a bit tiring, that's all."

"You don't like people, do you? You don't enjoy entertaining."

She frowned and looked out at the river through the tall casement windows.

"I like children," she said, and stroked the shiny surface of the mahogany chest of drawers. The light from the river and the sky caught the diamond ring he had given her. It was a pretty ring. Sarah had since sold it and everything else he had ever given her. She had put the money in the bank, with the other money she had saved during their marriage.

He fiddled with his cuff links. On the dark green wall were cartoons of dead British politicians. The whole house was decorated in an unremittingly masculine fashion. His two previous wives had made as little impact as Sarah had on the dark house.

"You must make an effort tonight. I won't have you spending all your time with Alice."

She thought his hair had receded a lot in the seven years they had been married. Perhaps his aging flesh was the reason he tried to seduce younger and younger women, just as he took on more and more challenging cases to prove his mind was still sharp. She knew by the end of the evening he would be walking with some woman or another down to the bottom of the garden, and through to the secret garden, where he would kiss like a teenager among the wild roses and return pleasantly flustered.

He squinted at her.

"The best thing you could do is get a decent job."

"I like being with Alice."

"I want you to get someone to help you with Alice. I want you to buy yourself some new clothes, buy some pictures. Women are supposed to buy things, but all you ever buy is clothes for Alice."

"That's what I like doing best."

"You two behave like lovers. It's unhealthy. You float around like a cloud or a piece of chiffon. In bed I think when I put my hand out, it'll go right through you as though after all you were just a river mist."

She looked down at her hand.

"You don't love me ... that's what I can't bear," he said.

"I think I probably do."

He shook his head.

"No," he said, "you don't."

With that, he left the room to go downstairs and check the food and drink and put on the music, and turned around to admire the weight of his material possessions: the damask chaise longue, the oil paintings dense with darkness and light, the antique books on the shelves which suffused the room with intelligence and the soothing permanence of the past.

When she went downstairs she found him standing, looking toward the Thames, in the wood-paneled drawing room.

Soon people began to arrive, and Sarah went

upstairs to say good night to Alice, who was sitting up in bed, drawing. They talked. Alice would spend days hardly saying anything and then would all of a sudden want to talk, usually at the most inopportune times. She had first brought up the subject of death, for instance, a few months previously while she was sitting in the bathroom, with Sarah standing by her, waiting to wipe her bottom.

"Do children ever die?" she had said, legs dangling, knickers around her ankles.

"Hardly ever," said Sarah.

"Not even if they put their heads in plastic bags or run across the road when a car is coming?" Alice had eyed her mother with an innocently calculated expression. It was hard to lie to Alice.

"Well ..." Sarah had been torn between the need to keep Alice alert to the physical dangers of such activities, and the desire to save her from the mental dangers of fear. "Of course, yes, they can hurt themselves very badly if they do anything silly."

"And if we die we can go to heaven?"

Sarah nodded.

"And what's heaven like?"

"Lovely," said Sarah miserably, who didn't believe in heaven or hell. "You meet all your relatives who've died. You'd meet my grandfather."

Alice had kicked her feet against the white porcelain.

"But, Mummy," she said, "nothing could be nicer than this."

And it was true for Sarah too. With Alice she never experienced that nightmare sense of distance, when everything moved away from her, leaving her stranded, as though all the objects around her were museum objects from another time and place, which she must on no account touch.

Again, before the party (their final party, as it happened), Alice talked and this time the subject was her career, which had given her considerable trouble since the age of two.

"You know, Mummy, I think I'm going to be a circus acrobat and ride either a tiger or a horse." She thought a little longer. She was sitting up in bed, her lips pursed. When she spoke, it was always after considerable deliberation, as though not one word was being chosen carelessly. "I'll probably wear a gold dress."

"It might be dangerous to ride on a tiger," said Sarah.

Alice regarded her with kindly disdain. "Mummy," she had said long-sufferingly. "You don't understand. When wild animals are trained, they love their masters and don't hurt them."

Eventually Sarah went down the stairs and noted that George was talking energetically to a girl of eighteen who reminded her of a magnolia flower, lush and inviting, with plum eyes and inordinate amounts of white skin. Her hair hung over her eyes like curtains about to go up on some dramatic performance. The girl, Stella, glanced at Sarah uneasily. Probably she doesn't even like him, thought Sarah, but if he tries hard enough she will in the end. He'll tell her all the things she most wants to hear—mostly that she is beautiful but also that she is mysterious, tempting, intelligent, funny, all of which she will be as he watches her with his flattering eyes.

And now Sarah was no longer allowed near Alice. Now Sarah had to sit out on a wall, in the rain.

This time she would take control, for once, she told herself. It would only be a matter of time. She would try to be less passive, more like Amanda. But the problem was she so often felt as though she'd stumbled into a foreign film she could make no sense of, but that somehow she was the star and that she was expected to know the lines. Nevertheless, this time she would know the lines. George was skilled at the games of lawyers and power. But love would win in the end, and the moated fairy castle where they kept Alice enchanted would vanish, ideally with everyone in it except Alice. Sarah wondered if George's latest girlfriend and putative bride, Trisha, told Alice fairy stories. This girl had a banal face, with a snub nose and something unkind in the back of her eyes which she tried to cover up with her giggles and flirting.

Sarah kicked at a puddle.

Sarah had met Trisha Hunt a few times. Trisha, she discovered, had studied mathematics at Edinburgh University, but at an early stage had clearly decided to make a living being flirtatious, which was less hard work than mathematics and anyway, it had, until recently, been a perfectly orthodox career.

Trisha had arrived at one of their dinners over a year ago with a strapping young man, but had spent most of her time flirting with George.

He had liked it. His skin became more glossy when a woman leaned toward him and trailed her voice over him. Sarah poured wine into the crystal glasses on either side of her and made polite conversation. She was good at polite conversation: she knew how to fill pauses, how to steer conversation in the right direction, how to make people feel they were enjoying themselves (by getting them to talk about themselves). She was, all in all, a gracious hostess while Trisha sat there wriggling on her tight little bottom wondering whether if she kissed the wealthy, impressive George Stewart, he would turn into a handsome prince.

Sarah laughed at someone's joke, a crystal laugh, with an edge to it, so that after the laugh had died away it seemed the crystal had broken, leaving splinters in the air. She pushed away her hair with her ivory hands, smiling. She had a swan's neck.

One wall of the dining room was lined with books, mostly in flaking leather. Even his books were prosperous. She had imagined she would spend her time reading in this house by the river, and talking to George about the books they read. But George only acquired books and learning as he acquired other possessions and the photographs of his former wives, which he kept in the top left-hand drawer of his desk.

Trisha laughed and touched George's shoulder. His skin shimmered.

Sarah watched Trisha's reptile eyes.

She had drifted out and up the stairs, to the room of her sleeping child.

Lying there, Alice had seemed for a moment much older than six, as she often did when she slept, a young woman with long limbs, and Sarah experienced the horror of any mother—that each day she loses the child she had, that each day time carries off in the night the child of the day before. The baby is soon gone forever, and only a few photographs and surprisingly vague memories remain, then the toddler rules, stomping through the rooms regally, and the mother is certain she'll never forget this as torrential day follows torrential day of discovery and storms and dogmatism. And then the toddler for whom everyone stopped in the street, whom everyone adored, is all at once gone, one night when the mother comes to see her child sleeping. It's gone in the night, carried off, and in its place is a changeling creature, entirely wonderful but bossy with more certainty, no longer with the uncertain, desperate bossiness of the toddler, who behaves like an emperor who might at any time be stripped of its powers. Here is another child, loved more uncomfortably, less simply, a child who plays with other children, a child who is no longer all yours but belongs to the world too.

Her bedclothes were all over the floor, her mouth squidged to one side and her little hands clenched anxiously. Her legs were tucked up in a fetal position.

It seemed sad that the young human form should have to lie alone in the darkness.

Sarah went over and kissed Alice's cheeks, and Alice murmured something dense and soft and sweet like roses talking.

The smell of her skin was far headier than any male lover's. It gave Sarah a sensation of absolute peace, whereas the smell of a lover was that of a hunter, something strong and disturbing.

The next time Trisha Hunt turned up, she arrived with a repellent grey Scottie called Rufus whom she stroked and caressed and kissed in an exorbitant display of sensuality. The Scottie belonged to Trisha's mother. Trisha kept trying to get Alice to fuss over the dog, but Alice stood back, close to her mother, holding on to her, watching Trisha and the dog warily. The dog trotted glumly over the lawn.

"It was a great idea of George's," said Trisha in her gossamer voice. "A picnic on the lawn . . . I so much wanted to meet Alice."

"Alice, why don't you go and sit next to Trisha on the blanket?" George said.

"No, thank you very much," said Alice, fingering the cotton of her mother's dress. In the damp air Alice's hair spread out all around her. Her pale green eyes watched Trisha from beneath her bangs. That day Alice looked healthy, with a slight tan and a nose sprinkled with freckles, but still her eyes were serious and still there was the wildness there which had been in Alice from the beginning.

"I won't gobble you up," laughed Trisha.

She tried to make a daisy chain for Alice, but her sharp red nails kept breaking through the tender stems. Meanwhile Rufus trotted around relieving himself on the phlox, the pansies, the foxgloves, all Sarah's favorite flowers. He wore a tartan collar.

"I don't like that silly woman," Alice had told Sarah afterward as she sat at the scrubbed pine kitchen table, trying to draw a picture of the dog, complete with fangs.

"No, neither do I," Sarah had admitted, stretching up to put a plate away in the cupboard.

"But," continued Alice, "the look on your face when Rufus peed on your purple foxgloves was quite funny."

Sarah laughed, and this time the laugh was carefree. She was glad to be exactly where she was—in the big kitchen with the old sink, with the walls hung with Alice's pictures, and the flowers they had picked together that morning in the center of the table, delphiniums and lilies.

That night Alice slept badly, dreaming of dragons gobbling her up.

It wasn't until the winter, last winter, just after Christmas, that George had first told her he was in love with Trisha Hunt.

She had laughed, she recalled.

"I pity you," she had said, which she did.

18

Kate wakes crying in the night, and Amanda gets up at once (noting that Tom doesn't even stir). She picks up Kate and strokes her, pats her, until she is still. Then the two of them go to the window and peer at the world outside, watching the cold dawn rising like the moon. The strangeness of early morning clings around the minutes, and it seems that Kate belongs to this period of day, after the blackness but before the gaudiness of daylight. Mother and daughter, awake in the sleeping house, are part of an older world, older than the bricks of this house, older than the oldest paintings here.

The two lovers go to bed, beside the giant's body. Amanda caresses her baby and feeds from her breasts, and as Kate feeds her face enlarges with a dopey, sleepy content.

An hour later Kate wakes her mother by pulling her nose. Amanda looks with surprise into the bright-eyed, grinning face of her bedtime companion.

Amanda laughs.

19

Breakfast was a daunting affair in Jonathan's house. It was dominated by silence. Spread on the wooden window seat was an array of newspapers, all in triplicate. Jonathan sat at his throne in the center of the table, sullenly reading the political pages. If anyone so much as glanced over his shoulder to read what he was reading, he would glare. At breakfast he was a cross between a square mountain and a bad-tempered old bear. He would grunt every now and again, and occasionally made a noise which sounded a bit like "Good morning," when someone appeared for breakfast. But he would not look them in the eye. He had his own personal pot of honey to his left, which enhanced the impression that he was a bear very recently emerged from hibernation.

On the other side of the room from the newspapers were cereal, milk and orange juice, and a hot trolley with a toaster on top and silver plates of sausages, bacon, tomatoes, and fried bread beneath. One of the most humiliating features of this breakfast was attempting to use the toaster, which rebelled if you cut the loaf of bread less than perfectly. An elderly American lady who unaccountably must have turned up during the night was struggling with the toaster as Amanda came to sit down.

"There we are," said the lady, and came back to her seat, next to Jonathan, and began to make perky conversation about the weather, which was indeed very agreeable. Jonathan managed to answer yes and no, but not to remove his attention from the newspaper. As she spoke, a smell of burnt toast interrupted the conversation.

"Oh, my God," she cried, "I've burned the toast."

Jonathan turned his head to watch the woman hurry across the room to save the toast, and then he turned his face again to the paper he was reading.

Amanda had left Tom struggling to put on Kate's diaper. He had the tempestuous expression of a gladiator as he tried to keep Kate still.

"You're learning," she said.

"Don't patronize me," he snapped. "I'm fine. Kate and I have an understanding. . . . Oh, my God, just as I got the diaper on—she's wet herself again. Kate, how can you do this to me, and in front of your mother?"

"I'm starving," said Amanda. "I'll just leave you two to get on with a little father and daughter bonding."

She swept out of the room.

"Fucking diaper," she had heard Tom say as she closed the door.

Amanda wanted a piece of toast, but couldn't face the moody machine. She noted that the Russian was sitting at the other end of the table waiting for his food. Nobody had attempted to explain to him that it was necessary to get his own. When she brought her cereal to her seat, Amanda caught his eye and pointed at the cereal.

He nodded.

"You have to get it yourself," said the kindly American lady. "Get it yourself," she said even more loudly to him.

Jonathan took another mouthful of coffee.

"Anything good in the newspaper?" said Amanda to annoy him.

He slowly lifted his eyes to her. He grinned.

"They are behind me if you want one," he said.

He stood up, put his napkin on the table, and slouched out of the room.

"Such a nice man," said the kindly American lady whose husband, it turned out, was the head of the CIA.

Later, as Amanda played outside with Kate on a rug, she noted that Alan, the young scientist, was wandering off through the vegetable gardens with Trisha. Today she wore jodhpurs and a barbaric red T-shirt. She had a way of standing close to men. Amanda noted with amusement that Alan kept trying to separate himself a little but that she kept veering in. Trisha was an inappropriately urban figure, although her outfit was clearly supposed to suggest an interest in riding.

Jonathan sat on the white ironwork two-seater talking earnestly to a handsome young man who had just arrived, a mercenary who had fought in Angola and various other troublesome spots in the world.

They were discussing a dangerous build-up of weapons.

The weather was hot for this time of year.

Sooner or later, everyone passed through Jonathan's house: soldiers, politicians, barristers, artists, scientists. It was all as it always had been: the woman on the rug with the baby, and in a way happy to be so, while the men sit nearby discussing the build-up of weapons in such a way as to suggest that nothing at all could be more exciting and delightful.

As Tom talked to the economist James Peterson, they walked up and down with their hands behind their backs, staring intently at the grass as though reading their lines. As she watched his strong face she thought again how much she loved him. He didn't seem quite to belong in the world, as she did.

Last night they had made love again, but she had felt embarrassed to be doing so with Kate's snuffly, sleeping presence in the crib beside them.

She tugged at a blade of grass. Kate wore a

bluebell blue dress today. It brought out the blue of her eyes. She had ocean eyes.

The house, enormous and lazy in the sun, sprouted spiraling chimneys and outbuildings.

She was aware that Jonathan was irritated that she had brought a rug for her and the baby to sit on. He kept glancing at it as though it and indeed the baby would be more appropriately situated in some suburban park, with a picnic hamper containing plastic plates. Indeed, his glance seemed to suggest, if he had desired a baby and a blanket he would have made sure that they were there.

He did not like things to be different from how he envisaged them. This did not mean that he was in the least narrow-minded or petty. Far from it; his imagination could encompass the most extraordinary events, including surprising couplings, drunkenness, catastrophic quarrels, but not, somehow, a squidgy baby sitting on a navy wool rug on his beautiful lawn which tipped so gracefully down into the rose garden.

He liked to set things up: relationships, jobs, political partnerships. He liked to be in control, a Prospero in his stately mansion.

He had been delighted to welcome the baby to his house, but had not expected the baby actually to become a guest, someone one had to converse with and make provision for.

Amanda played Round and Round the Garden with Kate. The only place Kate had lines was in her hand. Her life in her hand. Such a sweet little hand. Amanda kissed it. She felt so much better with Kate close to her. When Amanda was at work she had a constant sense that Kate was in danger. But of course that was absurd, something all new mothers experienced when leaving their babies to return to work. She thought of Sarah's long, watchful face and the way she tied her hair so tightly off her face, leaving it naked.

Every morning when Amanda saw Sarah, she experienced a shock: the naked face coming toward her, the tense smile, the way she held her bone white hands tightly together, the way her clothes flowed over her although she wore uniform clothes, in shades of navy. Once she had walked down the street with Sarah and Kate, and had observed the way workmen stared and whistled at Sarah as she walked with her head tilted upward, apparently oblivious to whatever charm the men saw in her. Amanda was not jealous of that. It was Sarah's relationship with Kate which made her jealous. She despised herself for having such absurd emotions and did her best to ignore them, to make a point of being nice to Sarah and to express her gratitude for her excellent care.

As Amanda lay on the rug, Kate lay on top of her, a terrapin, nuzzling her mother's face. And then Amanda felt something like the touch of warm water on her neck, a tiny, tentative kiss.

"Oh, sweetheart," said Amanda. "You're kissing me." Mother and daughter solemnly regarded each other.

"Hello," said George Stewart, who stood over them, blocking the sunlight.

"Oh," said Amanda, sitting up. "Good morning."

"Another gorgeous day."

"Yes."

"Aren't you lovely?" he said to Kate. "I love babies. I'd love another baby."

Amanda put Kate on her back. She kicked her chubby legs a bit, waving her arms.

George crouched down and tickled Kate's tummy. His glasses glinted like coins in the sun.

"You're quite brown," he said to Amanda, momentarily stroking her bare arm.

She was surprised by his touch.

He stood up, brushing the grass off him, his eyes invisible behind the shiny glasses. "It's so wonderful to see someone fulfilled and happy. You see, you're so content with your husband— such a wonderful man—and with your new daughter."

The warm words had little conviction; it was as though he were just trying them out, as he might try out a new pair of shoes to see if they fitted. He towered over her in her sunlight, watchful, and Kate grew restive.

"Do you have a picture of your little girl?" said Amanda, keen to remind him of his responsibilities.

From his jacket came his wallet, and from among the five-pound notes he took the face of Alice: a wide mouth with pale green eyes and a chin like an elf's.

"Lovely," said Amanda, puzzled by the face.

"I think so," said George. "I took the picture a few weeks ago. I worship children. That's why I find it so hard to see my daughter distressed."

He wandered off toward Trisha.

While Amanda intently made a daisy chain, Jonathan came to join her. Kate had fallen asleep on the blanket.

"You have that expression on your face, very amused," she said as Jonathan moved a white wrought iron chair close to her. He would never have done anything so undignified as to sit down on a rug. "I think you're machinating."

He grinned.

"I'm always machinating, sweet. You should know that by now."

"Who are you moving where, Jonathan? We're not your chess pieces even though we do come to sit and talk on your lawn with all the obedience of chess pieces."

"Chess pieces aren't obedient. You should know that. They are until they get on the board, and then they do exactly what they like."

"Well, I would like things to stay as they are." She threaded another daisy into the chain.

"Impossible. Everything has to change. It's the law of the universe."

"What is it you want?"

"I want Tom to be as successful as he should be. He's a brilliant man. He should take the Cambridge professorship."

"And what about my job?"

"You should give it up, or go part-time. What's

the point of two people trying to manage a baby and a job? It ends up with both people being mediocre in their work and as parents. Much better for one to rise to the full heights he or she is capable of, and the other to make sure the family works properly, with help, of course. You should be thinking of yourself as a unit, not as separate individuals."

She rearranged Kate's blanket, hoping she wasn't too hot.

"I find this amazing."

"It makes sense. You'd be much happier."

"I expect all that was fine in the days when couples remained a unit, but nowadays, when they divorce continually, a woman is crazy to give up her career."

"But maybe people divorce so much because of a woman's career."

She looked at him and shrugged. "Maybe."

"Besides, you and Tom will always be together. You adore each other."

"Tom adores his work, Jonathan. You know that. Kate and I are secondary concerns. Why do you want him to take the professorship so much?"

"Well, perhaps I want him to be a fellow in a Cambridge college so you'd stay in London and he'd never be home and then I could win your heart by my attentive presence. Or maybe I don't really want him to be a professor, but wish to appear to be someone who has his best interests at heart, or maybe I just like Tom, which I do, and want the best for him, and for you, because I like you too."

"What is best for someone's career is not necessarily best for their life, you know," said Amanda.

"You seem very keen on your career."

"Not really ... incidentally, Tom said something about you wanting your man in as politics professor."

Jonathan bent down, took two daisies, split the stem of one with his nail, and threaded the other through the glutinous stem.

"Well," he said, "there is that too."

Tom strode over and sat by Amanda. "What are you two up to?"

"Oh ... Jonathan's been telling me about his altruistic plans for us. I'm to be a nice little wife and you're to be frightfully successful."

"I don't think she'd like it, Jonathan. I really don't think she would." He yawned, and stretched.

Kate was smiling in her sleep.

"I wonder what she's dreaming of," said Tom.

"Probably just involuntary movements," said Jonathan.

"Oh, I don't think so," said Tom. He put his hand on Amanda's leg and she was reassured. "I think she can remember what it was like to be swimming around in Amanda's tummy. She thinks it was rather nice."

"It makes economic sense, you see, and sense for the family," continued Jonathan. "One person with everything behind him—or you might say her—can forge forward and get to the top, taking his or her family with him, if someone— a wife, for instance—is there to look after that family properly. However, if both struggle, both getting up at nights, both at times being available to pick the children up from school—why, neither achieves excellence, both stay mediocre, and the family trundles along drearily, with two unhappy, unfulfilled parents who neither put everything into their family nor their work. Tom is a remarkable man. Help him. He looks unhappy."

"What's all this?" said Tom. "I'm fine. Absolutely and utterly fine. Just need a drink." He rolled his sleeves up a bit more, and tilted his head back as if all he wanted to do in life was to sunbathe.

"Jonathan," said Amanda, leaning forward, "I do not want to be lectured on the future of the family. Besides—if our marriage ever fails—the male is, under your prescription, left valuable through this process and the female jobless, careerless, useless, and poor, relying merely on the magnaminity of her former husband."

"Well," admitted Jonathan, "I admit there is that."

20

Kate is attempting to get hold of her toes with her hands and put them in her mouth. Kate virtually never rests in the way adults do. She is always busy. She even resents going to sleep because it means she misses out on learning time, and she has so much to learn. While attempting to hold her toes, she is studying the movement of the cypress tree above her as its leaves keep changing in the breeze. She does not know what a tree is. She thinks it is probably something nice, since she is beginning to learn that life is nice, on the whole. At first she had been terrified of it. She hadn't known whether to trust anyone or not. She now accepts that people are on the whole benevolent. After all, for all she knew, she might have been being fattened up for consumption at three months by the surrounding giants. She is wise to treat everyone with suspicion, but she is also wise to begin to let go of that suspicion and enjoy the sun on her bare arms, and her round face framed by a white frilly cap, and the feel and taste of toes in her mouth.

21

Sarah had befriended some of the residents of the Sunrise Hotel. One of them, Beatrice, knocked on her door on Sunday evening.

"Do you want a kebab?" said Beatrice.

She pushed open the door.

Sarah looked up from the armchair where she was reading. The chair had a thin brown nylon cover splattered with holes through which could be seen the original orange tweed cover. The table lamp did little to illuminate the room, which was a mushroom shade and so damp it could well have grown fungi around its peeling walls.

"Christ. I thought my room was gloomy. Why don't you cheer the place up if you must stay here? Incidentally," she continued, "why do you stay here?"

The hotel rattled as a car went by.

"Oh, I used to see these places sometimes . . . in the past . . . and I always wanted to stay in them . . . I don't know why."

Beatrice had a polished accent which contrasted with her appearance. Her lion's mane of red hennaed hair shot out all around her plain face. Beatrice wore short black leather skirts and fish-net tights which only drew attention to her masculine legs. She was six feet tall. In the street everyone turned and stared at her. She liked to believe it was because she looked so splendid as a woman. She had previously been a man.

Today her makeup was applied even more unwisely than usual: dollops of Pan-Cake foundation, brushfuls of scarlet blusher, caked mascara, and enough eyeshadow for a clown. Her eyeshadow was green, a conservative choice for her. Sometimes she favored red.

"What are you reading? Dostoyevsky? You must be mad reading Dostoyevsky in a place like this." Beatrice marched over and took the book from her. "It'll depress you. You have to avoid things that depress you. You should know that. You shouldn't live here, for a start."

"It doesn't depress me. I told you. I feel comfortable here."

Beatrice chucked *The Brothers Karamazov* on the bed, where it lay, a black rectangle on the powder blue candlewick bedspread.

"Why do you live here?"

"I don't. I am temporarily staying here until I find something more suitable. The old chap takes pity on me, really. He lets me stay cheaply. He likes me."

Sarah stretched out her toes and yawned.

"I'd give anything for feet like that," said Beatrice. "Anything. Look at mine."

Sarah looked; they were as cumbersome as an ocean liner.

"Never mind," said Sarah.

"Come on."

"I'm not sure if I feel like having a kebab."

"It's just around the corner, it's cheap, and besides, you're too thin and peeky."

Sarah took her brush from the top of the chest of drawers and brushed her hair. The chest she dated from the 1800s, but it had been so kicked and battered it was probably pretty worthless. It had lost three of its brass handles, which made it hard to open the drawers.

Beatrice watched avidly.

"Do you have any nail polish on?"

Sarah shook her head. Beatrice was obsessed by nail polish, apparently considering it the very acme of femininity.

"What shade of lipstick are you wearing?"

"I'm not. What are you wearing?"

"Scarlet Dreams. I thought it sounded nice."

"Mmm," said Sarah.

Sarah locked the door behind her, and they walked down the creaky stairs and out into the warm streets.

"Where were you born?" said Sarah.

"Oh, Oxfordshire. But I went to university in Bristol."

They passed an old bag lady who was as usual sitting on the bench as though just about to get up. A drunken man wove his way through them, and then back again to gawp at the extraordinary sight of Beatrice.

"I studied Russian, actually," she continued. "I was Phillip in those days," she said, "in case you were wondering."

They sat across from each other at the Formica table of the kebab house.

"You know," said Beatrice, "you're very lucky. You're beautiful, bright, everything before you. And you have amazing green eyes. Look at the rest of us ..." She nodded in the direction of another corner of the room, where a man with hamster-red eyes and a chalky face was pushing a slab of meat around his plate as though it were a live rat. "He's a heroin addict," said Beatrice. "And Maria over there, with the lovely legs and shorts, she's on the game. Only seventeen." Sarah nodded.

Beatrice ate a gargantuan portion of doner kebab and three portions of rice. She gobbled it up, then wiped her mouth so that all the Scarlet Dreams came off, and nodded her thanks to Sarah.

"You want to go to a bar and meet some other people?"

"No," said Sarah. "I'm not really very sociable. I'm a bit ... reserved," she said politely.

"Look at your long hands, so lovely," said Beatrice. "Are you quite sure you're not wearing nail polish?"

Of course, tourists stayed in the hotel, but not

for long once they had caught sight of Beatrice. The landlord didn't seem to mind much. A fat, sad man called Mr. Smith, he dragged himself around miserably and told everyone his problems, most of which concerned the hotel's plumbing, but some involved the untimely death of his wife, who had been run over by a truck outside the hotel five years ago.

He would spend much of his time with his hands in his pockets on the pavement, watching the trucks go by, occasionally swearing at them, always wearing slippers.

He would shake his head.

"No one's got any money anymore," he would say as he served Sarah breakfast, wearing an apron stained with fat splotches. "I can't afford to employ anyone. I have to do this."

"Well, I only want cereal."

"I've made you bacon and eggs," he said. "The rich are as rich as ever, of course. Nothing changes that. But we lot down here scrape to find a living."

He shuffled out of the dining room, in his slippers.

22

Kate spends a great deal of time examining her hands and sucking her hands and generally experimenting with them. She is interested in their relationship with her, but also in the way they can bash other things and make them move. She especially likes to bash a multicolored ball which hangs above her crib. Sometimes, after careful deliberation, she misjudges the range of her hands and aims fruitlessly into the air.

She likes the effect she has on the world. She likes the way that when she cries, her mother comes rushing and extinguishes the cries with soft words and hugs.

She especially likes the hugs. They soothe her. They make her one with her mother—one bundle of softness. They take away the edges that distress—the loneliness in the curve of a cheek, in the bend of a knee, solitary outlines carved in space.

She practices her vowel sounds—*i,o*—bubbles of sound drifting through time.

23

At around twelve the following Friday, Sarah took Kate outside in her stroller down in the elevator, through the wide emerald doors, and down the narrow street of warehouse conversions that still smelled of cinammon from the days when the spices of the East were stored there.

They walked along the street on the way to Trafalgar Square, to feed the pigeons and look around the National Gallery, one of Sarah's favorite places. A pink candy wrapper gave a weary twirl in the breeze, a ballerina at the end of a long day.

The council flats she passed all had net curtains. Sarah heard the voice again.

"Oh, Mummy ... by the way, I bought some sweets yesterday and I ate the lollipop, but I put my best thing—the chocolate bar—in the fridge ... for later."

Alice displayed her remaining sweets in her open hand.

"If you were here, I would give you one," she said, a little crossly.

Sarah shook her head.

She thought of the games Alice played. They weren't sweet, sentimental games. Her dolls fought and kicked and punched, and then made up. Alice dressed them in splendid clothes, chiefly constructed of tinsel stolen from the box of Christmas ornaments in the attic of the Chiswick house. Nevertheless, the dolls looked scruffy, usually because they had mislaid an arm or a leg.

Alice had preferred playing by herself or with other little girls because in boys' games the people were of little consequence. It was the cars that mattered. The plane was the thing, not the person flying it. Whereas the little girls played games with people: complex, emotionally trying games in which orphans suffered and princesses swept down from castles to distribute mischief or love, or food, or games. It was nearly always the women who waved from the pleasure boats which chugged their way up and down the river. The men didn't seem to have that tiring sense of having to be themselves on the boat, of having to be the person waving.

The buildings and cars were covered by a loose scattering of dust. Poor Kate. What a place to live. There were no trees, only litter and dust.

Children should live where there were trees to climb and space to run in, not roads that send dust flying into their lungs.

Sarah and Kate passed a betting shop.

Farther on, two tramps sat on the road with their legs sticking out, drinking cheerfully.

They crossed Tower Bridge and walked past the Tower of London, which sprawled, a medieval dragon, its turrets marking the sweep of its body. It was old and surly like the river, full of time. The tall modern buildings stood around foolishly in their shiny uniforms: Sixties fashion models showing off their outfits, temporary structures.

Nearby, the Thames ran brown and mocking, bumping the little boats up and down, laughing at the intersections and the brisk cars and the ugly tall buildings.

Twentieth-century people popped up colorfully on the battlements, overpainted toys climbing unknowingly over the dragon which seemed at any moment about to roar and yawn and stretch and fling them all off into the Thames.

What was once the moat was now filled with grass and contained a tennis court and a rusty playground.

Cars and taxis bustled by, the masters of the city, involved in a complex, winding dance, up and down and across the streets.

She looked up at the tall buildings. The sun glinted on their windows.

Sarah could see Alice's bedroom window in her mind. She thought of Rapunzel, Juliet, trapped princesses.

Sarah and Alice had the same green eyes, delicate chins, and wide mouths. They matched. She and Alice matched. Alice's father had snipped them apart.

George used to shout at Sarah in front of Alice. She remembered Alice's frown. She'd never forget it. That was one reason she wanted to work for people who had a happy marriage—because of that frown.

In the last few months before Sarah left, Alice had begun to draw queer pictures, stick men in red and black who gestured and fought. She stuck them all over the walls of her room.

"Daddy, I'm trying to be good," Alice had said, standing at the door of the drawing room.

Sarah and George both turned toward the figure in her pajamas, with the darkness of the empty hall behind her. "If I'm really, really good, will you let Mummy stay with us?"

"Alice darling, you have nothing to do with it," George replied.

Her face was screwed up, someone staring at the sun.

Sarah slipped away from her frame of cushions and in a moment had her arm around Alice's shoulders.

"George, let's stop this," Sarah said. "It's not necessary. We are giving up too soon."

"Look, as we agreed, we should have a trial separation . . ."

Alice stood there, her hand stiffly by her sides, a picture of a nun.

Alice tried to be as much like her mother as possible, and when Sarah was putting on her makeup to go out in the evening, sometimes Alice would stand by her and watch.

"Mummy, you look beautiful," she would say in the hushed tones of someone entering Chartes cathedral during a service. Alice's biggest treat had been to be allowed to brush her hair with her mother's silver brush.

George wouldn't let Alice and Sarah be together. He guarded Alice in his house by the water, had his lawyers surround her. He knew the intricacies of the law rather in the way that spiders know spider webs.

Sarah could see in her mind Alice standing by the window, looking out at the brown river. She wore her faded purple nightdress with a stiff frilly ruff.

Elizabeth I had looked down at the river from the Tower of London before she became queen.

And Rapunzel had been locked up in a tower by a wicked witch, but the prince had seen her and cried, "Rapunzel, Rapunzel, let down your hair!" and the girl had lowered her plaits and he had climbed up.

George kept Alice from her with court orders.

The house was a grand Georgian one, one of those places apparently perfectly at ease with itself: the scarlet door, the brass numbers.

"At first," George had told Sarah before she left, "when I made love to you I thought I'd make you real. Then I thought if I married you you'd be mine. I was wrong."

He stood there in front of a portrait of himself

in a gilded frame, which made him into a figure of stature, a medieval pillar of the community with his suit, his smile, and his twinkling eyes.

"You know, darling," Sarah said seriously, looking up from the tapestry cushion she was working on, "you've always reminded me of Chaucer's Miller. At university I used to find him a fascinating but deeply unattractive figure."

He had pouted and drunk the rest of his sherry, wiping the amber liquid from around his mouth with the back of his hand before turning and leaving the room.

She had in fact found the Miller an attractive figure as she had found George, at first, with his greed for life and his insatiable desire to gobble up all its sensual pleasures, while remaining a respectable figure in society.

Sarah had chosen a run-down room in a shabby hotel as an escape from the terrifying prosperousness of her previous existence. The material possessions—the antique sofas, the oil paintings, the bronze statues—had surrounded her like the treasures of a pharaoh's tomb. They made a mockery of the very worldliness they exalted. At least the forsaken hotel reflected her state of mind: something ragged, incomplete. She needed Alice to make her complete, as Alice needed her. She knew Alice was lonely.

The sun shone on the pavement and sprinkled it with children's glitter.

24

Kate's nose is a tiny bit red, a little clown's nose, and she is well wrapped in an all-in-one checked suit with the hood surrounding her sleepy face. She wears soft turquoise leather shoes. Her eyelashes are big dippers, extraordinarily sweeping protruberances. The buggy has a green-striped cover and can be tilted back to form what was more or less a tiny crib, and it is this position in which Kate slumbers now.

Kate wakes, and kicks her heels and looks around with delight. She likes the big show that is being put on for her. She likes the noise and the movement and the colors.

She doesn't know what the tall buildings are—indeed, she doesn't know they are tall. She just looks straight in front of her and sees mostly the middles of people as they pass—perhaps the most boring part of most humans, but Kate doesn't think so. She likes the way the middles rush up and down. Her eyes are even wider than usual, as though everything that is happening is being poured into her eyes. Her brain can't file it all away because at present she has very few categories of files available. The files don't have names, of course, but essentially the major ones concern nice things or nasty things, although she has recently started a file on funny things.

One action she finds very funny indeed is when Sarah lets her hair loose, bends over so her hair hangs down, then throws her hair back so her head pops up. It is a more interesting version of peek-a-boo. When Sarah throws back her hair, her face pops up from an unexpected place. Although Kate is not yet four months old, she already has some idea of what to expect, and is amused when the unexpected happens.

Certainly babies arrive in the world well equipped to deal with it. Babies, for instance, recognize human faces from birth, have a sense of humor to cope with the unexpected, and fear to cope with danger. Most are instinctively afraid of dogs and of the dark, and rightly so; what wolves lie in wait?

It is curious how few words there are to express what babies are like. *New* isn't suitable: it suggests something just bought from a racy shop, something completely finished and rather shiny. Even *innocence* isn't right because babies aren't exactly innocent. They soon learn to smile, and with a smile they can bring strangers over to admire them and talk to them in that pleasing, soft singsong voice which adults instinctively use to please babies. Some babies are born with anger in them too: they scream with a rawness and rage which lacks any innocence. They know about sadness too, as though the world's sadness is in them from the beginning.

Kate has certainly been born very feminine. She looks feminine—all soft and pretty with cupid lips—and she already uses her sudden smiles to enslave, but of course male babies do that too; it is the way the smiles come, so curvaceous and soft, that make her so unmistakably female.

25

On a street corner an old man with a gray beard walked up and down with his head bowed, a sign around his waist saying "HUNGRY. I DO NOT DRINK. PLEASE HELP. GOD BLESS YOU," as though he were sending a desperate telegram to an old friend. But the notice was written on cardboard, and nobody looked at it as they waited at the traffic lights.

Slumped in front of a tourist shop in Whitehall sat a young, wan man with his head in his hands, and long limbs sticking out everywhere. He had a tin, and his notice read, "AIDS SUFFERER. PLEASE HELP." Above him in the window of the shop, obedient rows of mugs embossed with Union Jacks lay resting while people hurried by.

Sarah hurried on. Kate gleefully kicked her heels up and down and enjoyed the speed and the occasional (very occasional) tourist who dipped down and told her she was pretty.

Sarah stopped outside a women's clothes shop. She once had gone in here with Alice. She'd bought Alice a chocolate ice cream cone, and some of the residue was left around the child's mouth. Sarah had seen Alice vanish into a carousel of white dresses.

"Alice!" she had called.

Alice had emerged smiling merrily, with a clean face, to Sarah's horrified consternation.

As Sarah stared through the shop window she could actually see Alice, back at three years old, her head popping out of a carousel of dresses: radiant, grinning, a comedienne.

Sarah closed her eyes tightly. She blinked and thought, *I cannot bear this.*

Sarah arrived at Trafalgar Square and struggled up the stairs of the National Gallery with Kate and the folded-up buggy.

Sarah went straight to Renoir's *Les Parapluies*.

She sat on a black plastic bench and stared at the picture.

People passed by and stood in front of her murmuring in different languages. She sat for a half hour. Kate occasionally stirred, her full lips mouthing some secret message while her hands opened and closed. Her hands lay over the cotton blanket which covered her as an old lady might be covered as she was pushed in her wheelchair by the seaside. Occasionally she half opened her eyes, decided the place was of little interest, then fell back into sleep.

Meanwhile Sarah stared at the painting.

In the corner of the painting the little girl with a hoop reminded Sarah of Alice, although Alice was not as pretty. Where the fair-haired girl stood, everything was gentle and vibrant while the hard edges and gray shapes of the adult umbrellas filled the rest of the picture. The men had silly pointed beards and deferential mustaches. One wore nasty black gloves. The women looked nicer, but none could match the beauty of the child with her blue coat and lace collar and an inner light which made all the adults dingy. They were standing in the rain, but the child was bathed in perpetual sunshine.

After a while she walked on, through other rooms, and eventually stepped out onto the portico overlooking Trafalgar Square, where people were walking, some after lunching in Soho.

It was there that she saw in the distance, by the lions of Trafalgar Square, her husband, George Stewart, with his arm around Amanda Richardson.

26

Sarah walked fast with Kate. She hated Amanda, she decided. Amanda worked when she should be looking after her child. She embraced other people's husbands when she should be looking after her child.

Amanda didn't deserve a child, thought Sarah. She didn't deserve Tom either.

Kate cried as Sarah bumped her over the pavement.

Sarah was walking in the direction of King's Cross.

Amanda always pretended to be so pleased to see Kate, and so grateful to Sarah, and such an admirable person, but Sarah knew differently now. It was even possible that Amanda was the reason George had not tried harder to make their marriage work. She wondered how long the relationship had been going on. Maybe years. Maybe Kate wasn't even Tom's child. Poor little Kate.

She had a momentary, disagreeable, vision of Amanda's long, slim limbs wrapped round George's body.

It was unfair to Tom, decided Sarah. Amanda was trying to have everything: a baby, a job, a husband, maybe a lover. She thought of Tom's smiling, eccentric face made up of straight lines: a rectangular forehead, a square jaw, a strong, firm mouth. Only when he smiled did all the lines break up.

She carried Kate in one arm and the stroller in the other up the stairs to her room.

Kate sat, propped up by cushions, on the threadbare rug, watching Sarah with enormous eyes.

Sarah knelt down before her and took Kate's two plump hands in hers.

"Why don't you stay with me?"

Sarah sang to her. The voice was calm, and a little eerie, and Kate stared at her as she sang it. Kate furrowed her brow.

"White wings they never grow weary
  They carry me cheerily over the sea
  Night comes, I long for you, darling
  I'll spread out my white wings
  And fly home to you."

Once Sarah had completed the song, Kate began to cry, as though hurt that the song had not really been directed at her.

"There, there," said Sarah. "Never mind. You really are a very lucky little girl."

She continued to rock Kate, looking down at

her eyelashes, the rose texture of her cheek, the movements of her chubby hands.

"Chinese sandmen," she sang softly, stroking her forehead.

"Wise and creepy
    Croon dream-songs
    To make us sleepy.
A Chinese maid with slanting eyes
Is queen of all their lullabies.
On her ancient moon-guitar
She strums a sleep-song to a star.
And when big China-shadows fall
Snow white lilies hear her call.
    Chinese sandmen,
    Wise and creepy
    Croon dream-songs
    To make us sleepy."

27

Sarah was back late, thought Amanda uneasily as she stood staring into Kate's wardrobe. Already Kate had outgrown some of her vests, terrycloth sleep suits, and a purple gingham dress. The outgrown clothes sat in a pile. Kate had worn the purple gingham dress for her first lunch out at the Italian restaurant, and all the waiters had buzzed around her and had wanted to hold her and kiss her. The greenish stain on the top right of the dress's lacy collar was from some mashed spinach a waiter had tried to feed her. Kate had smiled and smiled, then yawned and, when the least attractive of the waiters kissed her, began to cry. She had fallen to sleep slumped, with an air of excess, in Amanda's arms.

It was eight in the evening. Amanda had been back over an hour. She was particularly tired, having drunk more than was sensible during her lunch with George Stewart.

On Kate's shelves stood the fat striped clown with red wool hair and tiny eyes, given to her by Amanda's mother. It had a bell in it, and Kate enjoyed knocking it over. Beside it, lying on its side, was a small pink clown which smelled of lavender.

Amanda picked up a yellow plastic teddy bear rattle, which had red arms and blue legs sticking out from its round stomach. Strange how most toys for babies exalted fatness. She shook the rattle.

Amanda had had to keep all the presents Kate had been given, including a giant-sized rubbery spoon, knife, and fork set which cried out when you bent them. The faces all displayed alarm, almost as though people had been imprisoned inside them. Her friend Caroline had given her these, saying her son loved his set.

Amanda wound up the music box to Kate's battery-operated mobile. It played the tune, but not the words, of Brahms' lullaby.

Kate's favorite toy, a Humpty Dumpty in the guise of a schoolboy, sat perkily at the bottom of her crib. She loved Amanda to put the Humpty Dumpty on the edge of the table, smile at Humpty Dumpty and say something nice to it, then knock it off violently onto the floor. This brought peels of laughter from Kate.

The nursery smelled of Kate's baby smell, the smell of new life.

On top of Kate's wardrobe was a picture of Amanda in early pregnancy surrounded by a silver frame. She observed how her face, usually sharp and alert, was in the picture blurred.

Amanda tried to think about sheets. She imagined a white sheet dotted with tiny rosebuds. She imagined a pillowcase to go with it. She imagined stroking the cold linen surface. She imagined the set in her linen cupboard, in a thick pile.

Amanda shivered, and wished Kate and Sarah would come home. The flat was so empty without her. She carried cheerful Humpty Dumpty by a leg as she went to the phone.

She called her mother.

It was dark outside, and she could see the lights of the boats coming past.

After she'd finished chatting to her mother, she picked up a white tissue from the floor.

The toys were scattered over the oatmeal carpet: a rattle, a soft ball, a teddy with a blue ribbon and a demented expression in his eyes. A half-full bottle of milk sat on the coffee table.

The only brightness in the room came from the baby's toys. Everywhere else the colors were muted, blending, shades of cream and beige and white. *I like the reds, blues, greens of her toys. Everything has been too tidy too long. Tom and I have always been such an ideal pair, blending together so well in our muted, intelligent ways.*

She bent down and organized the toys into a pile. She took the bottle into the kitchen.

28

Sarah stroked the back of the baby's neck—soft dandelion-seed hair. She smelled the baby smell. It obliterated the smells of King's Cross' dust and dirt and even the sound of the cars roaring outside.

Her room was still, as though no window had ever been opened. The curtains hung stiffly.

She wished the baby's face were older, more elongated, more like Alice's. She felt a moment's anger at Kate.

Sarah moved a strand of Kate's hair from her forehead. She put down the baby's bottle. Kate was slumbering now, contentedly moving her lips as though imbibing some sweet milk from her mother's breast.

Sarah ran her fingers over Kate's downy skin. Would Kate be brave like Alice, or someone like herself, always watching, thinking, observing?

Alice had been born brave. At the playground, even at four years old, she would climb frames which seven-year-olds approached with trepidation. Alice always wanted to swing higher, then higher.

She played games starring herself as a warrior princess, brave and resourceful, with a hairband which gave her the power to fly. Alice even forced herself not to be afraid of the dark and slime of the magic boathouse.

Sarah knew that Alice would have tried to phone her, but of course poor Alice didn't know her number just as she didn't know her mother's address or her own, trapped in the tower of childhood, playing games with dolls, not knowing what was real and what was fantasy, what was true and what was a lie, weaving stories in her head that she could not write down.

There was a knock on the door.

Sarah cradled Kate more securely, instinctively protecting her from the bizarre figure of Beatrice.

"What is that?" said Beatrice.

"It's called a baby," muttered Sarah.

Beatrice wore a jaunty black hat over her hennaed hair. It did nothing to soften the masculinity of her jawline. She seemed obscenely large, standing there, taking up so much room.

"You'd better take her back," said Beatrice gently.

Beatrice sat down on the bed. Sarah wouldn't look into her face, but concentrated instead on the baby's face.

"I don't know what you mean. It's my baby, my child. I told you about her."

"Your child is older. I've seen pictures. Who is it, Sarah? Is it the baby?"

"I don't know what you're talking about," said Sarah sulkily.

"You'd better take her back. It's getting late."

"You're not my conscience, Beatrice. I'd be grateful if you'd leave me and my child in peace."

"Your child is older. I've seen pictures."

"Stop nagging me."

"Is her mother out late? Is that it?"

"I'm her mother."

"Stop it, Sarah." Beatrice touched Sarah's shoulder gently. "It's not sensible."

Sarah looked straight at Beatrice.

"Sensible! When have you ever been sensible?"

"There are other people involved. The baby's mother, for instance."

"You make an odd conscience, I have to tell you. Sitting there with your thigh-length boots."

"You've had this in mind, haven't you?"

"Not that I've been aware of. But you have to admit, she is beautiful."

"No, I don't think it's beautiful. I think it's horrible. Look, it's actually dribbling."

Sarah smiled at the tone of disgust, and the room lost some of its stillness. She wiped Kate's mouth with a tissue. Kate smiled in her sleep.

"Babies are horrible," said Beatrice. She patted her hair, as she had seen middle-aged ladies do. She took out a powder compact from the black handbag she always carried about with her and often swung like a weapon as she walked.

Beatrice looked at herself in the little mirror and daintily applied powder to her nose.

"You'd better take her back," said Beatrice. "Her mother will be getting worried."

Beatrice put on more lipstick and pursed her lips.

"Yes, her mother will be worried," said Sarah.

"You'd better take her back now. It's getting dark."

Sarah sighed. "Yes, I suppose I'd better take her back."

"I'll call you a cab, shall I?"

"Yes, I suppose you could call me a cab."

"Sarah, are you okay?"

"I'm okay," said Sarah.

29

The next day Sarah visited the baby department of Harrod's. She bought a yellow chicken which tweeted: a present for Kate. She was angry. She wished she had kept Kate. Amanda had been coldly polite with her when she returned so late with Kate the day before. Sarah had muttered about bumping into old friends; Amanda had scolded her about not using the telephone.

So far she had been the ideal nanny: hardworking, loving, responsible. She had averted her eyes from Tom when he watched her playing with Kate. When he was at home she brought him a cup of coffee and then politely withdrew. She knew he found her attractive. Men did find her attractive, partly because of a certain incomprehensible quality they called mystery. George had understood that her mystery was a mystery to herself too, as most things were, and that had endeared her to him. Sarah thought that from now on she might not be quite such an ideal nanny.

Soft toys stared down from the shelves behind

the counter. Even the wicked Mr. Fox had his place there, sporting his fine waistcoat beside his prey, the beshawled Mrs. Puddle Duck.

The shop assistant bundled up the yellow chicken in tissue paper and shoved it into a bag. It let out a plaintive tweet. The shop assistant was a stout woman with a sour expression.

Sarah inspected the rows of dresses for children. She touched the pale gold smocking on a creamy white dress which would have fitted Alice.

A baby watched her from its buggy. The baby had the expression of an elderly gentleman who had seen life and found it a most amusing but saddening business. The baby's faint eyebrows were raised in what appeared to be mock astonishment.

The baby was bald and rather fat, a cross between Oliver Hardy and an egg.

He was strapped into his stroller.

His mother examined the extravagantly canopied cribs.

From a musical box came that persistent lullaby issuing forth sweetness and hope:

"May you wake when the day
Chases darkness away,
May you wake when the day
Chases darkness away."

She left the baby department and passed through the floors stacked with possessions:

leather handbags, leather purses, scarves waving from a distant corner.

She noted a shop dummy in a crimson velvet skirt. Its hands postured elegantly, suggesting that this velvet skirt and little frilly white blouse, with evening bag, was what life is about: something formal, perfectly realized, slightly ridiculous, and utterly tidy.

It was only the edges of London that curled up, places where, when the wind blows, litter chases down the middle of the road, helter-skeltering forward, as the streets seem to empty except for a few loitering men, almost as though the streets are preparing for a shoot-out. But in London the shoot-out never quite came.

She took a bus back to her hotel.

The hotel was near two stations, King's Cross and St. Pancras. Everywhere there were people with suitcases, people with knapsacks, people hurrying to the next place. A bag lady sat muttering on a bench with a blue woollen scarf. She held on to her shopping cart as though she were just about to stand up, only she never did. She just sat there. Her shopping cart contained an overstuffed black plastic bag.

Sarah wandered into King's Cross station and observed the men and women in transit: a chic woman in brown leather trousers and suede boots carrying two broken suitcases, two young men with union jack shorts whose faces were also painted like union jacks, a black man in a white suit. Only she looked at them; it seemed they were invisible to everyone else. This was, after all, not a place. It was somewhere between places.

The street where her hotel was led up to St. Pancras, the elderly, flamboyant sister to smug new King's Cross station, which crouched by her side. St. Pancras was a fairy-tale castle, turreted, coated with blackness, and adept at casting an atmosphere of unreality and the temporary all around.

Over the other side of the road from the stations was a misfitting selection of bookmakers, Georgian houses, hamburger joints, and amusement arcades, which gave the impression of being blown into position, willy-nilly, by some malfeasant storm. There was litter everywhere too: piling up in black bags outside shops, escaping through cuts in the bags to join other bits of debris blowing away, racing and tumbling down streets, across roads.

She walked briskly back to the hotel, passing shop windows gray with dirt. Many of the houses looked as though they should be bulldozed. Some were in such bad condition that a firm tap from an umbrella might well have had a similar effect.

The carpet on the landing was bare in patches, as though it were the fur of a mangy cat, and indeed the house did smell of cats, although they could only occasionally be glimpsed prowling over a window ledge.

She unlocked her room. On the only chair were

strewn clothes: a gray sweater, matching skirt, and thick tights. Polished gray shoes waited underneath the chair.

It was sometimes hard to imagine that this lonely room wasn't her real life, that she actually had a child who loved her.

In her mind she saw Trisha Hunt sitting on a blanket, her legs tucked under her, her lipstick neatly applied. She saw Trisha Hunt's sharp little teeth. She saw them biting into George's flesh.

In her room two pigeons sat on the windowsill, fat burglars waiting to enter.

She was comfortable in this run-down area. London was scattered with areas like this, places which haven't decided what they are, or perhaps have just forgotten. They conformed well to her state of mind.

In the room above Sarah's, where Beatrice stayed, some enthusiastic sexual activity was taking place now, and the ceiling shook a little.

30

Tom and Sarah stood over Kate as she practiced her push-ups. She liked to push up with her arms and stretch up her head like a sphinx.

"Strange, she won't remember any of this," said Tom as she stretched up.

"That's doesn't matter," said Sarah.

"Well, all this effort ... all the attention ... she won't remember it."

"We won't remember our lives at all after we're dead," said Sarah. "That doesn't invalidate our lives."

"No, I suppose not."

"This is life," said Sarah. "This is what it is. All this effort. All this struggle."

Kate pushed up again, frowning with the effort.

"It makes one want to weep," she said, turning to Tom and meeting his eyes.

She held a coffee cup in her hand.

He frowned at her.

"I'd better be getting on," he said, not moving.

"You should," she said.

"The book's a lot of work," he said.

She pushed her hair from her face.

Embarrassed, he moved clumsily from foot to foot. He turned and strode off.

She took a sip of coffee and wondered whether she could make Tom fall in love with her. If she married him she could possibly gain custody of Alice, and very likely Kate. She wouldn't be a woman alone anymore.

After all, she told herself, if Amanda was having an affair with George, she didn't deserve Kate anyway. Perhaps she should even find a way to encourage their affair.

31

Sarah sat thinking about her marriage, listening to a talk show about divorce. The radio rested pertly on the rickety bedside table of her hotel room.

"I just wish I'd never met the bastard," said a woman's vengeful voice.

"The only reason I married him," said another voice, "was because I wanted to screw him all day and all night. I was too respectable, you see. Had to marry him, didn't I? And one day I didn't want to screw him anymore, and look what I was left with—a scrawny man with no job and a drinking problem."

"She took the children away. They've gone to live in Scotland. My job's here. I never see them ... it breaks my heart." The man's voice trembled. Sarah turned off the radio, which crackled convivially.

Sarah couldn't wish she had never met George Stewart because if she had never met him she would never have had Alice.

She just wished that he no longer existed.

She'd met him when he came down to her university in the south of England to talk about libel law to a respectful collection of students. (Sarah was studying English, but occasionally she would wander into other lectures.) She had sat in the front row: white face, perfect features, long, straight hair.

He had stood there, puffing out of his suit, addressing his remarks to her, a frog trying to win the heart of a princess. The overhead lights made him sweat, so his skin glistened. His red bow tie clasped his plump neck.

At the time she was sleeping regularly with an unhappy young man, Martin, who worshiped her. He sent her love letters and poems and was particularly ecstatic about sex with her, which was odd, as she found it uninteresting but inoffensive. But it seemed to bring such pleasure to him that she continued with it, in a faraway manner. She had always felt she existed somewhere different than the physical presence of her body suggested—perhaps in a book somewhere, or in a picture, or around a corner she had not yet turned. So she let Martin make love to her, and her sense of separation made him even more desperate about her. In his college room he would kiss and caress her and shyly, ardently, confess his passion for the mounds and secrets of her moonlit body. To her he seemed not exactly childish but certainly incomplete: the reddish hair, the gawky limbs, the spikiness of his elbows.

George Stewart, on the other hand, was undoubtedly complete: plump, worldly, with a sparkle of good-natured venom in his eyes. His smile slipped over to her invitingly as he talked, it tucked itself around her, told her everything would be all right, he knew how the world worked, he'd show her, he'd handle taxes and taxis and mortgages and laws.

He spoke to her afterward and invited her to lunch with him, and they had walked together away from the lecture theater, down a pathway, and all around daffodils had been throwing their heads around and the world had seemed bright and innocent.

He had a Mercedes, and in its smooth black luxury he took her to a dark restaurant, lit by candlelight. He was unhappily married, he told her, and she believed him. He ate lobster, and gouged out flesh from the claws with a metal fork of a type they no doubt used in hell. Some of the flesh clung to his lips. He wiped it off quickly with a white napkin.

He laughed a lot, and made good jokes, and summoned the waiter with the slightest movement of his hand.

"My great sadness," he said, mopping his lips, "is that I don't have a child. Neither of my two wives got pregnant, although, God knows, we tried." He chuckled. "We had tests, of course. There was nothing wrong with me or them. I should love a child. Above anything."

"I should like a child too," said Sarah and realized, for the first time, that indeed that was exactly what she wanted, what she needed, more than anything.

"Ah," he said and nodded, almost as though the matter was finalized and only the paperwork—the courtship, the foreplay, the lovemaking, the marriage—was left to deal with.

"You seem a little ... sad," he had said, leaning over and placing his plump hand on her long, slender one. The waiters moved around them discreetly: the lovely young woman with the ugly older man, a familiar story, beauty and the beast, the princess and the frog.

She nodded and pushed away her plate of sole.

"Most people are sad, don't you think?" she said.

"Oh no, it's not necessary."

Her face hovered pale in the shadowy restaurant, but he could hardly be seen; his shape blurred into the shadows.

"I'm seldom sad," he continued reassuringly. "My marriage isn't working ... but I'm not sad." He put more pressure upon her hand. "When you're older, as I am." He paused, as though he was doing something magnanimous and open by admitting he was older. "You lose certain things—a certain quickness of movement, a liking for loud music—but you gain equilibrium."

She was an only child. Her parents had been older: distant, involved in card games, their garden, their quarrels, and somehow not able to give much love to her. Her mother had been forty-three when Sarah was born.

Sarah went through her life observing herself—ah, that is me talking, ah, now I am having something to eat, not feeling she belonged with her body or her parents, a changeling.

Her parents lived in Epsom, in a modern house with picture windows overlooking the Downs. While they had played bridge every evening, she had read and worked. While they gardened their flat rectangle of land with its green carpet of lawn, she read. She hated the neat fence around the neat lawn. She hated the light, a constant, bleak light from the Downs and their constant low-level bickering. She hated the whole death-less, lifeless, pattern of their lives. She would sit alone in her room, with its green-and-white-striped wallpaper, listening to the rise and fall of their voices downstairs, feeling puzzled.

She had a breakdown when she was sixteen. She quite enjoyed the stay in the hospital, where everything was as blank as her mind. She liked to stare at the glass of water on her bedside table. Various friends came to visit her.

But here was George Stewart, dripping with worldliness, someone who belonged in life, who had the hang of it.

He had a dashing smile. It was quick, confidential, and sexually demanding. It asked her to forget his double chin, his graying hair, his Pickwickian girth. It informed her that all that was a chimera; the reality was in his dark, approachable eyes and his thick, hot lips. With all this came a comfortable house, garden, and security.

Sarah felt that here was a man who might look after her and take away her sense of homelessness. Besides, she wanted a child, and the touch of his skin was not at all unpleasant. Indeed, there was something repellently attractive about George Stewart, and he was quite aware of it.

He ordered Brie and a little port.

"Well, I think the lecture went really well," he said.

She had a small espresso.

"When can I see you again?" he said.

When he first brought her back to his house, he cooked her steak, which she had eaten slowly, while watching the portly, confident man chew his food quickly, keen to consume whatever pleasures life had to offer.

He massaged her shoulders while she finished her food, and she watched the curves of the lettuce lying on her plate. His hands were strong and certain. On the dresser were decorative plates brought back from travels abroad. He loved beautiful things, and Sarah was beautiful.

"You're so distant . . . you haven't quite locked into life yet, have you?" he said. "You still feel at one remove from it, don't you?"

"That's right," she said.

Sometimes she felt transparent, some kind of moth fluttering around.

"I know I can help you," he said.

There was wind in the damp air, and it stirred the voluptuous flowers of the magnolia tree in the Chiswick garden.

32

Kate is in her crib chattering away to her rattle. She is lying on her stomach, her head held up in the cobra position. She lets herself down and rolls over so that she can watch the ducks waddling around the border of her room, a border bought for an unknown person.

She kicks: kick, kick, kick, as though she is on an intensive exercise course and has no time to waste. As she kicks she watches a felt horse, cow, and pig in the mobile above her. Kate frowns a little as she watches them twirl. She appears to be remembering those shapes from somewhere.

Kick, kick, kick.

The room was there, waiting for her, before she was born: the little clothes in the wardrobe, the soft balls and wooden jigsaw puzzles on the shelves, the ducks making their plodding journey around and around this room by the side of the river.

Even the music was there, ready for her, wrapped up in its tape.

33

During Kate's morning nap Sarah listened to her breathing and watched her dreams in her face. Kate murmured and frowned. Sarah stared at the photograph of Amanda and Tom, arm in arm, which sat among Kate's books. She tried to see if she could see deception in Amanda's face.

She wandered into the drawing room and took out one of the photograph albums from the bookshelves. The album was dedicated to Kate. There were rows and rows of her. Most hours of her existence had been chronicled: there she was having her first bath, first bottle, first pram walk. If she turned out to be an international star there would certainly be sufficient photographic material for the volume covering her early years. In many of these pictures Amanda was holding Kate, and there was nothing in her eyes which suggested betrayal, except perhaps for a certain anxiety, but that could have more to do with the pressures of having a new baby.

When Kate woke, indignant, Sarah cuddled her.

Kate turned her hands this way and that, frowning, a jeweler checking over a diamond.

Sarah thought about the country house where she had worked as a nanny in France before going to university; it had had trees all around the château, cutting it off from the present. On the grounds was a vegetable garden, a walled paradise of delphiniums, roses, rhubarb, lettuce, and an old brick shed with broken windows. She remembered the slight tarnish of the brows of a woman's portrait, the white at the center of a frilly pink rose, the violence in the marks of the marble.

"Oh darling, you and your imagination," her mother used to say as she walked away after Sarah had asked her to join in a game. She'd smile so gently, so amused, as though Sarah's imagination were some kind of absurd hamster to be tolerated but not encouraged. Sarah had had a small, damp room, and at night there were black shapes and blobs of strange color in the corner which terrified her. Once she told her mother, and she told her not to be so silly.

Sarah never thought of asking for a light on at night, and her mother never gave her one, so the strange, distorted shapes continued to dance and beckon in the corner of the room. Her parents put her to bed early, and that's when her imagination grew, in those long, terrified hours.

The world's a stage for adults, but it's during the rehearsals of childhood, thought Sarah, that some of the greatest dramas occur: the terrors at nighttime, the effort to discover what is real.

How absurd it all was, thought Sarah as she looked across the river: all the towers, all the money-making, all the self-important hurrying people. Humanity has had it wrong all these years. It's the puppies and kittens and lambs that are important. It's quite easy to see that a lamb is alive and a sheep is, well, more or less dead, as we adults are. Being an adult is a kind of limbo between the living and the dead, but of course we're not allowed to see this in case it makes us despair. This place, for instance, this city of adults, it's a city of the dead, like New York, like Tokyo, and the tall, flat buildings are its many tombstones.

Kate was wriggling, and Sarah put her down so that she could lie on the floor and kick. She kicked so hard her limbs were a blur. Sarah was standing over her, remembering how Alice used to kick like this.

Sarah bent down, took one of Kate's hands, and placed it on hers. A tiny hand in a big one. The tiny one, with its miniature nails, lay like a starfish. Kate took it away and continued to wave it as she kicked—hoopla, hurray, quick as possible into life, strengthening the limbs, doing the exercises, desperate to get into life.

She had desired George at first; they had made love day after day, tearing at each other, as though wanting to possess each other's flesh forever.

34

In bed Alice's hair stuck out in all directions, and her face glowed pale as white roses in the dark. She wobbled one of her front teeth. She wore her ruffed nightdress, which added to her air of formality.

"How long will it be before you come home?" she said. "Daddy and Trisha have a lot of parties. Their parties are very loud. There is a party on now. Perhaps that's why I can't sleep. They're playing music and talking and spilling out onto the lawn at the back like a glass that's been filled too high. When you and Daddy had parties, you used to come and sit with me, do you remember? And Daddy would come in all red and cross and ask you what the hell you were doing. And you would blink and look pale and say you were tired . . . and say something about all those people . . . and brush the hair from your face. And once he grabbed you by the arm and he was puffed up with crossness like a frog. You preferred being with me, didn't you? Trisha likes to be with other people. When will you come home?"

Alice took a sip of water.

"I get that lonely feeling I used to get when you kissed me good night and I knew I had to go into the blackness all alone. . . . I get that all the time . . . I have no one to talk to. Only my toys, and they're not real.

"Trisha and Daddy whisper about you to each other. You know that Daddy told me you were not a good person to look after me? Why not? I said. But he wouldn't say; he just looked vague as a newt."

35

"Darling, would you mind looking after her while I make dinner?" said Amanda, who was holding a wriggling Kate.

Tom snatched a furtive glance up from his computer.

"Well, look, I'm just at a really important part right now, and it's going really well. You couldn't just put off making dinner for a while?"

"Please, Tom, you say that every evening. I should like a pleasant family dinner before we're both too exhausted to do anything but grab a bit of bread and cheese. What I have in mind is a tomato and aubergine casserole. I have a vision of all three of us sitting together at the dining table, with some wine and candlelight, talking to each other, admiring our child, listening to some interesting music."

"That sounds terrific," said Tom, his eyes returning to his computer. He tapped in a word. "Thanks."

Kate grabbed at Amanda's nose and Amanda evaded the attack.

"Tom. I want you to look after Kate while I get dinner."

"Look," he said, spinning around on his swivel chair. In an exasperated gesture he ran his fingers through his hair. "I am busy. I really am. I am involved. You just have to put up with my book a little bit longer—and then I'll be free of it. Then, look, we'll go on a vacation."

He turned back to his book. A halogen cast a pool of light on Tom's desk. The rest of the room was in darkness.

"Tom, we have a baby. The baby uses up hours. I don't see why she should only use up my hours. I thought we had a deal, a partnership. I do work, you know. I do rather well in my work. I earn good money."

"I know all that."

"Well, I have to remind myself of it sometimes."

"When I've finished my book I shall—"

"You've been writing it for months and months. At this rate she'll be going through puberty by the time you finish."

Tom swiveled a bit.

"We married for better, for worse," he said.

"But not that I should put up with the worse and you the better."

He scratched his head and swiveled a bit more, casting longing glances at the waiting screen.

"You like looking after her. You're good at it. I'm not. I try ... but I put her clothes on the wrong way around, I don't know how to play with her, and I use up all the stickiness on at least three diapers before I get one to stick. I'm not made for it." He opened out his hands in a display of innocence. "Besides, she doesn't want me."

"Of course she does. Anyway, I want you to help me. Most of this baby business is slave labor. Why should I be the slave while you write and then don't even turn up for dinner because you're so busy working? I want a life, a cozy family life. I'm not interested in being Mrs. Mozart or Mrs. Tolstoy or Mrs. Dickens. I'm really not."

Tom swiveled a bit. He stared up at his chart of the heavens on the wall in front of him. His narrow room was plastered with posters showing different interpretations of the universe, and of the earth's place within the universe.

"Look," he said, pointing, "that's how Copernicus saw the universe. That over there is how the Egyptians saw it. Look all around ... if I could contribute my own vision, would that not be more important than looking after Kate while you get the dinner?"

"Not really," said Amanda. "It would turn out to be an impartial view, anyway. It would only be a step toward some future interpretation, whereas Kate is here now, complete. She won't represent some alleyway of thought in which you lost your way. Here she is." Amanda joggled her and noted she had a wet diaper. "Three-dimensional. Inarguably real. Not needing an equation to explain her. She is it. Life itself."

"Okay, okay," said Tom, suddenly laughing. "You win." With his feet against his desk, he pushed himself away on his chair. He stood up. "You win. I shall look after life itself. I shall be privileged to look after life itself."

"She has a wet diaper," said Amanda.

After he'd changed the diaper, he stood on the library steps in front of his bookshelves, which faced the wall of windows overlooking the river. He intoned some titles to Kate, as if he were repeating poetry: *Inflation and Time Asymmetry in the Universe, Bumps, Voids, and Bubbles in Time, The Red Limit: The Search for the Edge of the Universe,* and *An Axisymmetric Black Hole Has Only Two Degrees of Freedom.*

Kate sat propped up against the sofa, clenching a red rattle and watching him. She had recently acquired a puzzled expression.

Above his jeans he wore a frayed shirt with the sleeves rolled up. His shoes were scuffed. In the clear light a few stray gray threads crept over his hair. Every now and again he would lean out and seize a book and, using the library steps as a stage, read from it to Kate in a theatrical voice.

Amanda occasionally slipped into the drawing room, still in apron and oven gloves, check that they were okay, and slid out again. Amanda wished Tom was not quite so, well, extraordinary. She wished he could just play with Kate on the floor instead of turning the whole thing into a recital. But she could hardly complain. That was what he was like. He never walked anywhere, he always strode. When he watched television it was with astonished interest. When he ate, he would eat quickly, then stare surprised at his plate when the food was gone. It was as though everything he did he was doing for the first time.

They had met at a party in New York. Tom was standing right in the center of the room, his head jutting out above the rest. He saw her and she saw him, and he returned to his conversation. She had come with an actor boyfriend. Tom introduced his beautiful blonde companion to the actor. Tom and Amanda left together and so did the actor and the beauty, who later married. And that was that. Amanda was impressed by his brilliance; he seemed to like her competence and grace. Both came from the same middle-class, academic backgrounds.

From the moment Amanda had first entered the party, Tom's eyes had been on her. When she went to the bathroom she looked at her face, and it was beautiful in a way it had never been before, as though Tom's attention had in some way transformed it. Her face was thinner, her eyes bright, her smile slower, more sultry, more intelligent.

When she walked back to the room she knew she was walking differently, with more grace.

He asked her about herself, and she asked him about himself. He told her he was a scientist.

Tom had insisted on walking Amanda home, and he suggested coming up to her hotel room for a nightcap. They were both shy at first and then they made love. Afterward, she sat up on the side of the bed. She had a slim body, with freckles on her back. He kissed each of her freckles.

Outside, a police siren faded away and another one replaced it, as was the case throughout the long, hot night.

"You know, I—" she started to say the following morning.

"Please don't tell me you never usually sleep with a man on your first date . . . no, maybe tell me," he said grandly. "In fact, I think you could lean over and tell me that two and two make four, and I would find the statement scintillating and innovative."

In those days he still had the air of a clever schoolboy, someone trying out his phrases and attitudes, still slightly puzzled. Amanda's love had given him a confidence he had previously lacked.

"I like this new rug!" he shouted to her.

Amanda had bought a Persian rug in purples, reds, and deep blues, which she had spread out by the windows.

"Well, I felt this place was too stark now that we have Kate."

Kate's intelligent eyes watched her father.

He climbed down from his stage, crouched down, and pressed her button nose.

"I wonder, by my troth, what thou and I
Did, till we loved? Were we not weaned till"
    then?
But sucked on country pleasures, childishly?
Or snorted we in the seven sleepers' den?"

Amanda stood at the kitchen door.
"She's beginning to like you."
"Of course she is. She's going to be a great scientist. I am nothing to what she will be, am I, babe? What will you do—discover how to make time run backward? How to travel to Saturn for a day? How to have immortal life? Which of these will you achieve, chubby cheeks?"

Kate waved her rattle and beamed.

Tom took a sip of chilled white wine.

"Is there any more casserole?" said Tom. "I'm ravenous. I think I'll try to work really late to-night to get the chapter done."

36

Alice sat in her room alone, talking to her mother.

"Daddy is getting as fat as Humpty Dumpty," she said. "Some daddies get like teddies when they eat too much but, you know, Daddy doesn't. I don't want to hug him. He puts his arms out to me and I'm supposed to run into them. I try to do it. But when I get there he's not soft like someone is when they really love you.

"He pats me on the head.

"He always asks me to come to him. He should come to me sometimes, and bend down and talk to me.

"He had new sunglasses. They were big and blue and made him look like a pop star, one of those silly, fat ones.

"He smiles at me all the time. It looks as though someone has glued the smile on.

"We went to the zoo together today—you know, the place we used to go—and I patted the goats and stroked the lambs—and I didn't like it.

I kept thinking of you. Daddy and Trisha were standing there—with those smiley looks on their faces. I wanted to paste different looks on them. I wanted them to look sad.

"Afterward she and Daddy took me out to lunch. I was very silent. I only said yes and no and 'very nice.'

" 'She's always withdrawn,' Daddy told Trisha. 'Don't worry about it,' Trisha said.

"I could see Trisha was bored with me as usual. She drew me a picture of a cat on a napkin. She doesn't really know what age I am—to her I could be baby or two or ten.

"Daddy ordered me a salad.

" 'She loves salad,' he said.

"I've never eaten a salad *in my life*. They are full of worms. I heard an airplane flying overhead and I wondered if you were on it. The salad had cottage cheese on one side and *fruit*—something green and round and spongy—and *lettuce*. She told me I must eat up.

"I wouldn't. I just kept my mouth shut. She might be trying to poison me. I am always careful with strangers, just as you said.

"In the taxi on the way back, Trisha and Daddy started to quarrel; he was cross with her for having lunch with some man. When we got back I listened at the door of my bedroom while they shouted at each other in your bedroom. She let out a screech like a bird.

"I went into the bedroom. I saw her reach out and take Daddy's new sunglasses and drop them on the floor. She lifted her foot, then slammed it down. They crunched very sadly. I wanted to laugh. I ran back to my room. I laughed, and so did my dolls, especially Martha.

"When are you coming back?—just say soon."

37

Another long-term inhabitant of the hotel whom the landlord had taken pity on was Mr. Richards, a stately, formal man of around forty who wore torn clothes and an expression of despair. He bowed slightly whenever he saw Sarah, which was quite often, since he lived in the room across the hall. Four years ago his wife had thrown him out because of what she called mental cruelty. In fact, he told Sarah sadly one day, as they hovered in the hallway, she was just driven to distraction by his habit of drumming his fingers on the table, and by his pessimism.

"She called it pessimism, I called it realism," he said. "Tell me now, Sarah, are you a pessimist or an optimist?"

His head jutted forward in the manner of an emu whenever he asked a question, which Sarah imagined could grow to be annoying.

"Oh, a pessimist, I think."

The linoleum on the floor was broken here and there. A cleaner came every day and stared disapprovingly at any outbreaks of dirt.

"Personally," she would say, shaking her head, "I can't stand dirt." She would then wander upstairs to examine the dirt there. The landlord found her healthy disdain for dirt so impressive he continued to employ her although she did little to eradicate cobwebs, dust, the lingering smell of finished frenzy, of perfume and sweat and tainted pleasure which hung not unpleasantly over the corridors and rooms.

"What's a girl like you doing here? You're so poised and well put together," said Mr. Richards. "I'm surprised Mr. Smith lets you stay. He usually only takes to people, well, like me or Beatrice."

"He probably sees through appearances," said Sarah.

They paused as a bewildered tourist puffed his way up the stairs, followed by the landlord shouting, "Oh no, not that room. Farther up. Can't you see the numbers?"

They watched as the landlord more or less pushed the plump Japanese man into a room. The man emerged a few minutes later, wiping his brow and shaking his head.

He trudged downstairs again, still shaking his head, while the landlord followed, railing against him.

"There's nothing wrong with these rooms. Nothing at all. You lot just can't recognize civilization when you see it," he said.

The yellowish paint blistered around Mr. Richards's door.

Beatrice came traipsing down the stairs, wearing a red hat, of the kind Robin Hood might have worn. Her black vinyl boots came up to the middle of her thigh.

Mr. Richards gave a throttled snort.

"Beatrice," said Sarah, "why does Mr. Smith approve of us? Why does he let you two stay here so cheaply?"

"Well," said Beatrice, adjusting her oversized bra with a wriggle, "for one thing he's so grumpy no one else wants to stay here, and for another thing for some reason he likes people at the margins of life because perhaps he believes he can save us from falling off."

"Or he's waiting to see us fall," intoned Mr. Richards.

"Cheer up," said Beatrice, clapping him on the back so that he jumped. "Let's go to a pub—you too, Sarah."

They walked to a dense, smoky pub where the strange trio received intent scrutiny: the beautiful young woman, the drag queen, and the scrawny middle-aged man like something out of a black-and-white horror movie.

"It's the children I miss," said Mr. Richards, sipping his half pint of beer. "I really do. She has custody. That's what's made me so . . . nervous, not seeing the children. They're my future, you see. I did everything for them. Two boys too.

Made them paper airplanes. Bought them train sets." He sighed.

"Fight the bitch," said Beatrice. "You've got to fight back. Character is action. You discover your character, your fortitude, your strength, through taking action. That's your problem. You're too meek. You accept too much."

"I've tried to live a decent life," said Mr. Richards.

"It's not enough. Decency is not enough. If I'd just been decent—just considered others—I'd still be quiet Phillip Black, a computer programmer with an undersexed girlfriend who was happy to wait until we got married to have sex. I had a girlfriend, you know. On Saturday I'd go out with her and watch her try on clothes and I'd long to *be* her. Just long to be her. Those tits. That walk. That's what I wanted to be. So—I did it," he said with a flourish.

Sarah and Mr. Richards regarded Beatrice solemnly.

"It was very brave of you," said Sarah in the silence.

"Yes," said Mr. Richards, taking her remark as a compliment. "But the thing is, I don't want a sex change. I just want to see my children regularly—but she's always too busy, or on vacation. She has a new man now. Apparently he doesn't drum his fingers and he's very optimistic, but she thinks he may be very stupid."

"Take her to court."

"Oh, I haven't the energy," said Mr. Richards.

"Look at me. I've always been a quiet sort of person. I can't rant and rave. And anyway I haven't got the money."

"Oh, you can get the state to pay for it."

"Maybe," said Mr. Richards, taking a discreet handful of salted peanuts.

"I'm trying to get my child back through the courts," said Sarah. "Only my husband is a lawyer. It makes it hard. He knows all the tricks. Sometimes I feel it's hopeless."

"You discover your character through action," said Beatrice. "Take action. Go and snatch her if they won't give her to you. Rules are made for breaking. There's a strength in you. I can see it," said Beatrice to Sarah. "You should do the same," she said to Mr. Richards, more dubiously.

Mr. Richards shook his head. "I could never do that."

"I don't know if I could," said Sarah.

"Of course you could. Mothers are supposed to be able to do anything. I've read all sorts of sentimental claptrap about mothers because I adore mine. One book records how a mother lifted up a truck with her bare hands to save her child underneath. *Now,* of course," said Beatrice, "my mother would leave me under it."

"I'm sure she wouldn't," said Sarah.

"She probably would," said Mr. Richards.

"You've been looking a bit brighter these

last few days," said Beatrice. "Is anything happening?"

"Nothing very much," said Sarah, taking a sip of the Black Velvet, which, to the surprise of Beatrice and Mr. Richards, she had insisted upon ordering. They told her she'd get drunk.

"I don't get drunk," Sarah had said.

38

"Can I come with you on *The Princess*?" said Trisha.

Alice shook her head.

"But I like boats."

Alice shook her head again.

"She and her mother used to go out together on *The Princess*. They did the last day before she left. I expect she's sentimental about it," said George. "They had some special place they'd never tell me about."

"But Alice darling," said Trisha, bending down and holding Alice's arms. Alice glared at the hands touching her arms. "I so much want to be close to you."

Alice broke free of Trisha's grasp and ran off into the house.

"She's certainly willful," said Trisha.

"She'll get over her mother," said George. "Children adapt."

39

"It's too late now. We were brought up to have a career. You can't give up work and retire to Cambridge. It would be deathly," said Caroline to Amanda.

Caroline's blonde hair was swirled into two wheels on either side of her face in the style of Heidi.

Caroline either chose her dress to match the restaurant or the restaurant to match her dress. Caroline wore a salmon pink jacket over a white dress with angular lines. The restaurant was salmon pink, with white tiled floors and a white ceiling from which recessed lights peered curiously down.

"But I'm miserable. Tom's even more remote than usual with me. I'm grumpy. At the weekend in the country Jonathan went on and on at him about the job. And I don't like our flat anymore, and the river depresses me. It's so consistently dismal: all those little houses, all those factories, all lining the side of the river. People going in and out of houses, and the river somehow making a mockery of it all."

"Is this postnatal depression?"

"I don't know what it is. And I don't think I like my nanny, only I can't think of a single reason why I don't, apart from the fact that Tom likes her and Kate likes her, which is wholly unreasonable of me. I am not an unreasonable person. I don't like unreasonable people."

"You love Tom. Everyone loves Tom. You are the envy of the entire world. You'd better be nice to him."

"I know. It's just ... I try to be nice, and then I snap at him, and then I apologize, and everything's fine and then he goes on being preoccupied and vague, and I snap again. He's been even worse than usual recently."

"He's probably thinking about space."

"I expect so. I wish I'd married a bus conductor." Amanda sipped her Perrier. "I just wish I'd known I'd end up feeling like this. We were all misinformed, seriously misinformed about the whole business. I thought leaving my baby while I went to go to work would be fine. But I didn't know. I imagined my baby as—you know—one of those burping, horrid things."

"Someone else's baby."

"That's right ... although of course your Susan is a lovely baby and not at all—"

"Amanda, is there anything else? You seem very bothered."

"Of course not. It's just that it's all so difficult."

A thin girl over on the other side of the restaurant was flirting wildly with a man much older than herself. He had that desperate expression of eagerness tinged with fear that is characteristic of such situations.

Every now and again she leaned her head down so that her hair fell forward—and then in a sudden, exotic movement, she threw her long hair back over her shoulder.

Caroline stared at the girl in some puzzlement, as though seeing some archaic form of human behavior.

"Isn't it quaint?" said Caroline.

"What?" said Amanda.

"Those two over there."

"Oh yes," said Amanda. "Very quaint."

As Amanda walked back to her office, she tried not to think about George Stewart, who kept phoning. She had to admit that she was flattered by his enthusiasm, especially since Tom showed little for her at present. Everything had been so much simpler between her and Tom before Kate came along. In those days he had worked all the time, and she had worked all the time, and when they couldn't work any more they joined up together for some leisure activity so that their brains would recover to work some more. The idea of pleasure as a motivating force in life was not one she or he had found easy to comprehend. Within a few hours of meeting, quite apart from immense sexual attraction, they had recognized that each thought that life was for working. She found no problem with him working until three in the morning and bounding out of his study waving computer printout sheets and talking about ratios and equations she couldn't understand. But once she had become pregnant, she had changed. She was abruptly shifted to a role she had thought she had abandoned. She needed protecting.

"I just did a pregnancy test," she told Tom. "I'd been meaning to tell you that ... I'd feared ... or rather hoped, I suppose ... well," she continued. "It's positive. That's the good news." She had tried to smile. She wore a pair of flowery pajamas which were a size too big for her, and she was lost inside them. She blinked her eyes a few times, as if unable to see properly.

"So," she continued. "Well," she said. "It's possible ... well, we might be going to have a ... baby."

"A baby?"

"A blue circle appeared in a test tube," said Amanda. Her lower lip was jutting out slightly, as Kate's would stick out when she was upset. "That's how I knew."

"Oh, Amanda," said Tom in a hushed tone as he moved toward her.

"I shall have to buy lots of books on the subject. I shall have to find out all about it."

"Of course you will," said Tom. "So shall I. Aren't you *brilliant*?"

"I don't know about babies, you see," said Amanda. "And I don't know what I'm going to feel. They say it's possible to fall desperately in love, apparently, and walk about in a haze, and not recognize people you used to know. It sounds very alarming. I might not like it at all."

"I'm so happy," said Tom uncertainly.

"Yes," said Amanda.

Over the following days Amanda jogged rather more vigorously than she had in the past. But soon she felt too ill to run. She spent much of the early mornings being sick rather than jogging.

"It's nature's way of slowing you down," he said as she threw up in the bathroom.

She emerged.

"In case anyone ever asks you your opinion on the subject, pregnancy is not shared in any way with the male of the species. I thought you should know," she said as she walked by him. "In case you thought that by watching me being sick you were sharing my pregnancy."

They had wanted the baby, or rather, they had been trying for a couple of months for Amanda to become pregnant, but had somehow not expected it to happen. It was so implausible, really. She had imagined the painful struggles of childlessness far more easily than having a baby: the visits to the doctors, the reading of books on the subject, the timing of sexual intercourse, the special positions for lovemaking. Amanda had bought a fertility thermometer from the drugstore after the first unmissed period. It was as though there were a gap in their lives which they felt the emotional trauma of childlessness could fill.

Amanda had had a relatively easy life. She had

a good-looking mother and a rich father, which is more or less what the lullabies wish for children. She had been brought up in a timbered Elizabethan house in Kent, had been to a distinguished girl's boarding school, and had from there proceeded to Oxford, where she had done well academically and acted in various college productions, including a fine performance as Portia, which still lent a certain majesty to her bearing, particularly in board meetings where at any moment it seemed she might lean over to a recalcitrant male and inform him, in a wise and tender voice, about the quality of mercy.

During the first part of the pregnancy, however, she had not resembled a Shakespearean heroine at all.

She felt as though a monster were taking over her body and changing it: pumping up her breasts, exhausting her so she fell into a drugged sleep every evening the moment she came home. She woke up queasy every morning, and all her former appetites were altered: she no longer wanted alcohol or meat and had no desire to go to parties or to talk to people. She was too tired to go to the supermarket, and asked Tom to. He returned one evening, claiming he'd been unable to find it.

For the first four months she had been sick every few hours and had ended up in a hospital on a drip which injected her with the nutrients she could otherwise not hold down. She had been at an important meeting and felt sick. She had not managed to get to the bathroom in time. She had not moved quickly enough because it had seemed so unlikely that she could be sick in a boardroom with leather seats, in a roomful of men, with a big window overlooking the phallic towers around her. She could still remember, with some amusement, the horror on their faces. The managing director had turned a shade of putty when she stood up during his presentation, holding her mouth and retching.

"Amanda," he said.

"Oh dear," she said, and turned on her high heels and ran.

The secretary leaped up and opened the door for her.

Afterward, she had put her arm around Amanda. Then she went back and cleared up the sick from the boardroom before returning to see if Amanda was all right.

"No wonder men don't like employing women," she said. "No wonder they make it difficult."

"It'll be worth it," said the secretary, whose name was Margaret, and who longed for babies. She had very bad skin but a sweet soul.

Amanda's hands fought with her hair in front of the mirror. Her skin was chalky. Her lipstick was all gone.

"Men go into bathrooms and have a quick pee while we spend half our lives throwing up in them, or trying to dispose of blood in them, or at best gazing in the mirror trying to disguise ourselves."

"Wait until you have to keep taking your children to them," said Margaret, who wished she had skin like Amanda, which even when she was sick like this had a freshness to it.

"Children? This baby is it. The one and only."

"When you have it you'll feel differently," said Margaret. "I've noticed that the ones who resent the idea of a child most are often the ones who end up loving their children most. It's the romantic ones who get disappointed."

Amanda smiled. She examined her face in the mirror. She applied some disguise—lipstick, powder—and she practiced smiling. She was not very good at it that day.

"You're very kind," Amanda said as warmly as she could manage. "Thank you."

Amanda had checked there were no buttons undone on her shirt, which was tight because of the size of her growing breasts. She took a glass of water. She made herself return to the boardroom table and those seven men who all sat with composed bodies which would never have to put up with an alien creature growing inside them, altering their shape. They looked up as she returned.

What she actually wanted to do was not to stride into the boardroom but to retire weeping into a window seat somewhere in the country and stay there for the rest of her pregnancy reading light novels, looking at old photograph albums, and staring out of the window. She had a strong urge to try to assess her life up until now, make shape of it, almost as though she would be a different person.

When she told one of her neighbors, whom she hardly knew, that she was three months pregnant the woman had advised her to start doing her pelvic-floor exercises so that she would have tight vaginal muscles after the birth.

"A loose vagina," said the woman "can play havoc with your sex life." Amanda stared at her. This woman had seldom talked about anything more personal than the weather to Amanda.

It was all like *Rosemary's Baby*, she thought, smiling politely and thanking the woman for the advice.

And so the pregnancy had continued. As she got bigger, so the advice too had burgeoned. Females all around gave her advice, and men who usually would hardly dare flirt with her had the nerve to pat her bottom. The men were reassured. She was back in her rightful place. They opened doors for her again and called taxis for her, and the worst thing was, she liked it. It was like acting out the life of someone else, someone whose body was in command and not the mind.

Nevertheless, sometimes she envied her former self as she curled up on sofas, on beds, hardly having the energy to read.

Then there was the fear—supposing the child was abnormal in some way, or just plain stupid. Birth was, after all, somewhat of a lucky dip, a genetic tombola.

Tom and Amanda both looked into the looking

glass more than before, as though trying to readjust their self-images. He, the wild scientist, was to be a father, a figure of responsibility.

And Amanda, graceful, lovely Amanda, the businesswoman, the steadfast believer that men and women were equal and the same, was to be a mother.

She, who had spent thirty years becoming the person she wanted to be, was constantly being told that, whoops, you'll be different after the birth. Never mind all that education. It was all just a game. It would all be blown away as if it were all just a dandelion clock: one o'clock, two o'clock, three o'clock, and it'll all be gone. You'll be a lovely new person. Your hormones will change you, they said comfortingly.

Together they went to the hospital to see the baby on the ultrasound.

Amanda put on a green gown, and a female doctor in a white coat smeared jelly over her tummy. A machine was placed over her glistening belly, and as it roamed across her skin a picture of something vaguely resembling a baby took form on the television screen in front of them.

"Can you see the heartbeat?" said the doctor, pointing at a mark on the screen which kept rapidly appearing and disappearing.

"Yes!" cried Tom. "I can see it." He flung himself near the screen. "Good heavens. Isn't it marvelous?" he said to Amanda.

"And that's its head . . . it's sucking its thumb," continued the doctor.

Amanda smiled dizzily.

As they drove away in a taxi together, Tom's hand rested on her knee. "That was our child back there on the screen," he said.

She put her hand on his.

"It's not back on the screen. It's here, in the taxi, with us now."

Tom stared at Amanda's face and then at her tummy. "There are three passengers at the back of this taxi," he said, making the idea sound chilling.

Amanda laughed. Kate would one day have the same sudden, fresh laugh.

Just as Amanda had studied Chinese before visiting China, so she studied birth, babies, and baby care prior to the birth.

She attended prenatal classes and lay on the floor with twelve other pregnant women, pulling in her vaginal muscles when Mrs. Felicity Grey informed her class it was time to pull in.

She was addressed by Felicity Grey, along with all the other women, as though they were all exactly the same person, A Pregnant Woman.

"Now your waters could burst at any moment. When the time is due, if you are at all worried you could . . ."

Amanda dutifully made notes, as the other women made notes. If she made enough notes, and remembered them well enough, she would pass this exam as she had passed all the other exams of her life.

She had nightmares occasionally, of dead babies, deformed babies, unintelligent babies, but Mrs. Felicity Grey told them that nightmares were perfectly normal.

Somewhere in her head a voice shouted that dead babies, deformed babies, unintelligent babies, were all perfectly normal too. But she stared fiercely at Mrs. Felicity Grey's reassuring face, and the voice faded.

In the bath she used to watch with pleasure the undulations of her smooth skin scattered with pools and drops of water as the monster moved below it.

"Look," said Tom a month before the due date. "I really can't get out of this lecture in New York. It's two weeks before the birth. It should be fine."

"I'd much rather you were around those weeks."

"It's a great honor to be asked to give the lecture, Amanda."

Kate arrived two weeks early.

Tom sent Amanda a stupendous bunch of white roses from New York.

Mind you, she thought as she walked, she knew a lot of women who would have been absent at the birth of their babies, given the chance.

40

Over on the other side of London, Alice's father, George Stewart, stood in Alice's bedroom. Alice had on her knee the doll Matilda her mother had given her. She rearranged the doll's hair.

"Look," he said, approaching her. "I love you. You must know that."

"Then you should get my mother back," said Alice.

"That's just not possible. I know you can make it work with Trisha. I know we have difficulties, but if you were nicer to her I feel sure it would help our relationship work out."

He wore a pin-striped suit: a man at a business meeting. She thought he did not look as a father should.

Alice stroked the pink cheek of her doll.

"I see," she said.

"You will try?"

"Mmm," she said.

After he had gone, Alice went down the stairs and out into the garden, where she skipped and skipped with her rope, not missing a beat, by the magnolia tree:

"My mother said,
   That I never should
   Play with the gypsies
   In the wood—"

"Alice!" called Trisha out of the window. "Don't make such a racket. I was resting."

Alice stopped skipping. She dropped the rope on the ground. She walked back into the house and sat at the old pine kitchen table. On the walls were Alice's drawings of stick figures in black and red. Trisha had said she'd take them down when the kitchen was redecorated in "lovely floral chintz." Alice knew how Trisha would decorate the room, like the inside of the kind of cake that made you feel very sick, all frills and bows and icing.

Her mother had liked things to be plain. This kitchen still felt like their kitchen, hers and her mother's.

Trisha had had a decorator in to redecorate the master bedroom. The woman had been horrid, and had thrown darlings and sweethearts all over the place rather as she threw those frilly blinds that don't work and look like somebody's dress in an old film about history. That was fine for a dress, but not for a window. The woman had had an anteater's nose and red hair. If Alice had touched the hair, she knew the color would have come off in her hand like blood or tomato ketchup. When the woman gushed all over her like a fountain that had gone wrong, Alice just stood there with her hands behind her back.

"Such a pensive child," said the woman gaily. Alice didn't know what pensive meant. She thought it might mean ugly. Since her mother had gone, she had not felt the same. She had not been the same in the mirrors. Somebody else had looked back at her, a funny little child only about one half there, somebody incompletely sketched, somebody somebody had got bored with and pushed aside. She couldn't see any light anywhere. There was none in her face. Her mother had said that Alice lit up the world for her. But now her mother wasn't here to love her, she felt she was just a shadow moving around the house, moving to school, playing with her friends, learning her lessons.

Alice stood up. She walked through the still house, and up the worn carpet, past the paintings which watched her from the walls.

She had loved this house while her mother had been in it, comforting its sadness, making the shadows friendly, telling jokes to the darkness. Silly jokes, of course, but Alice had liked the silly jokes.

But now the house was different. It never seemed to sleep as it had in the old days before Sarah went away. Alice would lie awake much of the night listening to the house breathing.

Sometimes she would hear Trisha cry out. Alice was sure Trisha's presence disturbed the house.

Alice entered her room. She would never let Trisha redecorate her room.

She stood at the window. Of course, she had thrown two old bottles into the river with a piece of paper in each of them on which was written, in her wobbly writing, the words, "Mummy" and "love" and "Alice," but what was the point? Her mother knew where she was—she just couldn't come for her because Trisha guarded the house.

41

On the way to work Amanda was sitting bolt upright in the car as though meeting her last moments in an electric chair. Tom was driving.

One of Amanda's feet was positioned on a plastic book for the bath featuring a hairbrush, a teddy, a tube of toothpaste, and a car. Her black court shoe pressed onto the cover, which featured an orange and blue cat with a delinquent expression. The other shoe rested on a supermarket bag containing a wet diaper.

Tom had greeted Sarah this morning with unnecessary warmth, thought Amanda, and Sarah had smiled at him with a low, flirtatious look. When she mentioned this to Tom, he laughed.

"Don't be silly, darling," he said. "She's just being polite."

"I'm not so sure," said Amanda.

Amanda tried not to think about Sarah. Instead, Amanda thought about sheets, which usually managed to comfort her. When she couldn't sleep she thought about sheets, and sometimes pillowcases, still in their wrappers. She imagined pillowcases covered in little flowers, the kind her mother loved to buy. She occasionally tried to put stripes over her imaginary pillowcases, but the stripes simply did not have the same reassuring effect.

Amanda's mother had revealed a few weeks ago that she too thought about sheets to help her go to sleep.

Amanda had always disapproved of her mother's existence—her cupboards neatly piled with sheets, her flower arrangements, her baking.

"But darling," her mother once said, "it has been a good life. I have looked after you and your brothers well. I have given you good memories. Above all, I have given you something stable and dull to rebel against. I have also done charitable work. My peace has only ever been sullied by those younger than myself who seem to think life is for suffering."

"But you accept a role as a parasite," Amanda had said.

"I have worked hard, darling, I can assure you."

Her mother had smiled and shaken her head, and wandered out into the garden to pick lilac blossom.

Grudgingly, as Amanda traveled with Tom into the city which was waiting there about to engulf her, she thought how pleasant it would be for Kate to live somewhere like her parent's house in Surrey, with the lawn and the lilac trees and the little park around the corner and the sweet, clean air.

With both mother and father working, it was crucial to have a home near the office in order to be able to get back to it quickly. So not only did Kate not have her mother looking after her, she also had to live in the middle of a city, thought Amanda morosely.

Amanda imagined a white sheet with a lacy border. She imagined taking it out of a crinkly wrapper and feeling the cotton stiff and formal.

Amanda's mother's first action on hearing the news that Amanda was pregnant had been to shop, to make sure that this child would not come into the world naked, but equipped with a complete layette, a crib, and everything else she could think of.

When, a week after the birth, she saw the changing table Amanda had bought for Kate, she frowned and said, "I wish I'd bought her that," and Amanda laughed and put her arms around her mother, standing there so sadly, and hugged her and told her how much she loved her, which she did.

They were not used to hugging each other and her mother was stiff for a moment, and then she relaxed and Amanda could feel her pleasure. Her mother smelled nice, of scent and peppermints, as she had always smelled nice. As Amanda had hugged her mother, her daughter lay in the crib, rhythmically kicking her legs, and for a moment she felt they were all one: the little girl, the young woman, the older woman, a set of Russian dolls, the baby fitting into the woman, the woman into the older woman.

The car stopped at some traffic lights.

"Are you looking forward to this party of George Stewart's on Saturday?" said Amanda.

"Yes, except I've got a lot of work to get done. Really, I shouldn't go. I certainly don't know how long I'll want to stay."

"When you actually get to parties, you know you always want to stay longer than I do."

"Tell me," said Tom, "why is it that nowadays most of our conversations take place in the car?"

"It's one of the things that happen when you have a baby. I suppose it's one of the few times we get to be alone together. Anyway, I read recently that most severe marital quarrels happen in cars. At least we're not having a severe marital quarrel."

Out the window Amanda saw a girl in a short leather skirt which beautifully covered her neat bottom. The girl carried a briefcase and walked as though the streets were hers, the skies were hers, they all belonged in her lovely lungs.

They passed clothes shops, jewelry shops, they heard pop music blaring from the open window of the car beside her.

Amanda stared at a man with a mustache. There was a man with a frown. There was a man with a big jowl.

How comical adults were, she decided, in their suits and ties, hurrying along, as though all the mechanical toys in a giant's toy shop had escaped.

There was the Bank of England, where men counted out their money. There was a merchant bank where men spent their days watching flickering screens. There was the Stock Exchange, where young men shouted things at each other. All over the world, ticker, ticker, ticker, tap, tap, tap, chat, chat, chat, information scurried from the world center about bonds and stocks and shares and gilts and gold.

Back in the Houses of Parliament older men sat huddled in folds of skin and suits, listening to other men's opinions of the world and expressing their own.

By the world they meant, of course, the human world of politics and wars and housing, not the other world which was here first, not the seas and the desert and the way the sunlight falls through the leaves of forests.

"I wish I was at home with Kate," said Amanda. "I feel I'm abandoning her. They used to leave them on mountaintops. Now we leave them with nannies or child minders."

"You said last night you'd go crazy looking after her all day, every day."

"Yes," she said, "but it seems sometimes I'm going crazy not looking after her."

They drove on, and Amanda hated to see the dirt covering the buildings.

"You know, I wish I could go in front of Kate for the rest of her life with a dustpan and brush sweeping up the sly people, the spiteful, the wicked, the dirt in the streets, the men who might hurt her, the women who might hate her. But of course I shall have to leave her to make her own way and get dirty before she gets clean."

"You needn't worry about her adolescence quite yet," said Tom.

She stared at his shoe. He had vast feet. She used to find something consoling about the size of his shoes.

"Your shoes aren't very clean," she said.

"I couldn't find the black polish."

"It's in the drawer where it always is. You can remember the names of every known planet and star in the universe, and yet you don't remember in which drawer the shoe polish is kept."

She put her hand on Tom's arm and was disappointed by its size. She wanted something smaller, more of Kate's dimensions. The pores of his skin were huge, potholes she feared she might fall through. His body took up such a lot of space. There was so much volume in his body.

"I'm seeing a man about getting more life insurance," said Tom.

She stuck out her lower lip.

"I'm sorry to be moody. It's just I didn't know it was possible to love this much. I thought love was something one did in one's spare time. I didn't realize it was a full-time activity."

"You know you could just take a consulting job two days a week . . ."

"I've been thinking about Cambridge. In many ways it's very attractive. But I enjoy my job and I'm frightened I'll lose everything I've built up, my confidence, my authority, the respect of others, my salary, all my autonomy."

She remembered the conversation she'd overheard in the nursery on the private ward three days after Kate's birth. She had been sitting there feeding the baby, and had therefore been invisible, just a mother. The woman who spoke was thin and efficient, with painted nails. She held a red baby with a scrunched-up face, and it was feeding. But she appeared to be holding the baby as far away as she could while still allowing it to feed.

"Everyone sends me flowers," she said to her husband. "Roses and chrysanthemums. I can't stand chrysanthemums. Flowers. It's like a funeral parlor in my room. Everyone smiles sweetly and sends me flowers because they think my life has ended. They're saying, 'Oh, isn't it lovely that Vivien has a baby. She must be so happy.' But really they're gloating, that's what they're doing, just like they do at funerals."

The woman had rubbed her eyes, spreading black mascara over them.

"Cambridge is only about an hour and a half from London," said Tom.

"I know, darling. It is very tempting. But maybe it's the easy option."

"That's not necessarily the wrong one."

225

Tom drew up outside her office building. He kissed her. His lips felt hot on her skin.

"Good luck, darling," he said.

He hardly recognized the face which looked back at him with unfocused eyes. It was fuller than her previous face, and much softer. Even the eyes were softer.

"Thanks," she said, and got out clumsily.

42

Kate will not, of course, understand about sex and politics and wars and housing for a number of years. She will believe that the things that interest her, like the way the light falls, her shadow, the movement of a cat, are what matters. She will be impressed by a dog running into water. She will be happy running over grass, then sitting down on her fat bottom. She will live in the present tense, as adults do only in certain strange, intense moments of existence.

She will consider herself the same as cats and dogs, part of the same world.

Kate has so much to learn. She has to learn our customs, our manners, what is considered good behavior and what is considered bad.

Right now, back at the flat, she wonders where her mother has gone, and cries a little.

43

"One day she'll tell us she loves us," said Amanda to Tom.

"A new voice saying old words," said Tom.

Kate kicked some more and then, with a frown of effort, rolled over onto one side.

"Aren't you clever?" said Amanda.

Kate laughed, a clear, beautiful laugh, rejoicing at her cleverness, at the rate it was all taking place, at her sense of happiness, at her mother's smiling face. Oh, the smiles, how Kate loved to see smiles.

"You know, I still don't like leaving her with Sarah," said Amanda. "All day long. I'm nervous . . . they say a mother's instincts are good. Maybe I shouldn't leave her with someone who makes me so wary."

Tom shrugged. "Well, maybe you should find someone else. Whatever you think. Or take Kate to work with you. Why don't you do that?"

"Darling, perhaps you haven't noticed, but Kate's a great deal of work. Obviously, if I could dump her in a briefcase and take her to work, there would be no problem. Besides, I did take her one day. It wasn't a big success, if you recall."

She remembered how as her car had sped toward her office all those weeks ago, every now and then it had taken an excitable jerk to the left or the right which appeared to be in response to the young baby's cries. The same cries had a deleterious effect on the front of her dress, for milk spurted from her breasts and could not be contained within the copious absorbent padding with which her bra was stuffed. She had been trying to cut down breast feeding in readiness for her return to work, but her breasts had not yet got the message and were urgently producing milk.

Amanda had turned up the radio, trying to distract her mind from Kate.

Amanda remembered thinking fuzzily about the words. Since Kate's arrival most of her thoughts had been fuzzy and distant. Some had been so far away that she had never quite managed to reach them, and they had soon given up waiting around for some attention and disappeared.

She had tried to reach a thought about the irrelevancy of pop music to the lives of those with babies; there was simply no time for the themes of contemporary music, and that was the thought, she supposed, although she was aware that there was something far more complex and interesting available to think if only her mental apparatus had been up to it.

Amanda still recalled the day with some horror. She had parked in the garage beneath the forty-story office building where she worked.

She had sat listening to Kate's innumerable complaints while considering how she might manage to get out of the car with Kate, into the elevator, up to the tenth floor, and into her office without disturbing everyone with Kate's hungry cries. She was not sure she could carry it off.

Amanda tried not to consider the possibility that this trip to work was an error. She had been taught to think positively. She was on her way to the office, therefore it was a good thing she was on her way to the office.

She knew women who claimed that for the first six months their babies slept all day every day, so they could be taken anywhere. This did not tally with Amanda's own experience. Certainly Kate slept, but only a few hours a day. Perhaps there was something wrong with Kate, or with other women's babies.

After she parked haphazardly in the garage under their office building, she struggled to get the baby carrier out of the car while also holding Kate, who was wriggling, and whose limbs acquired a superhuman strength when she was cross. She considered putting Kate down on the seat, but had a vision of her rolling off and crashing onto the cement floor. She recalled as a teenager studying books which showed how to hold a glass of wine and a plate of food and a handbag while standing up at a party. She wished she had seen one about how to hold a cross baby while trying to wrench a carrier out of the car.

Prenatal classes, she decided, should have included at least one lesson in which each woman had to have her hand tied behind her back while completing various complex tasks such as cutting the top off a boiled egg.

Amanda dumped Kate in the carrier, locked the car, and raced for the door of the office building. On arrival at the door, she realized she had forgotten her briefcase.

She considered leaving the carrier by the door while she ran back to the car, but memories of stolen babies made her trudge back complete with the screaming baby and carrier, which really was far heavier than it should have been because she had bought a particularly sturdy and expensive model, not realizing this was a waste of money. Kate's toes had touched the end of it within eight weeks.

Certainly the arrival of a new human being on earth was an extraordinary wonder and mystery, she thought, but the purchase of its innumerable accoutrements was equally shrouded in mystery.

Her various shopping errors had added to the sensation of puzzlement which had beset her since having Kate. She was not used to making poor decisions. She was the kind of person who researched a subject thoroughly and then made an informed decision. She was simply not the kind of person to buy too heavy a baby carrier, for too much money, which outlived its usefulness in two months. And as for the problem of the high chair, she had received so much divergent advice, she did not know what to do. Some high chairs turned into a child's chair and table. This seemed sensible. But Caroline had told her to beware of anything that turned into anything else.

"Nowadays everything turns into something else. But proper chairs simply can't be turned into proper tables. Next thing they'll be telling us that the baby's crib can easily be converted into its first fridge when it leaves home."

Eventually, complete with briefcase, carrier, and baby, she proceeded to the elevator. Amanda's office was occupied by a solitary secretary studying *The Sun* meticulously, with her head lowered so as not to miss a word.

"Hello, Ann. Busy?" said Amanda.

She checked her correspondence while trying not to listen to Kate's little coos and grunts, which abruptly altered to whimpers.

Kate let out a scream. Her fists were clenched and red, as though about to take part in a boxing match.

Amanda took her to the lavatory to change her diaper.

Another partner in the organization, Cynthia, who was married, forty, and without children, watched Amanda struggling to change the diaper while kneeling on the floor. Cynthia had often remarked on her dislike of babies.

"It's great to see you again," said Cynthia. "Will you be bringing the baby regularly?"

"Perhaps," said Amanda fiercely. "There should be changing facilities."

She wished Cynthia would not watch her go through this undignified procedure.

"No one here has a baby except you. People just don't have babies," said Cynthia.

"Oh, really? That's an interesting theory," said Amanda crossly. "How do you think we all get here, then?"

"Actually, my secretary thinks she's pregnant."

"Is she pleased? She's married, isn't she?"

"What a conventional view of life. She's married, so she must want children. As a matter of fact, she is married, and she does want children, but she had in mind having them by her husband and not some chap she met in a pub one night when she hadn't eaten a thing all day."

"Does that make you pregnant?"

"It does if you drink too much and go back to sober up at his place."

"There should be a day nursery in a building as big as this. It's absurd," said Amanda. "And changing facilities. We women have never been efficient at organizing our own well-being, and we're no better now."

"I can't believe this is you talking. You used to be so professional."

"If by professional, you mean masculine, thanks a lot."

She washed her hands while Kate lay, kicking

merrily on the mat and, looking around, quite pleased at this change of environment.

"She's a nice-looking baby," said Cynthia grudgingly.

"Oh, do you think so?" said Amanda, looking down at Kate.

Fortunately, Amanda had managed to rock Kate to sleep before the meeting, which went reasonably well, once the other people arrived and the atmosphere of money and power gathered her up and made her forget about Kate for a few seconds every now and again as she sat with the baby in her arms, making the men and women uncomfortable.

"Ah, yes," said Tom. "I remember the visit wasn't a big success." His forehead cracked into a theatrical frown. "It's the twenty-four-hour existence of babies which is the problem," he said. He started to pace up and down the room, with his hands behind his back. "I wasn't prepared for it, personally. Nothing in literature or art prepared me for it. Of course, in films babies are produced as comic turns, but—"

"Tom, please stop pacing up and down."

"Of course," he continued, stopping abruptly where he was. "Friends like Howard and Andrew have babies . . . but they tend to bring them out like . . . I don't know . . . stamps . . . then put them away afterward. That's if one saw them at all."

"I know," said Amanda, looking at Kate, whom she now held in her arms.

Amanda pulled a face at Kate, who allowed herself a slight toothless smile, but she didn't seem quite able to coordinate the rest of her expressions and her eyes remained serious. She tried again, and this time the mouth swam up into a little smile and at the same time her eyes shone, and then the smile collapsed from the effort and the grave little face pondered Amanda's enormous one.

Amanda ran a finger around her tiny ear, a soft, intricate maze leading into an impenetrable mystery.

"Have you noticed how Kate looks like a distinguished politician, usually Gorbachev? Why do you think that is?" said Tom. He came over to Kate. "Perhaps all babies do. Perhaps it's because they are born very dominating, or maybe it's because they're continually troubled, in the case of babies by wet diapers or hunger, in the case of politicians by taxes and insurrections of one kind or another."

"Well," said Amanda, "neither babies nor important politicians tend to have much hair."

Tom laughed. His laugh was a surprisingly crude one, and it always came at full force, as though he'd been holding it back for hours.

"We should get to bed soon," said Amanda.

"I'll work a little longer," he said, going into his study.

44

Trisha Hunt reminded Alice of Snow White's stepmother.

When she'd seen the film, she had been frightened of the prince coming and carrying Snow White away, because Alice didn't want to be carried away from her mother. But now that her mother had gone, she remembered how the evil stepmother had kept changing, as Trisha changed, and how she had given Snow White a poisoned apple, and how long her nose had been, like Trisha's teeth.

Sometimes Alice thought Trisha Hunt was really a bird, one of those dinosaur birds with long teeth.

After school, Trisha had taken her shopping and Alice had stood, a metal statue, in the department store as Trisha riffled through the clothes, merrily calling out the appearance of each item like an auctioneer.

"Superb maroon velvet dress ... beautiful white lace dress ... tartan dress with a red sash ..."

Afterward, she took Alice to tea at Fortnum and Mason's, and Alice's legs dangled from a chair as she ate little sandwiches and looked around.

"Now, I want you and I to be great friends," Trisha said.

Alice bit into her cucumber sandwich, and looked down at her black patent shoes.

"If you're nice," said Trisha, "you can be a bridesmaid when we marry. I know you miss your mother. But I want us to be friends. I really do. I love children," she said, rearranging her flowery dress on her slender knees. She wore high heels.

Trisha chattered all the way home as Alice sat on the black leather seat of the taxi.

"Now, where would you like to go for your next holiday? Somewhere with a beach, perhaps. Children love beaches. I know I did. A bucket and spade and I was happy, even though I was afraid of the water."

"Were you?"

"Yes. I can't swim even now."

"I like the water," said Alice fiercely, thinking how foolish Trisha was not to be able to swim. Her mother swam beautifully, and could even do the butterfly stroke.

As soon as Alice got through the door of their house, she hurried to her room and shut the door. She wanted to draw, but she couldn't find any paper, so she went to the pink wall of her bedroom with a red crayon and she drew a picture of a bird with long, sharp teeth.

Then she climbed onto the bed and cried for her mother.

45

Trisha Hunt liked to read fairy tales to Alice before she fell asleep. Trisha sat on the edge of the bed, arranging her skirt, relishing the picture of the pretty young woman reading to the eager little child. She had always read out loud well, with plenty of emotion. The flower curtains were drawn. She had a gin and tonic by Alice's bed. Above the two females was a picture of Alice's name entwined with flowers. She was reading from "Jack the Giant Killer":

". . . But the giant showed fight and took up his club to defend himself; whereupon Jack, with one clean cut of the sword of strength, severed his head from his body, and would doubtless have done the same to the magician, but that the latter was a coward and, calling upon a whirlwind, was swept away by it into the air, nor has ever been seen or heard of since."

Alice listened avidly, her arm around her teddy bear.

46

Sarah was standing in the kitchen when Tom returned home early. Kate slept. Sarah thought of Amanda kissing George. She thought of how George had made love to her, Sarah, out in the garden one night when they had been first in love. His skin had always been hot.

Tom rambled in, greeting her and stretching out to open a top cupboard, out of which he dropped a coffee cup which shattered on the floor.

They both stared at it. The white pieces lay, a violent jigsaw, on the terra cotta-tiled floor. They looked at each other.

The narrow kitchen seemed smaller than before, as though the white walls were pushing them together.

The dim light from the river infiltrated through the window.

He stood there: untidy hair, round glasses, his body big and clumsy and oddly vulnerable.

"Fuck," he said.

She stooped down and picked up a triangle of

white china. As she did so, she cut her hand and a little blood showed up on her porcelain skin.

He took a step toward her.

On one wall hung a poster displaying first-aid techniques. One picture illustrated a baby with a finger in an electric socket, lying limply on the floor while her mother poked her with a wooden broom to push her away from the source ("If you touch your child you will become part of the circuit"). Another picture depicted an infant in flames and a brave mother flinging herself over the baby to smother the fire ("Keep a blanket in the kitchen to use as a fire blanket"). It showed a child hung from its toes ("Turn a baby upside down and pat its back if it chokes"). A third illustrated a child tumbling down some stairs, its mouth wide with terror.

He took her hand gently. The cut was on the palm of her left hand. His face was swimming, losing definition. She continued to look into his eyes. She was fed up with being good; it only made her crazy. It only made other people push her around. It only made her lose whatever she had. She had always been told to be good, to be kind, to be passive. And now she had nothing.

You had to be strong. She moved closer to Tom, who was blinking in a puzzled manner.

"It hurts," she said. One of his shoes was standing on a broken fragment of china.

His wide forehead frowned. The furrows were so deep, she could have walked into them.

His mouth was huge too. She could have

climbed into it and curled up somewhere in the red cavern.

Her head was too full of hiding, she thought.

He held her hand, and their hands were flaming.

There should be another chart depicting dangerous situations for adults, including one with a couple with their hands on fire, and another with a man and a woman shoved tightly together in a white coffin-sized kitchen.

"You have lovely hands," he said.

"Do you think there'll be a scar?" she said.

"Do you want a scar?"

"Yes," she said. "I'd like a scar. At least it would show I'd been hurt."

"You show it," he said.

He was still holding her hand, as though it were some unbreakable priceless treasure. He kept turning it over and frowning.

His free hand rushed through his hair.

"I don't get very hurt," he said.

"You don't try very hard."

She closed her eyes. She was only her hand. The hand was being caressed and everything else had withdrawn; the rest of her body ceased to exist. As for the noises of the kitchen—the hum of the fridge, the whine of the fan—they were distant noises. She swayed. He stroked her fingers and it seemed he was stroking her bare legs. He touched the center of her palm and it seemed he was touching the center of her. His touch kept changing: stroking, pulling, delicately kissing into her skin, pressing hard into her skin. His finger explored the crevices between each of her fingers. The hum of the fridge changed its tone and she jumped slightly, but his hand went on playing games in her hand, and she returned to her drowsy state of desire, not wishing the hand to stop its seductive pathways. The fan contributed a faint breeze to the still room. How still everything was. She was aware that boats were probably bobbing up and down, that people in offices and in houses were making practical decisions about what phones to buy, what lawn mower to choose, what to eat that evening, but it seemed that really there were only two hands making love there, in some unspecified space and time—one of the hands a rough hand with hairs over its back and the other a ballerina's hand, white as milk.

She opened her eyes and looked into his.

"I shouldn't be doing this," he said. His thumb pressed into the palm of her hand.

"You've done nothing," she said.

He wanted to kiss her. She could see the heat of his lips. She let her eyes close again and waited.

"I shouldn't be standing here with you." His thumb pressed harder. "I must get back to work." The thumb made a circle in her hand, then the circle became wider and wider, and as it widened she opened her eyes again and watched his hand leave hers.

"I have to go," he said.

"Go, then," she said.

She was watching his mouth. She wanted to touch his mouth. His mouth took up most of his face. She wanted to touch it with her fingers, with her lips, with her tongue. His big nose stood like a sentry over his mouth, and above it were the brown eyes, two guards peering through his skin as though armed with bows and arrows, catapults, all kinds of primitive warfare to protect him.

"I am happy as I am," he said.

"*Quite* happy," she countered.

"Quite happy is fine with me. I am a realistic person."

She looked down at her hand. It looked very lonely, a slight movement of flesh.

"Okay," she said softly. "You'd better go."

He left. He rambled off, bumping into the kitchen door and out through the front door. She heard his footsteps stop outside the front door, as if he was thinking of returning, but then they continued down the hall.

47

In her office Amanda sat with her head in her hands. She stared at a pile of paperclips. She stared at the phone. She thought how immense her desk was, and how small she felt, sitting at the edge of it, in her chair. The desk was black, and the paperclips glittered. She had envelopes too on her desk, and rubber bands, and thick white sheets of paper with the name of her company neatly printed on the top in bright green.

Outside, the clouds were beginning to fill the sky, elbowing their way in until nearly all the blue had disappeared.

It was four o'clock. She rang through to her secretary and said she had to leave early for a meeting. Yesterday Tom had behaved very oddly. He had hardly spoken to her. She felt insecure. She wanted to see Kate, who made her feel secure.

She drove across London with her radio turned up very loud.

She wondered if Kate's latest cold was better. She wondered what Sarah Adams would be doing with the baby right now.

She remembered she had felt like this when she used to wait for Tom to phone during the first months of their relationship. The mixture of panic and anxiety and bliss was the same.

Not so long ago the phone calls and secretaries and decisions had meant so much to her, and now it was as though work was a late-night party she was glad to leave. The people she had so enjoyed talking to earlier in the night, when the party was new, now she didn't care if she never saw again in her whole life.

When Jeremy Harris had asked her to go to New York for some meetings, she had pretended to be excited by the idea. What she had wanted to say was "Forget it. Find someone else. I have a child to look after." But if she said that, Jeremy would have looked at her in a way that would have demeaned her. He would have despised her. He, after all, could go where he pleased. Working women too were supposed to be able to tuck their children up in photograph frames for days on end.

The flat, even more than usual, did not seem to belong to her. Sarah's blue raincoat was hanging on the coat stand. Sarah had some choral music on, high, mournful choirboy voices. Sarah's empty coffee mug was on the table.

Amanda took off her coat. She stared at the photographs of Tom and her, and was almost surprised to see them there, as though by now they should have been replaced by those of Sarah's relations: slight, dark figures with fairy eyes, creatures who moved stealthily around rooms, spreading an atmosphere of sadness. Even the river had begun to reflect Sarah's moods. It was gray, running fast, and in the early morning a mist often rose from it which filled Amanda with a momentary despair.

She told herself how good Sarah was with Kate, and how grateful she should be. Kate seemed to like her. Indeed, Kate seemed to love her. When she was crying, she was quickly soothed by Sarah. Her reference from the job she had in France said that Sarah had a way with children. But Amanda felt that she, as Kate's mother, knew her best and was the one who should be with her. After all, she knew what each of her cries meant. She knew what to do. She understood her. She knew what Kate was feeling even when she wasn't with her. She was Kate's puppet. It was as though tight strings had been tied all around the various bits inside her—the heart, the stomach, the lungs—and Kate tugged all of them very hard whenever she left her. Besides, she would never let any danger come to Kate. She was completely attentive to her because Kate's well-being and hers were indissolubly linked.

Amanda felt herself to be no more than notes in a briefcase, a series of business strategies, a late-twentieth-century version of a woman, someone who was no more than the impressive curriculum vitae of her life, whereas a real woman's life perhaps happens *between* the words of the curriculum vitae, in the ordinary, extraordinary moments of existence, in the unwritten impossible history of a child's first giggle, a child's first joke, the breeze through an open window.

Maybe I shall live in Cambridge as Tom would like and grow sweet peas and blackcurrants, and Kate can sit on the step next to me shelling peas grown in our garden and stealing the little baby sweet ones, she thought.

Or maybe I can never be comfortable now I know both ways of life, both ruthless alternatives, both indescribably desirable versions of a woman's life. Instead I will have to hire another woman to sit next to Kate and shell peas and tell her about "The Three Billy Goats Gruff" and "The Three Little Pigs" while I tell men in suits about Business Plans and the Garment Industry in the Twenty-first Century. I am two people; it's just that I have to hire someone else to play the part of one of them.

The nursery door was closed. She shouldn't burst in. Perhaps Kate was asleep. But she wanted to see Kate and her wide, surprised eyes. She wished Sarah wasn't disturbing in such a complex and, well, sophisticated way.

The choirboys' voices sang of the temporary nature of love and of mortality, and Amanda's eyes misted over. *My eyes used to be blue and now they're turning gray,* she thought, *like the river. Why did we ever want to live by the river? Even when the sun does shine on it, it looks miserable, as though taunting me to say that the sun is only temporary, a sparkle, a trick of the light, that the reality is the gray constant waters underneath. Only the stupidly insensitive or the wise should live by rivers. For the rest of us, those in between, it really is too depressing.*

My daughter is mine. Tom, well, of course I love Tom, but he's not mine. He's not of my flesh. He could be replaced. But Kate, she could never be replaced. There is only this Kate here, my daughter, my darling, my hope. She is me, but a better version of me. I knew it the moment she was born and I saw her quick, intelligent, curious eyes. She is a blend of Tom and me, a perfect alignment of all that makes me like him and him like me, all the reasons we need each other, all that is complementary about us, all blended in her into a whole.

I don't know why I'm thinking like this. Perhaps it's the music, or the movement of the river, but something makes me think of people leaving each other.

The door to the nursery was slightly open. Through the opening she saw Sarah rocking Kate tenderly in her arms.

Sarah was singing to her in a sweet, high voice:

"Rock away, my little, rock little baby,
Rock away my precious, beautiful baby.
Lulli, rock away.
Wherever you may be, there will be your joy.

Lulli, rock away.
Strong little baby, wonderful baby,
Proud you make everyone as we rock your

cradle.
Lulli, rock away.
Wherever love is, there you will ever live,
Ever living, you fill our hearts with sweet love.
Lulli, rock away."

She then sang:

"White wings they never grow   weary
They carry me cheerily over the sea
Night comes, I long for you darling
I'll spread out my white wings
And fly home to you."

Sarah was so involved with her singing she did not hear Amanda.

Amanda was the intruder again, the outsider, the woman who worked out there in grayness, away from the warmth here at home.

Kate was dressed, Amanda noted, in an outfit she had not yet put her in. It was a present from a cousin, fuschia pink with big pockets. She looked lovely in it, but did not look like her baby. She seemed to belong to Sarah, as the flat seemed to belong to her.

Amanda would have liked to have been the first to dress her in that particular outfit. She wanted to be Kate's only guide to the world. She wanted to show her deep snow for the first time, to give her her first taste of ice cream, and to watch for the first time how her little nose squashed against a window. She wanted to be the first to take her swimming, the one to hear her first words.

Amanda stepped into the nursery. Sarah looked startled at the mother's entry. Without speaking, Amanda took Kate from Sarah and hugged her tightly. Sarah looked away, pretending not to notice the passion with which Amanda held Kate.

"Hello, Sarah. Has she been all right?" said Amanda after the first rush of love had subsided.

"Bit snuffly," said Sarah. "Oh, Tom was here earlier, but he had to go back to work."

Sarah got up to go. Amanda was torn between her businesslike self wanting at once to clear up matter of New York with Sarah, and her maternal desire to be alone with Kate.

"Do you have a minute? I must talk to you about something," said Amanda, and looked slightly surprised. She found herself surprised now by both her selves—the passionate mother and the figure who strode confidently down office corridors. She no longer knew who she was.

"I'm thinking of taking Kate to New York with me on a business trip I have to make the week after next."

Sarah stood at the door. She wore a light blue shift, almost a nurse's uniform.

"New York?" she echoed.

"That's right."

"She can stay here with me," said Sarah. "I'll look after her well. I don't mind the extra hours."

"I definitely would like to take her. I'd miss

her too much. But of course, she can't come to all the numerous meetings . . .

"Please, Sarah. I would be grateful. You're so marvelous with Kate."

Kate opened her eyes, stared at her, frowned, and closed her eyes again.

Amanda placed Kate into her crib.

She wandered into the kitchen to make herself some coffee. She realized she was trembling.

Amanda stabbed a teaspoon into a jar of instant coffee.

Perhaps I shouldn't go to New York, she thought. Perhaps I should be honest and just say I can't bear to leave Kate. Perhaps she should tell them to send someone else. Or maybe she should just leave Kate behind, with Sarah and Tom. It might even be good for Tom to have the responsibility. It was just that she didn't really trust him with Kate. He might go out and forget about her, or drop her, or forget to feed her. Besides, she somehow did not want to leave Sarah and Tom together.

Indeed, it might be invigorating to return to Kate at the end of a day in New York. She was always reading about women who perfectly managed the world of home and work. Why shouldn't she be one of those women? She brushed down her skirt. In spite of her smart clothes and confidence, she still looked almost too young to be a partner in a big consulting firm, and a mother. Everything she did, she did with an air of integrity, as though she were a head girl in a school play playing the part of a businesswoman. This made people at times take her less than seriously, to their cost.

She dreaded that if she said she didn't want to go to New York, she'd be patronized for it. People would be understanding, but would despise her. She did not want a reputation for emotional frailty. She had worked hard all her life. She had tried hard. Her mother and father had treated her the same as her brothers. They sent her to a good school, a good university. She had never felt that men were more important than she was. It had never occurred to her. But now she felt pressure not just to refuse to go to New York but to give up work, to execute the person she had spent her life becoming. She did not want to throw away all that she had tried for, all that she valued, just for the satisfaction of certain primeval urges such as holding her baby whenever she pleased. She should be stronger than that.

A magnet on the fridge helped secure a picture of the newly born Kate. For a moment, looking at Kate's picture—she looked so vulnerable, so pink and delicate—Amanda wondered how she could even think of taking her to New York City.

Sarah stood at the kitchen door, holding Kate, who had woken, in her arms.

"Okay," said Amanda softly, "it might be . . . dangerous for Kate in New York. She'd be safer with you here. I'll leave her here. You're proba-

bly right. It's just that ... I'll miss her so
desperately."

Although Sarah wore her neat, polished shoes
and had white buttons running down the front
of her dress, there was something disorderly
about her eyes.

She kept blinking at Amanda. She stood at the
side of the door, almost as though hiding, and
the recessed lights which illuminated the white
kitchen so brightly somehow missed Sarah, who
was an altogether more shadowy figure.

I have to stand in the spotlight, thought Amanda.

She smiled at Sarah as she went past her to
Tom's study. She slumped down on his chair.
There were books everywhere: *Realm of the Neb-
ulae; The Nature of the Universe; Space, Time and
Gravity*. She sipped her coffee from a thin bone
china cup. She stared up at the posters describ-
ing Copernicus's and Galileo's view of the heavens. On his desk was a picture of her early in
her pregnancy.

The choirboys' high cathedral voices trembled.

She had never wanted to be a maternal type.
She wasn't made for the role. She was slight and
girlish, and more suited to the tennis court (she
excelled at tennis) than the maternity ward. *But
I am trapped now, ensnared in cobwebs of love,
hopelessly entangled,* she thought.

Sarah knocked on the door.

*How extraordinary it is to pay for someone to have
this relationship with my daughter,* she thought.

It's like paying a mistress to make love to one's husband.

"I think she wants you," said Sarah. She put Kate into Amanda's arms. Amanda held her tightly. For a moment Amanda felt quite grateful to Sarah.

48

Of course Sarah had been to see a lawyer after realizing that George intended to keep Alice. But she had sat there in pain, unable to focus, hardly able to speak, noting how shiny his desk was but how the dust covered the window.

"Mr. Stewart claims you had lovers," he said.

"It's not true. I had an old friend who loved me, that's all. His name's Martin."

"He had letters—he also said you suffered from mental disturbance and provided us with psychiatric reports."

"I haven't had any mental problems whatsoever since Alice was born. The problem in the past was always that I needed her—I didn't know it was she I needed, of course—and then she came and I realized that all my angst had been because I needed her."

The lawyer sat back in his chair, his legs like two huge mountains and his face splotchy.

"You don't have a good case. You could fight it, but you might lose."

And she had felt immensely weary. She hung

her head and stared at her lilac handbag and matching lilac suit. She was dressed like some-one going to Henley.

How ridiculous it had all been. She had accompanied George to Wimbledon, to Henley, to cocktail parties, to all the events at the center of establishment life, and all the while she hadn't been quite there, it was true, and that was why George was angry with her. That was why he had organized this conspiracy of lawyers. She had smiled, and carried handbags, and made conversation, and not stretched over and grabbed the salt but asked for it to be passed, and she had poured a little on the side of her plate, but sometimes she got carried away and pour a small mountain of salt, and thought about Lot's wife being turned into a pillar of salt, while all around the intricacies of politics were being discussed.

"Oh, quite," she would say, "oh, certainly," and she would think about the way the river clung to the banks and was then swept away as though at the center of everything was this suffering, this separation.

She wore color-coordinated clothes. She went to the hairdressers. She wrote proper thank-you letters, but at night she lay listening to the rain slamming into windowpanes, wondering why she was lying in bed with this man.

And then she had given birth to Alice, and all at once her life had a meaning because it had created Alice.

After Alice's birth Sarah had not wanted to continue with the life she had. She didn't want to meet the people in suits and formal dress, and she didn't want to pass the canapes and pour the champagne. She wanted to lie in bed with her baby.

"So I found you at last," Sarah had said to her baby. "I looked for you in the faces and bodies of men, and here you are, quite different from all that. How could I have known?"

"She's your little doll, isn't she?" George had said nastily.

He had always been jealous of whatever it was that made her distant from him, and now that disengagement had a corporeal form, he was profoundly jealous of it—but in time he learned to be fond of the exotic creature, with her moods, tumultuous rages, and smothering kisses.

Sarah began to make excuses to avoid going out with George and leaving Alice behind. He would come back late with a rumpled sense of the world about him, and she would be glad to have spent the evening alone in the house with Alice, glad not to have been out there wearing lipstick and smiles. Instead she would sit reading in their drawing room, and every now and again would go up the stairs, past the oil paintings of the French countryside, expressing both peace and some profounder sense of disturbance, and up to Alice's bedroom, where she would watch the baby sleep, and then the child, as the body in the crib lengthened month by month. The house would be still except for the child's quiet breath.

In the drawing room she would finger George's silver trinkets and feel herself to be utterly detached from this house of his, a visitor at a country house hotel. Nothing here except Alice belonged to her, especially not the clothes in the wardrobe, which she and George had chosen for someone quite other than herself: someone positive, someone perfectly balanced on his arm.

At night she read Alice fairy tales of wicked witches and princesses, of people not being what they appeared to be, of giants and bad fairies, of dark towers, of revenge.

"Do you know my husband?" Sarah asked the lawyer.

"Everyone knows Mr. Stewart," he replied as the light pressed against the windows.

The lawyer had a callow face.

She stumbled out into the street. She considered going to her parents for help, but decided she couldn't bear it—she couldn't bear again standing at the picture window examining the flat lawn while her mother stood beside her, her breasts like cushions, telling her she had never managed to take control of her life.

"So clever," her mother would say, "and everyone always adored you. . . ."

Her mother wore snowstorms of powder and smelled of eau de cologne, of stifling odors. When Sarah was with her mother she felt as though she'd been packed up in an old box and couldn't get out. Her mother liked to touch her, as though perpetually wrapping her up.

She could imagine her mother swaddling her tight, horribly tight, as a baby, and still wishing she could.

As for her father, he went about his life as though the whole of his existence were a displacement activity. He played his golf, played his endless bridge games, did the washing up, all with a sense of guilt, as though there was something very important he really should be doing. He would jump if she interrupted him doing almost anything.

When Sarah had to go to the hospital during her breakdown, her parents were not much help. Her father stood at one side of the bed, looking twitchily over his shoulder, putting his hands in and out of his pockets, while her mother stood at the other side as though someone had overstuffed her with padding and she couldn't move. Her hair was crimped and gray, and peculiarly lifeless.

Sarah had lain there on the white sheets, in the private room, looking at the flicker of the tree outside her window.

When Alice was born, Sarah's parents were thrilled and flung themselves with enthusiasm on the lovely child. But Sarah didn't want them doing to Alice whatever it was that they'd done to her. She didn't like the way her mother breathed so closely over, swaddling her with her warm toothpaste breath. She didn't like the way her father tickled Alice with an extraordinary lack of concentration, as though he were mentally studying logarithms at the same time. She didn't like the colors of the clothes they bought her, or the sizes, which were always too small, as though they were incapable of adjusting their visions to reality.

The smell of her mother's cologne would make Sarah want to choke, as though doors were being slammed tightly all around her. In her mind she would see her mother's tidy dressing table, with its dusting of face powder.

She could perhaps have gone to Martin for help.

She had continued to see Martin during her marriage, but only as a friend. He was just a boy, really, although two years older than she. She had allowed him to visit her in a spirit of sympathy.

He was just an old friend, she had told George, which was perfectly true. Gangly, nervous, freckly, Martin watched her as though she were a miracle. He was a photographer and he would take endless photographs of her: of her at the window, of her in bed, of her combing her hair, as though if he took enough photographs he could capture the essence of her. But he never could capture it. It was somewhere, he knew, in the curve of a cheek, or the shape of her hand, or the way she moved when she was tired, and one day he would capture it, and then he would be all right and not feel as though all the time spent with her was some sullen dream.

Sarah would kiss him sometimes, but briefly, charitably, and she would advise him on what to do (he worked for a newspaper but wanted to be recognized as an artist). She had a good sense of what other people should do with their lives.

He told her she should leave George and come to live with him, and that they would be happy. But she didn't know, he was too young, too unfinished, while she at times seemed hardly to exist. She needed a hold on reality.

"Alice is your hold. You know that. Since you've had Alice you've been fine. He keeps you here like some . . . enchanter."

She laughed—that fine, distant laugh.

"Why do you stay with him?"

She shrugged. "I . . . like it here. He's the father of my child."

"He traps you with his possessions," said Martin fiercely.

"Oh, I don't know about that."

"He does."

"I think it's called giving someone a sense of security," said Sarah. "What's so wicked about that?"

"Because it's not real . . . there's no security to him. It's a pretense . . . all the material things are a pretense."

He looked around the drawing room where they sat.

"The Persian carpet . . . the comfortable, shadowy lighting . . . it's all part of him. You're not even in it. You appear to be in it. But you're not."

"Well?"

"You should leave him and come and live with me."

"But I like it here. It's very beautiful. And Alice likes it too."

"I look at the photographs of you all the time. When I take the photographs I think at last I finally have you, but then when the photographs come out I find they're not what I meant. I suppose," he said, "I'm not a good enough photographer."

"Oh, you're very good," said Sarah. "Really very good."

"I almost feel that if I had a photograph which captured you perfectly I wouldn't need you, but I suppose that's not really so."

"Probably not," said Sarah, stretching and yawning.

Since she had broken up with George she had not contacted Martin, and did not want him to know where she was. But George and the lawyers knew the number of her hotel, and called her sometimes.

49

"Early in the morning," read Trisha, sipping the wine she had brought up with her while Alice listened. She had been arguing with Alice's father and had already drunk rather too much.

"Gretel had to go out and hang up the kettle full of water, and light the fire.

" 'First we'll bake,' said the old dame. 'I've heated the oven already and kneaded the dough.'

"She pushed Gretel out to the oven, from which fiery flames were already issuing.

" 'Creep in,' said the witch, 'and see if it's properly heated, so that we can shove in the bread.'

"For when she got Gretel in, she meant to close the oven and let the girl bake, so that she might eat her up too. But Gretel perceived her intention and said:

" 'I don't know how I'm to do it: How do I get in?'

" 'You silly goose!' said the hag, and she crawled toward it and poked her head into the oven. Then Gretel gave her a shove that sent her right in, shut the iron door, and drew the bolt. Gracious! how she yelled! it was quite horrible; but Gretel fled, and the wretched old woman was left to perish miserably."

Alice smiled.

"You love fairy tales, don't you?" said Trisha, whose voice was slurred.

Alice nodded.

Trisha leaned over and planted a kiss on Alice's cheek. Alice flinched, but Trisha appeared not to notice. Trisha smelled of wine and scent.

"I did too, when I was little."

"You should let me see my mother."

Trisha held Alice tightly by the arm, so tightly it hurt. The next day there was a bruise, but Alice was too proud to tell anyone.

50

Again, Sarah tried to phone Alice, but again the nanny answered and said no one was allowed to speak to Alice. Sarah begged her, but the girl, knowing who it was, just put down the phone.

Sarah had written to Alice but knew the letters would be intercepted and that even if Alice were given them she wouldn't understand them.

Early that evening she went once more to see her latest lawyer.

They sat in his hunched little office. He was in his twenties but had acquired an air of enormous importance. He had a well-scrubbed face and rubbery lips.

"I feel Alice is miserable with this Trisha Hunt," she said. She took a sip of water from the glass in front of her. Pink lipstick stained the glass.

"I met little Alice once. She seemed a strong-minded little thing," he said.

"This is bad for her," she said. "She's terribly unhappy and lonely."

"And how do you know that?"

"I feel it."

"I'm sure Mr. Stewart is looking after her well."

"I thought mothers always got the children. I can't understand why I don't."

"Usually they get the children," he said, tipping back his chair and loosening his tie. "But not always. You are dealing with a clever man in George Stewart—a man who knows all the ropes. Plus, of course, the little girl is with him right now. You left the house. But long-term he can't win. You have justice on your side."

"I'm not interested in long-term. I need her now. She needs me. She needs me very badly."

He smiled. "I'm doing my best."

"You're failing."

"He's offering her security."

"I have plenty of money. I'm looking for a flat to buy, near her school. It's just at the moment, it upsets me to be too close."

They talked some more before she swung out of the room, watched by the men standing chatting in the hall, and ambled out into Gray's Inn Fields. The air was fresh and sunny. She tried to walk briskly, swinging her arms, holding her briefcase. That was how she'd planned her walk: confident, someone who could handle the law, someone who could handle anything, but then her legs began to give way under her and she sat down on a bench in her smart pink outfit.

Later that evening, finding Sarah alone, Beatrice took her to her room and eagerly showed her a catalogue of high-heeled shoes for size twelve feet. She also displayed her collection of gold and silver stiletto-heeled shoes.

"But don't you find it difficult to walk on them?"

"Oh, no. Well, yes. But I practice. Come on, dear," Beatrice said, tapping the bed. "Do look at this brochure. I'm saving up."

Sarah sat by her. The brochure featured a hotel in Brighton where cross dressers and transsexuals studied "How to Be a Real Woman." There were lessons on deportment, makeup, on dress, and on the last day, the group was taken out to drinks at a hotel as women, with a genuine female instructor. The illustration showed a collection of demure middle-aged women with curly hair and big knees, sipping wine in the lobby of a hotel.

"How do you earn your money?" said Sarah.

"Well," said Beatrice, "of course I have the dole and . . . oh, I write a bit." Beatrice rubbed her nose. "Some pornography, I'm afraid. Not that I approve of it. But you have to make a living. Of course, I'm not staying here much longer. I'm thinking of moving into a flat nearby. You could come too, if you like. You don't want to stay here."

"I feel comfortable here."

"But you're a charming, graceful young woman. You're so . . . self possessed . . . so pure, so clean—almost priggish. Really. I can't understand why you stay in a place like this." Beatrice jumped up. "Come and see my nail polish." She opened a drawer and Sarah saw rows and rows of nail polish in every shade, from Opal Dawn to Black Madonna.

"Very nice," she said.

"My dear," said Beatrice, "you're very quiet and you never see anyone. Are you okay?"

"Oh, I'm having a break from real life."

"This is real life," said Beatrice. "Don't let anyone tell you differently."

"I'm still upset about my little girl. I've been doing my best to get legal custody. I don't just want visitation rights. But it's going to be a long time before I win."

"You know what they say about possession being nine-tenths of the law? Why don't you just go and take her?"

"I can feel her calling me. Most of the time I feel her calling me. It's just if I go and grab her and I fail, I might never get her back."

"Something will come up."

Beatrice examined her large face in the mirror, then glanced quickly at Sarah. She fluffed out her hair.

"My dear," said Beatrice, applying scarlet lipstick on her lips and dabbing her nose with a sandstorm of powder, "do you think I need another wig?"

"No. That's . . . very nice . . . very colorful."

51

Tom's mother came to lunch on Sunday with her third husband, William.

Tom had put the *Messiah* on loudly and was standing near the stereo, conducting the music, while William stood beside him telling him about his sailing boat.

In vermillion socks, a threadbare pair of jeans, and a sweater covered in zigzags like a television gone wrong, Tom smiled to himself as he conducted.

"I'd adore a brisk walk by the river this afternoon. Can one hire a boat?" his mother asked Amanda.

"Not really."

"Mind you, I don't altogether like the look of it. It's filthy. Now, in Richmond ..."

Tom appeared behind her. He put his arm around her.

"Mother. My darling," he said. "It's the same river. It flows."

"It looks dirtier here, much dirtier. Do you

remember how we used to hire a boat in Richmond to take us all down the river?"

"I do, Mother."

Eventually they sat down to lunch. The new husband was a chatty man, with a double chin and a red face.

"Would you like to hold Kate?"said Amanda to Tom's mother.

"Is she quite clean now? I thought before, I detected . . ."

Amanda gave Kate to Tom while she got the salad and smoked salmon.

"What a lovely meal," said Tom's mother. "I suppose you don't have much time to cook—except of course, you have help, I hear. I do hope Kate doesn't prefer the nanny. I hear that can be the most awful trauma. But what does this young woman do all day?"

"Kate's a lot of work," said Amanda.

Tom leaped up, galloped to the stereo, turned it up louder, then swiveled round.

"That's better," he said.

"Little babies aren't much work," said Tom's mother. "They sleep all the time. I just used to put you in your pram outside, and you slept."

With her free hand, Amanda attempted to grind pepper on her salad.

"Nowadays people believe in playing with babies," she said.

"Are you going to put her in her crib now?" said Tom's mother.

"She wouldn't like that," said Amanda.

The new husband helped himself to wine.

"Adorable baby, that Katherine," he said. "She really is a splendid child. It's all genetics, of course. My advice to anyone who marries a woman of child-bearing age is: check out the ancestors. It's all in the ancestors somewhere. Watch out for mad aunts in attics. Early deaths in families should make one take care too." He took a gulp of white wine. "Unless the deaths are murders, of course, in which case it suggests no genetic health problem."

"Unless a member of the family goes mad and kills another member of the family," said Tom, his elbows on the table. "People usually only murder those they know well. It's a sign of breakdown in a society when people start going around murdering those they don't know well."

"Amanda, you're not getting anything to eat," said Tom's mother. "Why don't you let me hold Kate for you a while?"

"You just like holding the baby, don't you, dear?" said her husband. "I can see it. You like the feel of the baby in your arms."

His wife frowned at him, and Tom and Amanda smiled.

"She is very cuddly," said Amanda.

"And, dear . . . Amanda, are you finding it absolutely terrible leaving her to go to work?"

"No. It's fine. I'm finding it fine. I think it's good for children to be looked after by someone other than their mothers."

"How wonderful that the whole thing is so

simple. You just have a baby, find a nanny, and return to your well-paid work. In our day we were so hopeless about it all. We liked to look after the babies ourselves. We felt absurdly protective of them. Why, an area like this, south of the river, more or less the East End, we wouldn't have brought Tom here even for a day trip. Silly, weren't we?"

Tom's mind seemed to fly in from a long way off, and he frowned at his mother. "Mother, please. The area has changed a lot since then," he said. "Things are different."

"Ah, yes, and of course in those days we were all rather proud of our babies. I know how ridiculously proud I was of Tom. I liked to take him around to my friends. I do believe we actually enjoyed looking after our babies. Funny, isn't it? It wasn't anything to be ashamed of at all."

"Oh, stop it, Mother." said Tom. "You're giving me a headache." He rose and stretched, towering over them all. "You really can be absolutely relentless."

"I don't know what you're talking about, dear," said his mother.

Amanda sliced the bread with a black carving knife.

52

When Sarah arrived at the Richardsons, Tom was alone, playing with Kate halfheartedly while attempting to read the newspaper.

He leaped up, beaming.

"Oh, Sarah."

"Hello," she said softly. She hung up her coat. "Where's Amanda?"

"She had to go to work early."

"What a dreary day, don't you think?"

Kate waved her arm appreciatively at Sarah, who bent down before her.

"She has a sunny nature," said Sarah.

"It's true," said Tom.

"'You know," she continued, holding one of Kate's hands. "I believe I came here once, with a boyfriend, when I was about sixteen, before the warehouse was converted. It smelled of spices as it does now. We climbed through a window. There were desks everywhere with empty ink wells, and huge yellowing ledgers

with spidery writing. I think it was here, anyway. It could have been somewhere else. It
smelled damp too but exotic, as though all the
spices from foreign lands had affected the
atmosphere."

She kissed Kate's hand.

"My boyfriend and I . . . we made love, on the
floor . . . by a tall desk . . . and the window
through which we had climbed in was open, and
I could hear the sound of the river."

She looked up, a quick, dark glance. He was
watching her intently.

"I-I'd better be getting to work."

He put down his coffee cup.

"Oh, yes," said Sarah. "You should."

"I'm giving a lecture on the theory of Chaos,
how a butterfly flapping its wings in a rain forest can cause a storm in the Antarctic two
years later, and I have to give another this
evening. . . ."

"I wish I could come."

"I'll see you later," he called as he left the flat
with his briefcase.

At around five o'clock, the phone rang. Sarah
answered it, with an abrupt "Yes?"

The voice on the other end of the phone was
that of George Stewart's.

"Can I speak to Amanda Richardson, please?"
he said.

"She's at work," said Sarah in a voice as disguised as she could.

"I just phoned her there. My name is George Stewart. Tell her I rang, will you."

When Amanda arrived back a few minutes later, Sarah passed on the message from George, and Amanda reddened.

53

"There's someone downstairs for you," said Beatrice late that evening. "Someone tall, handsome, overdressed, and nervous."

Sarah came down the stairs and at the bottom, in the hallway, stood Tom.

"Come up," she said.

He bounded up.

"I was just passing by . . ." He examined his watch. "I know it's late."

She opened the door of her room for him.

"I was just at a dinner around the corner. Astronomy, you know. Discussing black holes and red dwarves and chaos. In Islington. Enormous amount of disagreement on all sorts of fundamental things."

He surveyed her room, with its peeling wallpaper and chipped paint.

"Is this where you live?"

She nodded.

"It's not what I imagined."

"What did you imagine?"

"Oh, I don't know. Some castle somewhere.

Some manor house. Some island. Certainly not this. Although, of course . . . it's very nice." He glanced dubiously at the torn armchair. She laughed.

The landlord knocked on the door, at once put his rosy head in, grunted, then withdrew.

"He's making sure I'm all right," said Sarah. She crossed her arms. "And am I?"

Tom's bulky body took up most of the room. His evening suit and tuxedo made him stand even straighter than usual.

"I . . . just wanted to see where you live. I was in the area. It was a formal event. We all gave speeches."

She took a step toward him, her head tilted to one side, her jeans tight, her hair loose over her shoulders, her eyes laughing at him.

"What did you give a speech on?"

"The first three minutes of the universe."

She smiled. "And now you're standing here, in your shiny shoes, with your bow tie at an angle."

He straightened his bow tie.

"I thought," he said, "you might like to go to the pub or something . . . for a drink. I . . . didn't feel like going home right now . . . and as you were so close I thought . . ."

She raised her eyebrows. "The pub?" She shrugged. "If that's what you want."

"I do," he said.

She sprayed herself with scent.

"Tell me . . . just supposing . . . what would you do if Amanda was ever unfaithful?"

The room smelled of his alcohol and her scent.

"We should go out. There's something peculiar about this place," he said.

"I know."

"I think I find it easier to cope with black holes," said Tom, the lines of his broad face broken up into a puzzle.

"Because they don't have emotions and desires? How do you know?" she said, picking up her coat from the armchair.

In the pub, they talked and laughed and drank too much until the pub closed and he kissed her goodbye on her hand, outside the hotel, in a courtly gesture.

54

"You're back late," said Amanda as Tom came banging and crashing into the flat like a gang of hooligans.

Curled up in her armchair, a biography of Henry VII in her hands, a glass of water on the coffee table, in a white Laura Ashley nightdress, she was trying to present a portrait of wifely calm.

"Oh, I know. I think this flat must have moved. I took the wrong turn."

"Tom, are you okay? Your limbs look as if they've been put on differently, and you've changed your eyes."

He laughed and slumped in one of the oatmeal armchairs, stretching out his legs so far that they seemed to be in another time and place.

"Black holes. I dream of black holes. Perhaps we're in a black hole. Old Professor Roberts insists on the many-universes theory, you know. He discounts chance, he discounts God, he believes there are many universes where the laws and constants of nature are different from each other. He believes that every logically possible universe that could exist, does exist.

"So, for instance, in another universe you could be talking to me now with your hair off from your face with a hair band. And in another, we could already have had a son called John."

"I find even God a more plausible theory," said Amanda.

"I wish you could take me apart," he said wearily, "and put me away in a box for a year or two."

"We don't spend enough time together as it is, Tom. I certainly don't want to put you in a box."

He leaped up, flung open the French windows, and stared up at the night sky with his arms apart.

"Look at the sky. You and I spend too much time gazing at that river. That's the past . . . liquid history. I'm fed up with the past. Tonight, for once, you can see the stars. Their names! They have such glorious names! Vega! Betelgeux! Mira! Sirius! Where does our future lie? In which planet or perhaps which star? Poetry!"

Amanda uncurled herself.

"You should come in," she said. "You'll wake everyone up."

"Why—why shouldn't I shout into the heavens? Why shouldn't I? Maybe someone in some other universe will hear me. Maybe I'll hear myself crying out." He leaned on the rails.

Seconds later he slipped around behind Amanda, pushed her out onto the balcony, and pointed out star after star. "You see there . . . there's the North Star . . . now to the left of that . . .

"Imagine," he said, "in another universe there might be creatures living on the North Star pointing at us. We mustn't get so caught up in the here-and-now."

"Look, this is the universe we're living in," she said. "It's no good you trying to distance yourself from it . . . and anyway I'm cold standing out here in my nightdress."

"It's a pretty nightdress."

"I was going to seduce you tonight. We don't seem to . . . get around to it much."

"You're always too tired."

"I know," she said.

The white cotton nightdress with the frilly collar did not flatter Amanda, who suited sleeker clothing. The collar surrounded her neck as though her head were something about to be served up at a grand dinner. She shivered.

"Oh, we're so lucky to be alive," he said, hugging her waist. "So terribly lucky. In all of space and time, we made it here at this moment."

"I don't know if I've quite made it. I seem to have left all kinds of things behind."

"Nonsense." He turned her around. "Look, a nose, a mouth, two green eyes, two arched eyebrows, two arms." He bent down. "Two legs. Even feet with sweet nails on every toe. What more could you want? Why, you're even more than you are—you've cloned yourself. You have Kate, too."

"I feel sad, Tom, and I don't know why."

"Tiredness, darling. It changes everything. Why, when I get back from traveling I'm always puzzled by how tired I am. And with a baby— why, you're on a long journey every day. Time is different to her. A minute is an hour, a day a week."

"You don't see me as just her mother, now, do you?"

"Of course not. You're my wife."

"I know. It's just the whole thing. Sometimes I feel like a frumpish, middle-aged woman."

"You don't look it. You're beautiful. You know you are. Like an intelligent gazelle. Maybe," he said, "in another universe there are intelligent gazelles and they rule the world. I think I'd like that—to chase you over the plains."

"Or beetles," said Amanda gloomily.

"What?"

"Maybe in some other universe beetles rule the world and we'd be beetles."

"Or birds."

"Or birds," admitted Amanda, watching the seagulls.

"How's Kate?"

"She screamed most of the evening. But she's sleeping now."

He took off his bow tie, put it around her neck, and kissed her nose.

"I love you. I'm glad we're so happy together. Life is wonderful." He sauntered inside. "By the way, on the way back from the party I passed by the hotel where Sarah stays . . . in King's Cross. I couldn't resist popping in and seeing how she lived. Such a strange girl."

"Are you joking?"

"No. I passed by it in the car, saw a parking space, and stopped. I was curious. She's looking after our child, after all."

"I see," said Amanda, in the doorway, a cold wind blowing behind her. "And how does she live?"

"Oh, in a grim little room."

He vanished into the bedroom. She closed the French windows and, shivering, followed him. He sang in the shower. His clothes were strewn over the floor.

"Don't worry. It was all perfectly proper," he shouted.

"You like her," she called out.

He stepped out of the shower and shook himself like a puppy. He grabbed a towel.

"Of course. She's a good person to look after Kate."

Amanda stuck out her lower lip.

"I don't think I shall go to New York, after all."

"Oh, really, Amanda. You should go. Don't be silly."

He dried himself while humming, "I was a big man yesterday . . ."

He embraced her before he was dry, and she drew back a little, not wanting to get her new nightdress wet.

"In the old days, darling," said Tom, "we used to make love in the shower."

"Well," said Amanda bravely, "why not?"

It was at that moment that Kate began to cry, as though sensing there was something going on not wholly to her benefit.

By the time Amanda returned from ministering to Kate, Tom was spread out asleep naked on the bed. She covered him over and curled up in what space was left beside him. She fell asleep thinking of Sarah's raw face coming toward her.

55

"Oh, Caroline," said Amanda, "I don't know what to do. Tom was horrible all morning. I think he had a hangover. He told me I was obsessed by Kate. Well, why shouldn't I be? I felt very hurt. She's only four months old. Mothers just are obsessed by their children. Doctors are obsessed by medicine, cricketers with cricket, boxers with boxing. I don't want to pretend I only have mild interest in my child. Well, I do pretend that when other people are around, but it annoys me."

Caroline laughed. "Haven't you understood yet? Female skills are considered entirely menial and oddly humorous, from child care to knitting. I thought you knew. Everyone else knows."

"I'd never been interested in any female skills before, so I didn't know, actually."

"What you have to do is pretend you don't have a baby. If anyone finds out, pretend the subject doesn't interest you ... and only ever discuss your baby with really close friends." Caroline laughed again, a sharp little laugh. "It really is funny: all over London, women meet secretly and talk in low voices about their babies when they used to meet secretly and talk in low voices about their lovers."

"Caroline," said Amanda. "By the way, you wouldn't think Tom the type to fall in love with . . . our nanny, would you?"

"Of course not."

"Good. I just wondered. If he was the type."

"Amanda," said Caroline, wide-eyed, pushing aside her half-eaten plate of vegetable mousse, "what are you talking about? Are you going mad?"

"I don't know. I expect so," she said cheerfully. "I mean, I expect everything's fine. It's probably me just feeling a bit insecure. You know how it is."

"You're never insecure. You don't honestly think that Tom has fallen for your nanny?"

"No, of course not," said Amanda.

"I'm sure it's just your resentful feelings about your nanny. People do feel jealous, but I have no doubt it's her relationship with the baby you're jealous of . . . and you're transferring your feelings to Tom, if you see what I mean."

"Probably," said Amanda, noting that this time Caroline had worn a plain white dress to go with the plain white restaurant and that she, Amanda, found the restaurant so white and desolate she could weep, and wanted to. She stared at the glass of water.

"Put it out of your mind."

"You haven't met her. She's not like other nannies. She's very grown up. Rather poised. Very pretty. Rather well educated. I was a fool to employ her. But I don't spend my life seeing other women as threats."

Caroline reached for some bread.

"Oh, Christ," said Amanda.

"Are you going to New York?"

"I don't want to leave Kate."

"Or, it would seem, Tom."

"I feel like a fool. I'm sure I'm imagining it."

"I'll come and meet her if you like. I'm an excellent judge of character."

"You'll probably like her. You'll probably start going out to lunch with her. I don't know why I don't just move out now."

"Oh, Amanda, that sounds like self-pity."

"Well, I do feel a bit sorry for myself," said Amanda. "Even Kate . . . I think she likes Sarah better."

"Sack her. If I were you, I would definitely sack her. If she's upsetting you this much, I should ask her to leave. Tell her she's overeducated."

"But Kate loves her."

"That's why you want to sack her."

"It's not a good reason. It's a terrible reason. I can't do that."

"You're too decent, Amanda."

"If we got someone else and Kate didn't like her, I'd feel terrible. I'd never forgive myself."

"So you'll even put up with Tom possibly

being infatuated by your nanny . . . if your nanny makes Kate happy."

"Well, more or less."

Amanda took another gulp of wine. She hadn't eaten anything. She felt somewhat drunk.

Caroline shook her head and poured Amanda some more wine.

"You can be very endearing," said Caroline.

56

Amanda and Tom left Kate with Amanda's mother on the day of the boat race party at George Stewart's house.

Tom meandered happily through the crowd in George Stewart's back garden, knocking off someone's lighted cigarette ash here, knocking Pimms over someone else, waving to someone over on the far side of the lawn, brushing his head against branches of trees so that soon his hair was scattered with raindrops and leaves. Every now and again he would swoop down and converse with a cluster of people.

The pewter sky let out a little rain intermittently.

A team of waiters in black kept filling up their glasses, and the rain released the garden's smells of wet grass and lavender.

There was an excitable tone to the afternoon, and as Amanda talked to an old friend, she noted a man's hand resting on a woman's waist; both the man and the woman stared at it with puzzled expressions. Certainly the man seemed to feel he had no responsibility for the recalcitrant hand.

Jonathan came by and kissed her warmly. "Hello, Amanda," he said. "You're looking very lovely as usual. Whose side are you on?"

"Sorry?"

"The boat race. Remember you came here to see the university boat race?"

"Oh, yes."

"Have you and Tom made up your minds about Cambridge? I shouldn't leave it too long."

His eyes glittered. She introduced Jonathan to her friend and moved off, winding like Tom through the clusters of people in the garden with its solemn rose bushes, talking to someone here, someone there, not staying to talk with anyone for long, standing alone for a moment by the rhododendron bushes at the end of the garden to survey the scene. Every now and again someone brushed against a tree and some drops of rain came tumbling down and people laughed.

The waiter refilled Amanda's glass with Pimms, and the light amber liquid glittered in a snatch of sunlight. A man pushed by her and she moved back, stepping on a clump of bluebells. She looked down and saw how her heel had squashed the glutinous stems.

Trisha Hunt undulated toward her in a sleek black snakeskin of a short dress, entirely inappropriate for the occasion, except that her straw hat with the black band gave her outfit an afternoon freshness, which she needed. For in spite

of her youth, Trisha did not have any freshness
in her worldly-wise face, with the cruel, thin
lips disguised by too much lip liner.

"Hello . . ."

"Why, Amanda," said Trisha, "how marvelous
you could come. That was a terrific weekend at
dear Jonathan's. Have you seen him? He's here.
What a spectacular house that is, and of course
what a darling man."

Trisha gave Amanda a harsh smile.

"You had lunch with George, I hear. He thinks
the world of you," said Trisha.

"Isn't that nice? How flattering."

"George adores all women. It's his downfall,
of course."

Trisha adjusted the tilt of her hat, and as she
did so the rings on her short fingers flashed.

"Oh, Amanda, you're treading on the bluebells!" cried Trisha. "Would you mind awfully
if you moved? You see, George's first wife just
loved wild gardens, so we have all these bluebells and primroses and climbing roses. George
is a little sentimental about them."

Amanda stepped off the bluebells.

"How is the little girl?" said Amanda.

Trisha was examining the state of the party;
noting who was with whom and where. She appeared to have an almost scientific attitude, as
though studying the social habits of ants.

"I see Sir Edward is talking to Lord Snow-
fort," she said.

Trisha's high heels sunk deep into the grass.

"The little girl. Where is she today?" said Amanda.

"Alice? Her nanny took her out somewhere."

"I'd love to meet her."

"Oh, she's perfectly sweet."

"You like children?"

"Look, I mustn't hog all your time . . . I must circulate. A hostess's duties!"

In the slight wind the leaves of the trees stirred, and Amanda could smell the river. It seemed to her that the smell of the river had not left her since Kate's birth.

"Hello," said George Stewart, placing his hand lightly on her arm. Dressed in black trousers, red suspenders, and a flouncy white shirt, he resembled an aging poet.

"It's a good party," she said.

He leaned forward and whispered in her ear: "And you are by far the loveliest woman here."

She smiled slightly, choosing to ignore his remark.

"Your house and garden are magnificent," she said.

"I've made so many mistakes in my life," he said in a low voice, shaking his head. "You know, you'll hate me for saying this, but sometimes I wish it were you, someone like you, sharing it all with me. Someone like you, someone poised and cultured, a woman with a career." He smiled, and his eyes crinkled up.

Amanda allowed herself to laugh. "You don't

mean any of it. I think that's what I approve of so much about you. You're so wonderfully insincere."

"Insincere? Oh, I'm very sincere."

"You've been married three times," she said.

"That's correct. I fall in love easily."

"And out of love, it seems."

"Not really. I still love my third wife. It's just that she didn't love me. She put up with me. She fell out of love with me. She became separate from me."

"Oh, I'm so sorry."

George looked sad, as he had throughout most of lunch, and she felt sorry for him.

"Did she work?"

"Oh, no. She never worked. She wasn't the type to work. She drifted through her life. She never made decisions; she let decisions make her."

"And where do your ex-wives go? Do you keep them in the cellar somewhere, like Bluebeard?"

"My first two have married again. We see each other amicably. My last wife is the only problem. She's trying to fight me for custody of our daughter. I thought she might have given in by now. But I suppose I never quite understood her. She was always a blessedly mysterious creature."

"It sounds as though you almost miss her."

"Does it? We used to have a good relationship, you see, a very . . ."—he looked shyly up—"passionate relationship, before Alice came along. I miss that, certainly."

Somebody called out that the race was about

to begin, but she and George continued to talk and drink in the garden as the sky darkened and everyone left to watch the race on the front lawn, until finally they were alone.

"Can we have lunch again?" he said.

"I don't think that would be a good idea. And I'm afraid you really should stop calling me."

"Oxford! Oxford!" cried a clutter of voices. "Come on."

"Cambridge! Cambridge!" called some others.

"Shall we go and watch the race?" she asked him.

"I think I love you," he said.

He stretched out his two hands, cupping her head tenderly in them, and kissed her on the lips.

At that moment Amanda saw Tom standing behind George, and her eyes opened wide.

"Oh, darling . . ." she began to say, pushing George away so that he walked backward into Tom.

"When you're ready," said Tom, "you might consider coming with me to see the boat race."

"Excuse me," Amanda said to George, backing away. A bird scuttled away in the tree above, and a leaf fell down on her head's disordered bob.

"Gosh," said George, "why, the boat race has begun! I'd better be off." He hurried across the lawn.

Tom seemed taller than usual.

"It was nothing, Tom," she said as they walked away.

"I know," he said without looking at her. "Don't worry about it. It's just that he's a wily man and he quite clearly finds you attractive."

"You still look cross. You can be very intransigent."

"Intransigent?"

"I'm not having an affair with George Stewart."

"I know that, darling. Let's not talk about it anymore. Let's forget it."

They watched the boat race in silence.

57

Alice's little red suitcase was still hidden at the back of her wardrobe. It wouldn't be long now before her mother came to get her. She knew it wouldn't be long. If her mother didn't come soon, she would have to work out her own way to escape.

It was raining, and the rain threw itself against her window like pebbles.

She watched the umbrellas of the people below: was that umbrella hiding her mother, or that one? The tenth one would be her mother, she told herself. One, two, three, four, five, six, seven, eight, nine ... ten ... but the tenth one passed by like all the rest.

She was frightened at night because now her favorite flowered curtains had horrible faces in them which only appeared at night. She didn't dare tell anyone because she knew if she did, the face would punish her.

She told herself to be brave, to be like Jack in "Jack the Giant Killer." He wasn't afraid. He wasn't afraid of anything. He outwitted the giant.

Perhaps her mother was dead, squashed on some road like an orange.

58

"George," said Sarah breathlessly, "I called to speak to Alice."

"You shouldn't try to do that," he said.

"Look, I'll come back to you . . . I'll love you."

"You won't, Sarah. I don't want to live with someone who doesn't love me."

Sarah stood at the pay phone by the front door of the Sunrise Hotel.

"Is Alice okay?"

"She's fine."

"Is she eating well?"

"Oh, yes."

"And her vitamins? And fluoride?"

"Fine."

"Let me speak to her."

"She's in bed."

"Get her up. Please. I don't want money, or anything. I just want Alice. I know how she needs me."

"She has school tomorrow."

"Trisha Hunt is not a suitable mother."

"She's fine."

"She caused all this."

"You did—when you grew so ... separate."

"I was being a good mother. She needed me. She'd been sick. You're a grown man. You didn't need me."

"I did. I was crazy about you."

"You had affairs."

"They were nothing. I loved you. I just couldn't get through to you."

"I used to feel sorry for you. In spite of all your possessions and your position and your prestige, you seemed so vulnerable. I should have known better."

"Anyway, that's over—although, of course, I miss what we used to have."

"You miss me pottering around after you."

"I don't want to continue the conversation. It's better we converse through our lawyers."

"Please, George. I can't bear it. You loved me. Please. At least for Alice's sake."

"She's better off without you. Here she has everything she needs. She has to adapt ... she has to grow up."

"George, fuck you ..."

She slammed down the phone and stomped up the stairs, where Beatrice stood, leaning with one foot against the wall, with her hands folded in front of her.

"You were listening," she blazed at Beatrice.

"Of course, my dear," said Beatrice, putting her arm around her. "I make it a point to eavesdrop as much as possible."

Sarah brushed away her arm.

"He's a monster. He seems so nice at first, but he's a monster."

"Go and get her, dear."

Sarah turned, walked down the stairs, called Amanda, and told her she was sick and wouldn't be in tomorrow. Amanda sounded quite pleased, to Sarah's surprise.

"Will you bring your daughter here?" said Beatrice.

"No, I won't. I'll take her to France. To live in the country. I have friends there. I'll miss Kate, but I'll get over her once I have Alice back. We'll be happy."

"What about the overdressed man?"

"I'll have Alice."

"Well, you can have my car if you like. It's a broken-down old thing ..." said Beatrice. "I never use it. Can't afford the gas."

"I'll buy it from you."

"Okay. It's a deal."

They shook hands.

59

At ten o'clock the next morning Sarah drew up in a side street near Alice's school with a screech and a clatter of brakes. Beatrice's Mini was noisy but spirited, although it's appearance was as eccentric as its former owner's: it had a chunk out of its front, scratch marks on both sides, and had been sprayed shocking pink: hardly an ideal car in which to make a getaway. Still, Sarah patted it as she got out, noting the suitcase in the back.

She ran up the stairs and rang the bell.

She'd dressed in a tan suit, tights, polished court shoes, and pearls. Alice's school was a respectable little private institution housed in a Victorian building, and she wished to conform to their idea of what a mother should look like. When Sarah had left the Sunrise Hotel, she had been laughing and hopeful, having paid her bill and booked tickets to France.

"Why, Mrs. Stewart!" said the school secretary, Joan Smith, and blinked. Her gray hair was arranged in a series of Brillo pads, and her face had a reassuring rubber quality, as though if you pressed her nose it would go in and not come out again until released. Her skin glowed with the pink flush of a pure life dusted over by a little powder. She had mole's hands which huddled together as their owner decided what to do.

"Come in," she said, standing back.

Sarah stepped into a smell of overcooked peas and mince. All along the walls of the hall were plastered papers with small hand prints in all different colors—orange, aquamarine, navy.

"The kindergarten," said Joan Smith. "They dipped their hands in paint and made hand prints—on pieces of paper, of course—which we then secured to the wall with Blu Tack."

"Oh, dear," said Sarah, looking at one of the hands in black. "How strange. All those little lifelines."

She gazed up the dark stairs toward the classrooms on the floor above.

"I'm afraid," said Mrs. Smith, "you can't go up there."

"No. I was going to ask you to get her. Alice has a doctor's appointment."

Mrs. Smith's lips thinned. "Mr. Stewart didn't tell us about that. She's not supposed to leave the building except with him or his . . . friend, Miss Hunt . . . or the nanny. We had express instructions."

Mrs. Smith fiddled with her brooch. "I'll speak to the principal."

"Okay," said Sarah, about to ascend the stairs two at a time the moment Joan Smith left her alone for a moment.

A diminutive figure with plaits and a green-checked uniform appeared at the top of the stairs and clumped down.

Sarah recognized her as Susan, a girl from Alice's class.

"Susan, could you—" Sarah began.

"Perhaps you'd like to come in," said Joan Smith, guiding her into the office and shutting the wooden door firmly behind her.

Joan Smith's desk was a castle of papers, with turrets about to topple. Official forms and type-written documents hung from every space on the yellowing walls. The calender featured Eagles of the World.

The school's golden retriever lay with its head between its paws, watching Sarah with mournful eyes in front of the empty fireplace. The hearth had fir green tiles with a tendril of a young plant in their centers.

Around the top of the walls hung years and years of little girls—long school photographs with eager faces and solemn uniforms. In the most recent one Alice's face looked down at Sarah, puzzled.

"Excuse me a moment. Do take a seat," said Joan Smith, entering the principal's office but leaving the door open so she could keep an eye on Sarah.

Sarah didn't sit down. She moved restlessly around the room, glancing repeatedly at the picture of Alice. She listened to the hushed voices in the room beyond.

"Well, I don't know . . ."

"We really should . . ."

Finally, Joan Smith emerged, playing with her brooch, her face more squished up than usual, as though someone had been trying to roll it into a ball but hadn't quite succeeded.

"We'd love to help you, but we made an agreement."

"To keep me from Alice?"

"Well, yes."

"I don't need your permission."

Sarah walked toward the wooden door.

"My dear!" called the principal, a formidably large woman in a gray suit, as she lurched toward Sarah and seized her hand. "How wonderful to see you. Do take a seat."

She plonked Sarah in a swivel chair. The principal's suit was stiff, and had an existence quite separate from its owner. The skirt's design was based on that of a barrel.

"Look," said the principal, her hands behind her back. "We unfortunately made an agreement with your husband. I have no idea of the rights and wrongs of the whole business. Nor do I wish to know them. I know that legally you are not supposed to see your daughter at the moment. Personally, I shall recommend strongly to Mr. Stewart and his lawyers that you do. The girl is disturbed. I believe she needs to see her mother. But, alas, I have no power."

She opened out her oversized hands to express her powerlessness.

"But you see, Alice has a doctor's appointment this morning," said Sarah, "with a specialist at Great Ormond Street Hospital for Sick Children. It's about the urinary infection she had as a baby. As you know, she nearly died of it. They want to check her blood count, and make sure she has no more blood in the urine. She suffers from mild hemeturia."

Sarah stood up.

"I have an appointment with the specialist, Dr. Barnet. You can check if you like."

"It's odd Mr. Stewart didn't mention this appointment."

"I always dealt with her health. George doesn't like hospitals and didn't feel it would be right for her nanny to take her to the hospital. She'll have to have a scan. Nothing serious, of course. It's all routine. But it can be worrying for Alice."

"We should have had a letter."

"Here's the phone number of Great Ormond Street. Phone them. Ask to speak to Dr. Barnet."

The principal took the number and returned to her room. A few minutes later she returned.

"I called your husband. He insists I must not let you near Alice."

The principal towered above Sarah, and all at once Sarah felt small and exhausted.

"I told him I thought the child needed her mother. I told him how upset she seems. She's not working properly or eating properly. I shall be contacting the lawyers. But I have to do things in an aboveboard manner."

Sarah felt she was back at school again, in the headmistress's office. Her nails dug into her hand.

"I'm sorry, Mrs. Stewart. I'm sorry about this."

The principal took out a handkerchief and mopped her brow.

"I . . . must see her . . . you don't understand. It's essential."

"I do understand," said the principal. "I shall do my best to help. You have always seemed a good parent."

She patted Sarah on the arm.

She guided Sarah firmly to the door.

"I shall recommend you have visitation rights. Most certainly. We principals have some power in the community."

Sarah stumbled down the stairs, out into the uneven sunlight, and along the street. The houses loomed up all around her. A woman walking an Afghan hound stared. Sarah came to the ridiculous pink car. She opened the door, climbed in, and sat with her hands leaning on the wheel for a long time before she drove off back to the Sunrise Hotel.

When the bell rang for the end of class, Susan whispered something to Alice, who at once ran fast down the stairs and into the empty hall.

The school secretary emerged.

"Where is she?" said Alice.

The principal appeared, even more rumpled than usual, with swerving eyes.

"Who, my dear? Now get back to your class."

"My mother," said Alice fiercely. "My mother. Tell me where she is. What have you done with her?"

The principal took her by the arm and returned her to her classroom.

60

"Sarah called to say she's not coming back," said Amanda that night, standing in the door of Tom's study.

Tom was at his computer terminal, his elbows splayed out and his shirtsleeves rolled up. He ran his fingers through his hair. On his computer screen a picture of a galaxy swirled like a Catherine wheel.

"What?" said Tom.

"She says she's under too much emotional stress. She was crying. She said she didn't know what to do."

Tom rubbed his nose. "What emotional stress? Did she say? Why was she crying?"

Amanda took a sip of wine. "She said something about her daughter."

"What daughter?" He switched off his screen, and the room grew darker.

"She said her husband had her daughter. I tried to get her to explain. But she was rather incoherent."

"A husband? I didn't know she had a husband." Tom brushed paper clips off his jeans. "Do you think she really has a husband—and a daughter? She never said anything at all about a husband. She seemed . . . too young. I think she should have told us if she really has a husband."

Amanda sipped her wine. A pink hair band kept her hair from her face. "We never asked her," she said.

"You're taking this very coolly," he said.

"I might not be able to go to New York next week," she said, "if she's not back. She sounded very upset."

"I thought you wanted to go."

"I suppose I could go for just a couple of days . . . and you, of course, could look after Kate. If she isn't back."

"But Amanda, I have lectures to give . . . and what about my book? I can't just walk out on all that. Besides, I wouldn't know what to do with her. How would I get her to sleep? Supposing she screamed for you and Sarah? I couldn't stand it."

"What are you afraid of?"

"Of dropping her, partly."

"I'll trust you not to drop her."

"You don't, you know," he said.

"I can't just chuck another nanny at Kate. She'll need a period with us. She'll be missing Sarah, and someone new would only upset her."

"Look, I've said before, when I've finished the book, I'll have ample time to spend with Kate."

"You can't continue to put your life off. It

won't go on hold. This is it, darling, and you can measure the minutes passing by how Kate is changing. This is it. It won't come around again."

He stood up. He ran his fingers through his hair again.

"It really is so terribly inconvenient," he said.

He had an ink stain at the front of his shirt.

He strode out of the study and spun around. "Well," he said, "we'll have to make a determined effort to make sure she comes back. Offer her more money or something."

"I don't think money's any part of her problem."

He marched to the kitchen and made himself a gin and tonic.

Amanda followed him in, carrying Kate.

"You seem very distressed, darling," she said.

"And you're very calm."

"Of course, if we went to Cambridge and I gave up my job, we wouldn't need anyone to help with Kate. This kind of thing wouldn't arise."

He shoved more ice into his drink.

"She's a terrific nanny. She's good for Kate," he said.

"She's quit, Tom."

61

Sarah lay with her head buried in her pillow. She listened to the sounds outside: the roar of the cars, the brakes. She went to the mirror and put on some red lipstick, a red gash in her white face. It was three in the morning.

She had, of course, always been on the edge of things. In the hospital she had identified with the characters who staggered around the corridors, lost souls with dark eyes.

She had in a way been wise to turn to George with his robust sexuality and his sanity. At least Alice had inherited some of George's toughness. Alice had had a grasp on the world from the beginning. Early on she had asked how electricity worked, where exactly the water in the taps came from originally, how phones were made. Her studious little face was always asking questions, watching faces attentively as they answered, trying to piece together the way the world worked. Whereas Sarah still had little idea about electricity and London's reservoir system.

Sarah dressed in black.

She walked up the stairs and knocked on Beatrice's door.

A grunt came from inside.

"Who is it?"

"Sarah. I want to go for a walk."

"A walk? It's three in the morning. Hold on."

After about five minutes, Beatrice let Sarah in. Beatrice's wig was put on at an angle, and her makeup was even more in the style of Jackson Pollock than usual. She rubbed her face and her mascara smudged so that she had panda eyes.

"What is it? Why do you want to go for a walk at three A.M.?"

"Why not? There are fewer exhaust fumes."

"That's true," said Beatrice.

They walked out. Beatrice strode off and Sarah tried to keep up. In spite of her bizarre appearance and air of dissolute living, Beatrice walked like someone on a hike in the Lake District: head up, best foot forward.

"You've been crying," said Beatrice.

"I felt lonely without Alice."

"How's that overdressed man?" said Beatrice, walking straight out into the road. Sarah followed. A driver honked his horn at her and called out.

Sarah walked on.

"Fine, as far as I know. Please. Let's just walk."

"You looked pretty pleased to see him that evening."

"I think you read too many trashy novels."

"I write pornography. I thought there was something definitely pornographic in his eyes when he saw you, and in yours."

"Oh, stop it, Beatrice."

They walked in silence.

"Do you want to go to a bar?" said Beatrice after a while.

"Yes," she said. "I want to go to a bar. I want to get very drunk at a bar."

"Okay," said Beatrice, and promptly turned down a dark side street. Sarah followed.

That night as she finally began to fall asleep Sarah saw Alice's face, her eyes wide open, lying on her little bed, her hands repetitively stroking the ribbon edge of her favorite blanket.

She could see, piece by piece, the scenes Alice was compiling in her imagination.

What shall I wear? said Trisha.

Something warm. It's cold on the boat, said Alice.

Sarah could sense Alice's fear. Sarah sat up.

Off we go, called Trisha a few moments later from the top of the stairs.

You look nice, said Alice.

In Sarah's mind, Trisha came down, swinging her arms, in a fluffy white sweater and tight black trousers.

And you look like the Michelin man in that life jacket, laughed Trisha, putting on a white anorak with a fur collar. *I'd never wear a life jacket,* she said.

314

It would certainly spoil the look of your nice jacket, said Alice.

Sarah could feel Alice's hands opening and closing with fear as the child lay on her bed. Her palms were warm. Alice moved some strands of hair from her face, and turned onto her side.

Come on! cried Alice.

Alice and Trisha went out side by side, across the road to the boat house. Alice unlocked the door and, together, they heaved the shabby little motorboat out onto the water where it began to tip around. Trisha was careful not to dirty her coat. Alice held on to the rope while Trisha climbed in, using her arms to balance herself, a bird in flight.

Alice jumped in.

Alice hugged her teddy to her. She had thrown off most of her bedclothes but she was still hot and restless.

Now, you're sure you know how to steer? asked Trisha.

Oh yes. Mummy always let me steer.

Alice turned the key in the electric motor. She took the wheel and *The Princess* puttered off across the Thames, which was growing darker by the second as clouds gathered.

What fun! Alice cried out. *I love the wind.*

The wind blew Trisha's hair around. She used one hand to protect her hairstyle as though she were wearing a wig she did not wish to blow away. Her nose and cheeks were growing red from the cold.

Above them the seagulls soared and screamed. The river was choppy.

Alice saw herself as wild and brave, her hair flying around her like a heroine from a book of Greek myths or maybe Gerda saving Kay in "The Snow Queen." She would not give up. She would not be afraid. She would do what she had to do and destroy the wicked witch forever.

In bed she sat up, and hunched her knees up to her chest. Her dark eyes seemed to have taken up her whole face.

You don't need to go so fast, Trisha shouted as they hit the wake of a pleasure boat. *I'm sure you're not supposed to go so fast.*

Oh, replied Alice. *It's fun to go fast. Mummy and I always go fast.*

It's rough! shouted Trisha, holding on to the sides of the boat. Her hair thrashed like snakes. *Stop this!* she shouted. *You're not allowed to go so fast. What about the ... river police. They'll stop you. We'll be in trouble.*

Too busy in storms! yelled Alice.

Storms? Is this going to be a storm? I'm getting wet. Stop it, you horrible child.

They sped through the water, the water spraying out all around, and Trisha, the witch was small and terrified in the boat, her face green, the snakes writhing about her head.

Thunder and lightning, sang Alice. *The way you love me is frightening.*

Slow down. Trisha tried to stand up, and

waved her arms as though trying to hit out at Alice.

Alice lifted her foot from the pedal. The boat sprawled to a halt. The witch toppled over and fell back with a splash and a scream.

Lightning flashed across the sky.

Alice drove off.

The hands of the witch waved from the water.

Alice smiled and kissed her teddy good night. Sarah could see her lying in her dark room, pale skin glimmering like some nocturnal moth. Around her, from the walls, her queer, childish drawings watched and from the shelves watched her disapproving dolls. Alice tossed and turned, pushing off her covers, her nightdress rumpled up, her thin arms flaying, her lips mouthing something.

Sarah also found it hard to sleep. Her pillow felt hot to her face. Sarah closed her eyes tighter to shut out her fears of what her daughter was planning.

62

That morning Amanda sat in a boardroom on the twenty-sixth floor of an office building. The carpet was gray with a red stripe around the edge, and the walls were decorated with abstract pictures which seemed to be suggesting some kind of vigorous exercise: strong lines and violent splashes of green and purple and red paint. One whole wall was made up of a vast window overlooking London.

She took her place. She examined her agenda. She spoke eloquently when it was appropriate for her to speak.

Amanda enjoyed the meeting, as she usually enjoyed meetings, because she was good at taking control. She began to sit up straighter, and to come up with ideas she didn't know she had.

But as soon as she stepped out of the room, her former unease returned.

63

Tom tried to read while Kate played on the carpet.

Amanda had had to go to work for an important meeting, and since he had planned to write at home today, he was left minding Kate.

Tom stared hard at Kate lying winningly on the floor, and wished she wasn't there.

Tom propped Kate up against the sofa and turned on the television. A man and a woman shouted at each other.

"I hate you!"

"I love you!"

The woman, satuesque in pink, had a flawless face apart from the tears running down her cheek. The man curled his lip.

Kate waved her arms around approvingly.

"Oh, I don't recommend it," he said to her. "It's an exhausting business. But already you can't wait, can you?"

After about twenty minutes, during which Kate joined in the more dramatic scenes with goos and whoops and appreciative grunts, the soap opera program ended. Tom noted it was an American series, with oversized characters making overblown statements, and that he would recommend it to Amanda for watching with Kate. He concluded that his child had an innate knowledge of human behavior which allowed her to appreciate human interaction. He wandered into his study to make a note of this, but became tempted by his computer screen. He was trying to compile a new brief history of the universe for the front of his book, starting with the Big Bang theory and moving from second to second after the Big Bang up to the first hour, then the first year, up to the arrival of Homo sapiens about six hundred thousand years ago. The cursor was flashing impatiently after the words "One hour after the beginning of time . . . the Universe has cooled. Most nuclear processes have ceased."

He heard a yell, and ran out to find that Kate had managed to pull the cord of an iron so that the iron had fallen on the floor beside her. He rushed over. Kate was beaming with pride. The cry had been a battle cry, not a yell of pain. The iron had been cool and had just missed hitting her.

"No," he said to her firmly and she laughed.

"It's all very well," he said, "but there is a school of thought which maintains men are genetically incapable of child care, something many men eagerly subscribe to. Now, I am not of that opinion. I am perfectly able to accept that women can do what men can do, and the other way around. But I do not wish you to ruin it all by breaking open your head while in my care, do you understand me? It would not further the course of male/female relations and the liberation of the female from the often tedious business of being the sole care giver. You get my drift? Good. Try to have some sense. I don't want it said that men are only capable of doing one thing at a time whereas women can put the things in the dishwasher and know what their baby is doing, while listening to the radio, while waiting to see if the washing is finished, while conversing with their business adviser on the cordless phone, while writing some poetry on the back of a shopping list."

Kate yawned.

"Would you like to go to the park?" he said.

In the park Tom stood as Kate watched the older children fight and run and climb. He was expecting something to happen. It struck him as odd that he was investing all this energy, and not much was really happening except time was passing. He hadn't written a word of his book. He hadn't made any decisions. All that was happening was that Kate was being kept alive, and that Kate was growing infinitesimally. Kate wasn't exactly enjoying herself, that was clear. She was restless and Tom guessed she was disturbed by him, if amused. She would rather have had Sarah's lovely face leaning over her than Tom's big one.

What he found most disturbing was the fact that he couldn't actually think when with Kate. Even now, although she was safely strapped into her buggy, he felt his emotions beginning to be tied up with hers in a worrying way, almost as though he were her.

He tried to remember the date he was using for the beginning of sex in the world. He thought it was probably nine hundred or seven hundred million years ago. He wanted to go and check it, but here he was in the faint morning sunlight, at a children's playground, watching prototypes for different Kates prancing over the jungle gyms.

Very like monkeys, he thought; then Kate began to struggle in her padded throne, and tentatively he let her out and placed her on the grassy slope beside him. He put his arm around her to make sure she didn't fall. She fought it off, sticking out her lip petulantly.

A woman smiled at him. *I clearly look hopeless,* he thought, *or perhaps it is still the sight of a father on a weekday with his child that amuses women.*

Kate stared up at him. He looked down at her.

"You two look very alike," said Sarah.

She was wearing a black coat, and was almost lost in it. Her hands hung by her sides as though she were uncertain of where to put them.

She dropped to her knees beside Kate.

"Kate. I've missed you."

Kate cooed and smiled and Sarah hugged her. The woman and child melted into one.

"I had to come back," she said to Tom. "I love you both. I do."

Tom ran his fingers through his hair.

"Come with me, Tom." she said. "Bring Kate. Help me. I need you."

He knelt down too, and made her meet his eyes while the toddlers rushed around throwing sand, shouting, their noses running. He took her face in his hands and kissed her on her wide lips.

"You don't need me," he whispered.

She plunged her hands into a recently abandoned pile of sand and watched it run through her fingers.

"I do," she said.

He shook his head.

"I love you," she said.

"Maybe," he said.

64

Amanda sat staring into space and chewing the end of her pen. She was trying to work out when she and Tom had been happy. He was behaving as if they never had been. But surely . . . she frowned. She remembered their first dinner out after Kate's birth (her mother and father had baby-sat). They had gone to a new Italian restaurant.

"You know," Amanda had said dreamily (too dreamily perhaps, she now thought) to Tom, "Kate justifies everything I've done. If I hadn't chosen to cross the road in a certain place on a certain day I might not have had a certain thought, and that thought might have led me to not meeting you, and if I hadn't met you there would be no Kate. If we hadn't made love that particular day, we might have had a quite different baby. Not Kate. Imagine not having Kate!"

"Quite terrible," Tom had said, staring at the menu. "What are you going to eat?" (Had she been excessive? Had he been irritated with her even then?)

He had grabbed a roll, dismembered it, covered a fragment with butter, and shoved it in his mouth.

"I'm starving," he said, with his mouth full.

"I think the liver might be good for her, and some spinach and broad beans. And first of all, some fish would be healthy. What about the prawns? No, too garlicky . . ."

The waiter stood over them.

Tom grinned. "We're ordering for a baby," explained Tom. (He'd been amused, and not cross, surely?)

"Ah," said the waiter in a puzzled tone.

"Yes, the liver is definite," announced Amanda.

The waiter was surreptitiously looking around for the baby. When he seemed to be staring overlong at Amanda's handbag, as though a baby might be secreted in there, Amanda smiled charmingly up at him and pointed at her breasts.

"Breast feeding," she whispered conspiratorially.

The waiter had reddened, and Tom had laughed. He had definitely laughed. He must have been amused by her enthusiasm, not irritated by it.

When they had got home after dinner, they had watched Kate asleep. A ripple had crossed her pink skin. The ripple had been something like a frown—new expressions in skin so soft that it seemed more like water than skin.

They had held hands that evening looking

down at Kate. She was sure they had held hands.

They had been happy then, and other times too. On their vacation to Italy, before Kate was born, they had behaved like new lovers. She was sure they had.

They had stayed in Tuscany, in a magnificent former nunnery with tall fir trees and a pool. It was the middle part of her pregnancy, and she was in a constant state of placid desire, so they spent much of their time making love in one of the stone-floored bedrooms while the smells of the firs crept in.

They had always been enthusiastic and moderately skilled love makers when they found the time, and in Tuscany, for once, there seemed plenty of time. All she wanted to do was to lie in the pool and watch her belly, or to lie in bed with Tom.

The family from whom the house was rented had a collection of art books, and when she wasn't making love or eating or floating she would sit in the cool main room and gaze at lush paintings by Botticelli or Rubens. A few times they drove into Florence, but it was crowded, and the paintings in the gallery with other people around were not so peacefully exotic and erotic as those she enjoyed in the curious house surrounded by dusty roads and vineyards.

She chewed her pen some more.

Amanda wondered what had gone wrong. Ev-

erything had started so well—the love, the birth—
and now Tom was distant and difficult.

She thought of George Stewart. At least he
was pleasant to her, she considered.

65

Alice tidied her hair. Above her jeans and over-size shirt, her face was white, and her eyes enormous. Her hands trembled, and so did her voice, as to calm herself she told her dolls, word for word, a story her mother had told her:

"Far away hence, in the land wither the swans fly when it is cold winter with us, there once lived a king who had eleven sons, and one daughter named Elise. The eleven brothers were princes, and used to go to school with a star on their breast and a sword at their side. They wrote on gold slates with diamond pencils, and learned by heart as easily as they could read; one could immediately perceive they were princes. Their sister Elise sat on a little glass stool, and had a book full of prints, that had cost nearly half the kingdom to purchase.

"Oh, these children were happy indeed! But, unfortunately, their happiness was not to last.

"Their father, who was the king of the land, married a wicked queen, who was not well disposed towards the poor children. This they perceived from the very first day. There were festivities in the palace, and the children were playing at receiving visitors; but instead of their getting, as usual, all the cakes and roast apples that were to be had, she merely gave them some sand in a teacup and told them they could make believe with that.

"In the following weeks, she sent their little sister, Elise, to a peasant's cottage in the country and before long, she spoke so ill of the poor princes to the king, that he no longer troubled himself about them.

" 'Fly out into the world, and pick up your own livelihood,' said the wicked queen. 'Fly in the shape of large birds without a voice.' But she could not make things as bad as she wished, for the children were turned into eleven beautiful wild swans; and away they flew out the palace windows, uttering a peculiar cry as they swept over the park to the forest beyond.

"It was still early as they passed by the peasant's cottage where Elise lay asleep. They hovered over the roof, and extended their long necks, and flapped their wings, but nobody heard or saw them; so they were obliged to go on. And they rose to the clouds, and flew out into the wild world until they reached a large, gloomy forest, that shelved down to the seashore.

"Poor little Elise was standing in a room in the cottage, playing with a green leaf for she had no other toy. And she pierced a hole through the leaf, and looked up at the sun, when she fancied she saw her brothers' clear eyes; and every time the warm sunbeams fell on her cheeks, she used to think of their kisses."

Alice went to the window, and drew back the curtains. It wouldn't be long now before she'd get her mother back.

She checked once more the contents of her red suitcase: a toothbrush, her passport, a pair of pajamas, a book. . . .

She returned to the window, then smiled into her dressing table mirror.

Alice secured a pink barrette on either side of her hair to keep her bangs from falling over her face.

She smiled again.

She put on a pair of old sneakers and pulled the laces tight.

The dolls watched her.

The teddies watched her.

She kissed Martha, who lost her straw hat as she did so. Alice didn't pick it up.

Around the walls of her room the red and black stick figures waved their arms goodbye.

Alice had photographs of her mother hidden in the dressing table drawer: her mother aged six, looking very much like Alice; her mother aged twelve, solemn and beautiful. Alice had an old passport of her mother's, with the corner snipped off, and in it the photograph showed a different mother at around the age of fourteen, with a sweet grin in a homemade dress.

Alice walked down the stairs. One, two, three,

four. She used to believe that if, after pulling the toilet chain, she didn't get down the stairs before the flush stopped, something terrible would happen.

Alice entered her father's study.

"Excuse me," she said.

He sat at his desk, a bulky figure, fountain pen in his hand, wearing a green velvet jacket, which he liked to wear when he worked at home.

"Yes, dear," he said to the child standing in the doorway, the light falling behind her.

"Daddy," she said, and she hung her head a little, and then she looked up. She tugged at her hair. "Can I go out on *The Princess* with Trisha?"

George frowned and put the top on his fountain pen. He rearranged his papers.

On the study wall were photographs of George with various politicians, and cartoons of British prime ministers. The room smelled of cigars and old leather books.

"Of course," he said. "If you want to. I suppose it would be a way of you getting to know each other better. Can you and Trisha manage to get it out?"

"Oh, yes," said Alice. "Mummy and I often did it."

He tapped his fingers on the desk. "It's not very good boating weather though, is it? Bit cold."

"Never mind. I don't mind. It will be an adventure."

George lifted himself up slowly, and adjusted

his round glasses. He came over to Alice and put his arms around her. She stiffened.

"Well," he said, "I'll go and ask her."

Alice followed him up the stairs.

She stood in the doorway of the room that had been her mother's as Trisha sat at the dressing table, doing her makeup. George had put his arm around Trisha and was whispering something. She shook her head, and then she shrugged and glanced into the mirror at the child standing by the door.

Trisha stood up.

"Okay, Alice, darling. I'd love to come out on *The Princess*."

"Thank you, Trisha," said Alice.

George smiled rewardingly at Trisha, and left the two females alone.

"No, what shall I wear?" said Trisha.

"I'll be downstairs," said Alice, as Trisha stripped and stood there, her small breasts sharp and pointed.

"Off we go," called Trisha from the top of the stairs. Alice looked up.

"You look pretty," said Alice.

Trisha came down in a sweater and jeans.

"And you look silly in that life jacket," laughed Trisha. "I'd never wear a life jacket," she said.

"It would certainly spoil the look of your nice sweater," said Alice.

George was talking on the phone in his study.

"Do hurry up," Alice said to Trisha. "I'm so keen to get going."

66

Amanda had a drink with Caroline after work. She felt she had to talk to someone.

"I'm going to advise Tom to take the Cambridge job," said Amanda. "He'll be much happier. I think we'll all be happier."

"But what would you do there? It's cold and damp. It's not all sunshine as in the photographs of all those magazines about country living. You'll be shut indoors, in some rickety old house with no one to talk to and a bored child. They probably don't even have play groups there."

"Of course they do. It's only Cambridge. It's an hour and a half away from London."

"I bet that's what Tom said to persuade you. You know it's not an hour and a half. With traffic, it's more."

"It's a town."

"A small town," said Caroline. "Personally, I like big towns."

"Well, I thought I did but I feel I should accept the possibility of change. I might find I like small towns."

"You might find yourself, say, preferring Dieppe to Paris?"

"Cambridge is a fine old town. Tom would be taking a distinguished job."

"I suppose you like reflected glory. 'Oh yes, my husband is a professor. Oh no, I look after my child. I gave up my job. I used to be in management consulting.' Oh yes, you'll love that. They'll ask you all about *his* work. They'll wrack their brains for something to ask you. They'll dread it if you start talking about small children."

"I don't care," said Amanda.

"Did you sack your nanny?"

"She left. She said she was under too much emotional pressure."

"I see," said Caroline, after a pause. "How's Tom coping?"

"He's minding Kate today."

"Willingly?"

"Unwillingly."

"You won't have any money."

"I might work part-time."

"Doing what? Making quilts?"

"I'll work here part-time probably."

"Part-time work is a figment of a mother's imagination. There is only work, and work done less well."

"I'll do it less well then."

"You won't be able to bear it. You'll be back full-time within six months."

"Well, at least I can try."

"You can."

"I'm not being self-sacrificing, Caroline. I actually want to be with her. I like it. I am being selfish."

"Oh, well, at least *that's* something," said Caroline.

67

Tom rang the doorbell of George Stewart's house.

Trisha opened the door.

"Why Tom! How wonderful to see you!"

Trisha threw her arms around Tom's neck and kissed him on the cheek. Trisha smelled of some deceitful scent.

"I hope we haven't caught you at a bad time," said Tom affably.

"Only that George is here," she said softly.

The little girl stood intently on the stairs, in a pool of light, and all around it seemed the house was in shadow.

Outside, a boat left a trail like a bride's through the river and the wind ruffled the water, as if searching for something.

The wind was creeping up, twitching the leaves, making the flowers sway, rustling the paper in the streets.

People hurried by, trying to get home before the rain began.

"We were going for a walk," said Tom, "and I thought it might rain and realized we were just around the corner from you, so here we are."

Trisha glanced at Kate in her buggy.

"Oh. I see. Why, you are a good father."

Bundled in her hat, Kate's querulous little face looked up at Trisha's towering over her. Her lips quivered.

"Come in! What am I doing leaving you standing in the cold? And do bring in the baby too. If I seem scruffy, I'm ready to go boating with Alice, but I can stand the disappointment."

She grinned at Tom.

"But Trisha," said Alice.

The little girl's arms dropped to her sides like toothpicks. Only her eyes were huge. Angry eyes.

"It wouldn't have been a good time to go out," said Tom. "I think there's going to be a storm."

"Really?" said Trisha, patting down her hair. "Although I grew up in the country, I'm hopeless about weather."

Tom tussled with the buggy to get it through the doorway, while Trisha hovered in front of him. Kate's lower lip stuck out.

"Why don't you leave the baby in the buggy?" said Trisha, once Tom had maneuvered Kate and her transportation into the hall. "Maybe it'll sleep."

"She slept on the way here, I'm afraid. No, I don't think we're due for much peace," he said.

Trisha shut the front door and secured mammoth bolts at the top and the bottom.

"What are you afraid of?" asked Tom.

"Oh—burglars. And the girl's mother."

Trisha took his coat, and tossed it on a chair in the hall. The hall was papered in a dense ivy pattern, and the brown chair reminded Tom of the foot of some old established garden.

"Can we please still go?" said Alice. *"Please?"*

"I'm sorry, Alice. Do you hear? Mr. Richardson said there might be a storm. I wouldn't have known."

"I like storms," said Alice, reproachfully.

"George!" yelled Trisha. "George, it's Tom Richardson!" she said. "He's working in his back study at the moment with his music on full blast. *George!"*

The little girl scowled. She was just like Sarah, Tom thought; the bone-white skin, the strange pale green eyes, the fragile structure of the face, the beautiful mouth. She tipped her eyelids down, then up again in the same disturbing movement which Sarah often made. She had Sarah's air of tension too, as though at any moment the delicate creature on the stairs would change into something altogether fiercer.

She was dressed all in dark green except for the fluorescent orange life jacket—green corduroy trousers, green duffle coat. Two barretts kept her bangs from her face, revealing the dome of her forehead.

"Shall I help you off with the life jacket?" said Tom.

"I can manage," said Alice, dipping her eye-

338

lids down then up again, with a quick smile. "But thank you."

Alice crouched by Kate.

"What splendid shoes," Alice told Kate. Kate waved her arms around, and a smile swept over her face. Alice took Kate's two small fists and kissed each in turn.

Kate watched with immense blue eyes.

"What's her name?" said Alice.

"Kate."

"Pretty Kate."

Kate struggled to get out of her buggy. She was part of the world now, not a creature from another one. When she was first born, her movements were slow, as though she were trying to push soft cobwebs away. When she fed, her little feet moved ecstatically, all curling and red, and once she was full, her face had a dopey expression of contentment. The blue veins had showed under her soft skin.

Even at one month, when she lay on the floor, her feet had fought and kicked. Life was there in all its power, showing that in one way or another it would continue kicking through the centuries, whatever other forces battled against it.

"Okay," said Trisha, "let's go and have drinks now."

Alice stood up and as she drew away, Kate cried out.

"She likes you," said Tom.

"You'd better grab yourself something to eat," said Trisha to Alice.

As the child turned away, Kate cried out again and her cry was a robust, hopeful, grand cry, a declaration of her bright presence in this house of shadows.

It unsettled Trisha. She pushed back the hair from her face.

"Off with you," she snapped at Alice. "I'll just go and get George. I don't know why he has those silly operas on all the time."

Trisha stalked out, and the little girl stared at Tom with Sarah's eyes, and he stared back.

Tom stooped down and whispered something to Alice. Her solemnity disappeared at once and she bounded upstairs.

The loss of her admirer, combined with Tom's inept unfastening of her strap, made Kate angry. She sniffled for a little while, as George appeared, hurrying along the dark hallway by the stairs. He was rubicund, patrician, welcoming, his arm outstretched, and wearing his smoking jacket. Kate let out a yell of indignation.

"Tom. What a surprise! What a delight! I hope you'll stay for a drink," said George.

"Thank you," said Tom.

George shook Tom's hand. Tom was startled by George's entry. Meeting Alice had so jolted him, he didn't quite know where he was.

George led Tom, holding a wrestling Kate, into the drawing room—a long, formal room with windows on one end overlooking the river, and on the other, the garden. This had an air of complicated profusion, the bare branches tangling with each other to suggest some insoluble maze.

George pulled the faded velvet curtains closed.

Trisha sat on a Victorian sofa covered in damson velvet, cushions all around her, while Tom's large frame filled an armchair by an inlaid mahogany desk. Tom helped Kate off with her snowsuit. Kate's face was red and cross, but she was enjoying her crying bout. Just as her laughter was pure and fresh and strong, so were her cries; they were the other side of laughter.

The rain began to hit against the window.

"Well, I must say," George said loudly as he poured them drinks, "I love it when people drop in. It stops you doing all the awful things you're supposed to be doing. Why, the case I'm working on now is actually quite intriguing."

"Oh, really," said Tom. He looked earnest, a picture of intelligent interest as he joggled Kate up and down on his knee. George talked on and on, pompously, even though he could hardly be heard over Kate's yells. Kate was dressed in a black-and-yellow terry romper; a deformed bumble bee. What little hair she had fluffed in wisps around her head.

After a while, Tom gave a surreptitious glance at his watch and a moment later tried to stand up holding Kate. Eventually he succeeded and, to Trisha's open-mouthed horror, came over and with a generous smile said:

"Trisha, darling, you couldn't just hold Kate

for a minute, could you? Just need to wash my hands." He nodded at George. "I expect George knows a few tricks to pacify a crying baby. I remember you saying how much you loved babies, George. I bet you are as good with babies as you are with everything else in your life."

George smirked. He levered himself from his chair, loomed over Kate, and began to make terrifying faces, which were no doubt meant to amuse. Every now and again he straightened his bow tie.

Tom could hear Kate yelling with gusto as he slipped out of the room. Her magnificent cries drowned the sound of his unbolting the locks on the front door.

He looked around the ground floor, from still room to still room, until he saw the child, a little red suitcase at her feet, at the dining room window, with her hands pressed against the glass.

68

"Oh, baby," said Sarah as she saw Alice at the window. She stood on tiptoe and put her hands flat on the glass, and Alice put her smaller hands, shyly, against the windowpane on the other side.

They smiled at each other, the same sudden sideways smiles.

"I'm ready," mouthed Alice.

The rain ran down Sarah's face and her hair.

69

Later that evening, when Amanda walked through the front door of the flat, she couldn't see Tom and Kate anywhere. Without taking off her coat, she ran into the nursery where she found Kate sitting up alone with a victorious expression in her crib.

"What have you done with Daddy?" said Amanda.

"Boo," said Tom, emerging from behind the door.

"Oh Tom," she said, relieved.

He put his arm around her and kissed her. "You're late. We were expecting you earlier."

She was shivering.

"Are you okay?" he said.

"Yes . . ."

Kate was giving her mother and father a tooth-less grin.

"She's been crying and crying this evening, haven't you?" he said.

"But you made it," she said.

"Well, just about."

He stuck his tongue out at Kate.

Kate laughed a fresh laugh without guile, without scorn, without foolishness, then stuck her tongue back in imitation.

Amanda picked her up, and Kate wrapped her fist around Amanda's finger, and laughed again.

"I love you, you know," said Tom, putting his arm around her.

"I know," said Amanda. "Of course, I know that."

70

At breakfast in France the next morning, Alice kept laughing too, for no particular reason.

"Who was that man?" she asked as she ate her second croissant. "The one who unlocked the door to let me out?"

"I looked after his baby, Kate."

"I liked Kate. Especially her screaming."

Sarah smiled.

"Yes, I did too."

"Perhaps we could visit her one day," said Alice, wiping her jammy chin with her napkin.

"Perhaps."

"Only I definitely prefer France to England. Definitely. So maybe we won't."

"Maybe," said Sarah, putting out her hand to touch her daughter's soft skin once again.

27 million Americans can't read a bedtime story to a child.

It's because 27 million adults in this country simply can't read.

Functional illiteracy has reached one out of five Americans. It robs them of even the simplest of human pleasures, like reading a fairy tale to a child.

You can change all this by joining the fight against illiteracy.

Call the Coalition for Literacy at toll-free **1-800-228-8813** and volunteer.

Volunteer Against Illiteracy.
The only degree you need is a degree of caring.